C000099541

WINTER MAYHEM

A 1920S HISTORICAL COZY MYSTERY - AN EVIE PARKER MYSTERY BOOK 14

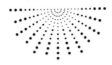

SONIA PARIN

ISBN: 9798426141834

CHAPTER ONE

A partridge in a pear tree

The drawing room, Halton House
December, 1921

*E*vie turned the page of the fashion magazine she had been perusing and stopped to admire a dress she thought would look quite becoming on Millicent.

She knew the local dressmaker, Mrs. Green, would have no trouble producing something similar.

She was about to suggest paying Mrs. Green a visit when she remembered she needed to employ a great deal of tact, not only with her timing but also with her choice of words.

Smiling, she glanced at her lady's maid. Or, rather, her new secretary.

How would Millicent react to her suggestion?

A short while ago, Millicent had been instrumental in exposing someone as a fraud. That *someone* had been the secretary Evie had hired.

Then, while investigating the death of a woman who'd been poisoned, Millicent had been the voice of reason, helping to settle her muddled thoughts.

All this had prompted Evie to make an official offer and promote her lady's maid to the role of secretary.

Caught by surprise, Millicent had been speechless.

Evie remembered delivering the news right in the midst of a hectic week during which she had entertained several houseguests, organized and hosted the annual hunt ball and, in-between, had attended several village fairs.

With everyone so busy, it had taken them an entire week to realize the *something different* they'd all sensed had been the absence of Millicent's exuberant chatter.

Even Edgar, Millicent's secret beau, had failed to connect the odd atmosphere at Halton House with Millicent's silence.

Finally, after a week of letting the news sink in, Millicent experienced a delayed reaction—a reaction of mammoth proportions.

Instead of expressing her astonishment at the offer of a promotion, Millicent thought it appropriate to respond in a demure fashion, one befitting her new role. During that torturous week, she employed all her willpower to contain her exhilaration. However, her raw emotions had been frayed to the point of turning them into live wires, sizzling with excitement.

Evie closed her eyes and recalled the moment the dam burst. Right in the middle of the night, Millicent had rejoiced... at the top of her voice... in her sleep, *"It's all my Christmases come at once."*

Everyone in the entire household had been jolted awake, rushing out of their respective rooms, down the stairs and into the hall, wearing their nightgowns and slippers, to see what the commotion was about.

"Has someone been murdered?" Cook had demanded.

The next morning, Millicent had been red-faced and quite apologetic. Once her shock had worn off, she had stepped into her new role, pretending as if nothing had happened, her focus fixed on displaying the utmost efficiency and discretion in her new role as secretary.

After that episode, Evie realized she needed to deliver her news with greater care...

Of course, as Millicent stepped into her new role, Evie now had to hire a new lady's maid. At least, she had Millicent to assist her. She would be doing the preliminary selection and vetoing all unsuitable candidates. That meant she couldn't afford to lose Millicent to another week-long silence.

Turning the page of the fashion magazine, Evie decided to delay making her suggestion about the dress until they decided how to go about hiring a new lady's maid.

Winter had well and truly settled in, so they had sought refuge from the cold in the drawing room where they had spent part of the morning looking through several fashionable publications in search of new ideas.

As far as Evie knew, if anyone needed a new lady's maid they simply advertised in *The Lady* or contacted one of the many agencies in town. However, she wished to investigate a different approach...

Evie turned the page of a periodical and remarked, "Oh, this is a surprise. Lotte Mannering is continuing to cement her position as the favored lady detective. Look here, she's advertising in *Dress and Vanity Fair*. The fine print promises the reader they can rely on absolute secrecy and exceptional abilities."

Millicent leaned in and hummed, "You missed a bit, milady. It actually reads *rely on a lady's touch*." Straightening, Millicent mused, "I think she's promoting your services, milady."

"Oh, how so?"

"A lady's touch. Surely, that means you."

"Heavens, I think you're right. But she never asked me about it. I wonder how efficient these little advertisements are."

"It's bound to be noticed by someone, milady. They'll hire you and then, word of mouth will spread and soon you'll be inundated with appeals for your discreet services."

Evie tipped her head back and laughed. "Discreet services? That sounds rather risqué." Almost salacious, she thought.

"What sounds risqué?" Tom asked as he walked in, rubbing the cold out of his hands.

"My discreet services."

Tom walked over to the fireplace to warm himself. "You tend to stand out, Countess. I think you might need to work on being discreet."

As always, Evie smiled at his use of her title as a sobriquet. "I'm not sure I want to change." As he continued to rub his hands, she asked, "Is it that cold outside?"

Tom shivered. "It's moderate, or so I keep telling myself."

"Is that your attempt at self-delusion?" Evie asked.

Tom shrugged. "I'm sure you're the one who told me the mind thinks what I tell it to think." He took a step closer to the fire. "Right this minute, I'm telling it to enjoy the balmy weather."

Millicent murmured, "I'll bring out your winter coat with the fur trim, milady, as well as the mink muff, of course. You won't want to travel with anything less than that."

"Anyhow," Tom continued, "the tree is all packed and Edmonds is about to leave. He wants to know if you have further instructions."

"Does he have the baskets?" Evie asked. "I'm sure there are several of them. Cook's been preparing them for days now and they've been multiplying at an extraordinary rate. Oh, and the new coat Mrs. Green made. Please make sure he takes that. There's no point in Nanny Fulham waiting for our arrival to receive the coat. She'll appreciate it now, I'm sure."

Ever since Evie had confirmed their visit to Nanny Fulham, everyone had been eager for her to deliver one thing or another, mostly Christmas gifts.

Realizing they wouldn't be able to fit all the parcels in the roadster, they'd decided to send Edmonds, the Halton House chauffeur, on ahead in the Duesenberg.

This would be one of their first festive season visits and the one which had required the greatest amount of strategic planning, with several delays along the way as people had hurried to complete handcrafted items.

The much-loved Woodbridge family nanny had recently moved away from her small cottage in the Halton House estate to take up residence in a house left to her by her widowed aunt.

The house was located in a village nearby and Evie had decided it would be a nice touch to visit her rather than rely on the post to deliver the gifts. In any case, when she'd moved, Nanny Fulham had forgotten to take the small pine tree she used as her Christmas tree, something that wouldn't fare well in the postal service.

The little tree had been planted in a large pot by her husband Nicholas when he'd been young and cared for throughout the years by their gardener, making sure it always looked its best for Christmas.

"Oh, I nearly forgot. Nanny Fulham asked if we could rummage through the attic for some old sheet music. It's in a folio with a picture of... oh, I can't remember what exactly. I'm sure it will come to me. Anyhow, the sheet music has some sort of sentimental value. When I asked if she wanted anything in particular, she didn't even have to think about it. I don't know why she waited so long to ask for it."

She looked at the stack of fashion magazines. They still had quite a few to get through. "We'll leave those for now, I think. It might be best to make sure Edmonds doesn't leave anything behind."

Tom nodded. "If you're thinking of going up to the attic, I recommend wearing a coat. I'm sure the heat doesn't quite reach there."

"I'll get one, milady."

"Oh, Millicent..." Evie drummed her fingers on the stack of magazines. "If there's nothing else to discuss this morning..."

Millicent hesitated. "Actually, milady, there is something else. I'd been clearing out the back of your wardrobe and found a box." She dug inside her pocket and produced a dainty card. "The box didn't have a label but I found a stack of these inside it."

"What is it?"

"It looks like a calling card, milady. Except... it has your old name on it. Evangeline Parker."

"Oh, heavens." Evie knew there were still some people who referred to her as Evangeline Parker because they refused to accept she had landed herself a titled gentleman. "How many are there?"

"I stopped counting at one hundred, milady. I'd say there are several times that number."

Evie rolled her eyes. "Heavens. I remember them. In fact, they are quite ancient. My mother had entertained high hopes of me becoming a social butterfly. Those were printed before we left America, well over ten years ago."

"What shall I do with them, milady?"

Evie waved her hand in a dismissive gesture suggesting they should be disposed of.

"Such a waste," Millicent mused. "Couldn't you use them as your lady detective calling card?"

Evie tilted her head in thought. In the next breath, she looked up at Millicent. All along, she had been struggling with the prospect of exposing the name of Woodridge to possible ridicule and perhaps even scandal. As a lady detective, she really didn't wish to have the family name associated with something others might disapprove of...

"My goodness, Millicent. You are a genius."

Millicent's cheeks colored. "M-milady?"

"Of course, when I'm out and about, sticking my nose where I shouldn't, I could revert to my maiden name and be Evangeline Parker." She knew Toodles wouldn't object, nor would her family back home. In any case, she didn't think they'd ever have reason to find out... "Thank you, Millicent. You've solved one of my problems. You are a true genius."

Millicent's lips parted and her eyes widened in surprise. Scooping in a breath, she clammed up.

Noticing this, Evie panicked. "Oh... Oh, dear. Millicent. No."

Millicent took a step back, followed by another step and another until she bumped against the door.

Tom chortled. "Countess. I believe you've sent Millicent into a week-long silence. Then, she'll explode and announce to all and sundry..."

Giving a silent denial, Millicent gave a vigorous shake of her head, swung around and dashed away.

A moment later, they heard what sounded like rapid footsteps. Except, they did not recede.

Tom walked up to the door and peered out. "Yes, just as I thought. Millicent is jumping up and down on the spot performing some sort of celebratory dance. I believe you have made her quite happy."

"I didn't mean to," Evie exclaimed. "That is... I didn't mean to send her into one of her long silences. I merely wished to compliment her."

Tom laughed. "There you go again, coddling your servants." Tom stepped away from the door and lowered his voice to a whisper. "She's coming back."

Millicent walked in. Holding herself upright, she said, "My apologies for my outburst, milady." She collected the magazines and carried them off, saying, "I'll be down momentarily with your coat."

Tom waited until he heard Millicent reach the top of the stairs to turn and say, "You really must be more sensitive."

Evie's eyes widened in disbelief as she whispered, "But I merely complimented her."

"That's precisely what you must stop doing. Stop pampering her. It's too much for her."

Shaking her head, Evie jumped to her feet. "For the life of me, I shall never understand..." She huffed out a breath. "I need to tell her to pay Mrs. Green a visit and outfit herself with some new dresses. How am I going to do that?"

"By small increments. Try hinting."

"What?"

"Show her a picture of a dress and ask her what she thinks about it."

"And then what?"

Tom slipped his hands inside his pockets and shrugged. "I'm sure it will come to you."

She straightened her skirt, tipped her head back and sighed. "I hope she grows out of... whatever this is."

Holmes, her little French Bulldog, stirred awake and yawned.

"Are you coming, Holmes? We're going on an adventure to the attic." When he wagged his little tail, Evie scooped him up.

They made their way up the stairs and met Millicent halfway.

"Your coat, milady."

"Thank you, Millicent. I'm sure I won't need it. You might want to take the lead. Anything above this level begins to look like a rabbit's warren."

"Yes, milady. I don't know why we call it an attic. It's merely a large room on the top floor. At some point, I'm sure it was used as a nursery and school room, but that was probably over a hundred years ago."

Millicent led them to the top floor and along a corridor to a set of double doors. Evie had ventured inside only once before and suspected the vast room stretched the length of Halton House and stored several generations worth of hoarded knick-knacks.

Most of the windows were blocked by large pieces of furniture and the only visible light came from a set of windows at the far end.

They wove their way around, inspecting boxes and trunks. Suddenly, Millicent stopped and put her finger to her lips.

"What?" Tom mouthed.

Shrugging, Evie walked up to Millicent who whispered, "I think I hear someone."

Listening, Evie nodded. She could definitely hear a conversation. No... more like an argument.

They continued on their way through a labyrinth of old furniture and trunks until they saw a couple of people standing in front of a wardrobe. With the curtains at the end of the room drawn enough to allow some light to spill in they could only see their silhouettes.

"I can't tell if it's a man or a woman," Millicent whispered. "They're wearing funny looking hats."

"Oh, they're bicorne hats." Using a couple of trunks to hide behind, Evie drew closer.

The soft light from the windows outlined a figure. Evie couldn't be sure, however, despite the man's hat, when the figure swept a hand out as if making a point, Evie recognized it as a typical hand gesture made by...

Henrietta?

As for the other person...

Hearing a snort of disdain, Evie shook her head. "Toodles."

Tom and Millicent came to stand behind her and they all leaned in to listen to the conversation.

"I put my hand up for the ghost of Christmas past first," Henrietta declared. "Therefore, I claim the right to select the costume and I say this fine gown suits me."

"So why are you wearing a man's hat?" Toodles demanded. "Admit it. You saw me reach for a hat and decided you wanted one too."

"There are two of them. I fail to see where the problem lies," Henrietta argued.

"You are wearing a gown. Why do you want a man's hat?"

Henrietta lifted her chin. "I am playing an eccentric ghost."

A third person emerged from the clutter of furniture, reciting, "It was a strange figure, like a child, yet not so like a child." That had to be Sara, her mother in law, Evie thought.

Sara continued, "In case anyone is wondering, I am narrating and playing the ghost of Christmas in the future. You can both squabble over the other roles. These ones are mine."

Toodles and Henrietta produced unladylike snorts with Henrietta asking, "And you think the ghost of the future is going to wear a long dress?"

Sara defended her choice of clothing by saying, "Well, they can hardly become shorter than they already are."

Toodles nudged Henrietta who then nudged Sara.

"I told you we would be found out," Sara whispered.

Henrietta stepped forward. "Evangeline. I thought you'd already left."

Emerging from behind the trunks, Evie said, "We are leaving soon, Henrietta. And, for the record, we didn't come up here to spy on you. We are searching for some sheet music."

Henrietta pointed in their general direction. "There's an abundance of sheet music in a trunk... somewhere. Behind you, I think."

As Millicent proceeded to rummage through several trunks, Tom whispered, "What do we do?"

Whatever Toodles and the dowagers were up to, Evie knew they wished to keep it a secret. So she turned her attention to trying to identify the sheets of music Nanny Fulham wanted.

"We can help Millicent."

"It seems such a wasted opportunity," Tom whispered. "We have them cornered."

Nodding and smiling at Toddles and the dowagers, Evie lowered her voice and suggested, "Best to leave them be. At least we know we won't have to worry about them getting up to mischief while we are away. In any case, Millicent will keep an eye on everyone, but I'm sure they'll just keep themselves busy."

Tom laughed. "Countess, you say that with so much confidence."

"They must be planning a surprise for us. Actually, I'm rather hoping they're working on a theatrical entertainment for us. I do enjoy those, especially at Christmas time."

"Could this be the sheet music, milady?" Millicent held up a folio with a picture of a partridge in a pear tree.

"Oh, yes." Evie peered over her shoulder and saw the dowagers and Toodles huddled together and whispering.

"They're definitely up to something," Tom murmured. "Why am I suddenly thinking of Macbeth?" Lowering his voice and adding a croak, he recited, "When shall we three meet again? In thunder, lightning, or in rain? When the hurly-burly's done..."

"Please, let's not tempt fate," Evie whispered back. "Perhaps we should leave them to it."

Grinning, Tom asked, "And bolt the door behind us?"

"Come on, we have what we came for. They're entitled to their secrecy."

"I'm sure you meant to say privacy. Or was that a slip of the tongue?"

Millicent grabbed the sheet music and held it against her. "I think I'll just hurry out of here. I'm feeling a chilly draft."

CHAPTER TWO

Turtle doves

Several hours later...

After a light and uneventful lunch during which everyone pretended they had not been to the attic, Tom and Evie drove the short distance to the small village Nanny Fulham now called home.

Despite a recent downpour, the roads had dried up enough for them to drive along without any hazards. Although, it was slow going for a while.

At the first sighting of a few farm houses dotting the landscape, they knew they were close to the village of Thornbridge. When they came up to it, they were not disappointed.

It looked welcoming with its pretty cottages lining the street, the mullioned windows catching the rays of sun when it peaked out from behind the clouds.

In one of her letters, Nanny Fulham had explained some of the cottages dated back to the 1500s and had been built using stone from a ruined 12th century Abbey giving the village a unique look which set it apart from other villages. Although some aspects remained similar to most villages in the area.

Driving along the main street, they came across a couple of stores and a pub in a corner. At the end of the main street, they saw a patch of green leading to a church and, opposite that, a village green with a memorial.

Tom leaned toward her and said, "We'll have to stop and ask for directions. What was the name of the street?"

There were several streets but none of them had signs.

Evie dug around her handbag and drew out a leather-bound notebook. "Old Salter Lane."

Tom stopped outside the pub. Rounding the roadster, he leaned in. "Staying in the car or coming in to warm up?"

"You're only asking for directions. I'll wait here." She tucked Holmes under her chin and watched Tom go inside the pub.

All too soon, he emerged, a puzzled expression on his face.

Evie watched him as he rounded the roadster and settled in before asking, "Should I be worried?"

"I'm not sure." He turned to her. "I've never actually met Nanny Fulham. Going by everything I've heard you say, she sounds like a lovely person."

"Oh, she is. She's been retired for a number of years

but that never stopped her from helping out at the school-house to offer extra reading lessons and when someone fell ill, she's always been the first to volunteer to help. Everyone in the village loves her and not just for her generous spirit. She's simply lovely and uncomplicated."

He signaled to the pub. "When I mentioned her name and asked for directions, the fellow in there grunted, and a couple of people shook their heads. Perhaps Nanny Fulham's popularity hasn't spread here."

"That does sound odd." As they drove off, she noticed a couple of people stop and turn to look at them. It didn't really surprise Evie as they were most likely curious to see the roadster in their village.

Continuing on their way, she turned to see if they were still looking at them.

They were!

Again, it didn't really surprise her as she assumed they were curious to see where they were headed. She then imagined it wouldn't take long for word to spread about Nanny Fulham having visitors.

After a short drive along a treelined lane, Tom pointed ahead to a detached house with a yew hedge, a large oak tree and rose bushes that would no doubt bloom in the summer. "Here it is."

"It's larger than I expected," Evie said. "In fact, I wouldn't call this a cottage. It's more like a small manor house. Nanny Fulham's Aunt must have done well for herself."

They also found the Duesenberg right outside the front gate.

"I'm glad to see Edmonds arrived safe and sound."

Tom held the door open for Evie. Tucking Holmes in

one arm, she reached for her handbag and the sheet music Nanny Fulham had requested.

As she straightened, she looked across the laneway and saw a farmhouse in the distance. Then, turning toward Nanny Fulham's house, she saw the rose bushes had been pruned and would no doubt be a sight to behold in the summer months. So far, Nanny Fulham's new circumstances exceeded Evie's expectations.

Even before they walked up the path, the front door opened and Nanny Fulham appeared, a welcoming smile on her face.

They greeted each other and Evie introduced Tom because, as he'd pointed out, despite Nanny Fulham living on the estate until recently, they had never met.

Nanny Fulham invited them in, leading the way to her spacious drawing room where they found Edmonds sitting down with a cup of tea, taking a well-earned rest after making his deliveries.

The small Christmas tree he'd brought from Halton House had been placed on a table next to the window. Edmonds had also brought in the dozens of parcels sent to Nanny Fulham from appreciative villagers who clearly missed her and wished her well.

"Oh, my. It's already beginning to look a lot like Christmas." Glancing around the drawing room, Evie saw it was well-furnished with several pieces of beautifully crafted furniture and comfortable chairs. Far more furniture than she remembered Nanny Fulham owning so she assumed they had come with the house. "And this room is splendid. You must get some lovely sunshine in here."

Nanny Fulham smiled and nodded and that's when Evie noticed something about her looked different. It took her a moment to put her finger on it. Finally, she realized Nanny Fulham's smile didn't quite reach her eyes.

Had they arrived at a bad time?

"Do please sit down. I'll get a fresh pot of tea ready," Nanny Fulham said and swung away to organize it.

Edmonds took a sip of tea and, noticing them looking at him, he set it down and made a move to get up.

"I was just on my way, my lady."

"Oh, no. Do sit down, Edmonds." Lowering her voice, Evie added, "We'll only stay long enough for tea." That had been the plan all along. Especially as Nanny Fulham had already written to say she'd settled in and had made many friends who kept her rather busy. Her letters had been cheerful and full of stories about the villagers she'd already met giving Evie the clear impression she had landed on her feet.

Edmonds looked toward the door and then lowered his voice to a whisper, "I think you might want to speak with Glenda."

It took a moment for Evie to make the connection.

She had only ever referred to her as Nanny Fulham. Although, the nanny had invited her to call her by her Christian name.

"Is something wrong?" Evie whispered.

Edmonds nodded and was about to say more when they heard footsteps approaching.

"Here we are," Nanny Fulham chirped as she walked in carrying a tray. She set it down on a small pie crust table and poured Evie and Tom a cup each, all the while chatting about how happy she was to see them again.

Glenda had already asked Edmonds to take back some gifts for her friends. Signaling to the little parcels on a table by the tree, she said, "Everyone's been wonderfully thoughtful." Eager to hear news from the village, she went on to ask about everyone, including the dowagers and Toodles.

Evie told her about various events taking place without any unusual disruptions and about being busy entertaining several houseguests as well as attending a couple of village fairs. Glenda appeared to soak in all the information, almost as if she'd been denied for too long.

"The village looks pretty," Evie remarked.

The change of subject had Glenda smiling but, once again, the smile did not reach her eyes. She must have become aware of this because she lifted the cup to her lips and looked away.

What if Edmonds had been right in his observation? Evie found herself entertaining a dilemma. If she didn't ask Glenda about it, she would feel quite negligent and if she did ask...

Well, what right did she have to delve?

Hesitating, she then decided she had the right of a concerned friend. However, she would have to be discreet and that, Evie knew, could be quite problematic as, despite Lotte Mannering's claim, she wasn't necessarily known for her discretion.

"Did your aunt enjoy living here?"

"Aunt Marjorie lived here during her entire married life."

Evie didn't press her for details but she did notice Glenda hadn't actually answered the question. "Did she marry a local?"

Glenda nodded but did not offer more information, something Evie found unusual as she was known for her cheerful willingness to chat at great length about any subject. All except one. She had never been known to gossip about anyone, hence her popularity in the village.

"Have you given any thought to what you will do to keep yourself busy?" Nanny Fulham had always enjoyed helping wherever she could, either at the school house helping children improve their reading skills, at the small lending library helping to sort the books or by visiting elderly villagers and reading to them.

"I think I might enjoy a full retirement, my lady. The house is more than I can really cope with and I'm sure it will keep me busy."

Evie wanted to ask if she would get someone in to help her. She knew there had been a girl in the village who'd helped her with some cleaning a couple of times a week...

Instead of prodding for more information, she considered moving on to another subject, but then changed her mind. The only way to set her mind at ease would be to get to the bottom of the problem, whatever that might be. "Will you have help looking after the house?"

Nanny Fulham had always been a practical woman, wearing her hair brushed back and gathered in an unfashionable bun at the back. She had never had a hair out of place. Yet, there she was, brushing an imaginary stray lock. Almost as if she needed to do something to distract herself.

Or, perhaps, to distract Evie.

"Your tea must be getting cold. I'll get a fresh pot." Glenda surged to her feet and disappeared down the hallway.

"Countess, I think you might have touched a raw nerve," Tom suggested.

Sounding worried, Evie said, "Yes, I agree, but I don't see how or why."

Edmonds set his teacup down. "I suspect she might be exaggerating about settling into the village."

"Really? What makes you say so?" Evie asked.

He pointed to a flyer on a table by the fireplace. "It's for the church Christmas choir. You know she's always sung in the choir. Well, they won't have her."

"What?" Evie couldn't hide her dismay. "Is that what she said?"

Edmonds shrugged. "Not in so many words, my lady. They're asking for more singers and yet when she approached them about it, they said they had all the singers they needed. I know they still want more singers because I saw the flyer when I drove through the village. I stopped to ask for directions and saw the flyer on one of the windows."

Evie hoped the flyer had been left there as an oversight. "Maybe they forgot to take it down."

Edmonds shook his head and went on to explain how he had walked in and had heard a couple of people talking about the choir with one of them saying the *more the merrier*.

Evie's mind flooded with questions.

Why would Glenda suggest they didn't want her?

Had Glenda exaggerated her enjoyment of her new life?

Why would she?

Evie sat back and looked toward the hallway.

If Glenda didn't like it here, she could always sell the house and either return to her cottage or buy a house somewhere else.

Then again, she'd only been here a short while. It could be a case of everyone needing to adjust and make allowances.

What if Nanny Fulham had already done everything she could? Would she try to save face and put up with her unhappiness? Or would she remain as practical as ever and eventually realize she should abandon this new life and return to her old life?

Evie wondered if she should broach the subject and assure Glenda she would be welcomed back with open arms and warm hearts. Nanny Fulham would always be entitled to the cottage on the estate.

She glanced at Tom as if making eye contact would help her come up with the proper course of action.

Everyone who lived and worked at Halton House came under the protection of the chatelain. Or, as was the case at the moment, the *chatelaine*. But Glenda no longer lived on the grounds of Halton House.

Regardless, Evie didn't feel that should exclude her from offering friendly advice.

On the one hand, she didn't wish to pry. Then again, if Glenda suddenly found herself living in a place where she didn't feel happy but had too much pride to do a quick about-turn...

Well, someone needed to reach out to her. On the bright side, owning a house of her own certainly gave her more options.

Evie heard her approaching. If she said anything to Glenda, she should at least try to lessen any embarrassment she might feel.

"I'm sorry I took so long." Glenda gave them a brisk smile. "Edmonds brought in so many baskets, they've filled up my little kitchen. I can't believe how thoughtful everyone's been."

"Brace yourself. Tom needs to bring in some more parcels." Evie looked at Tom and gave him an encouraging nod.

"Oh, yes..." Tom stood up. "Perhaps Edmonds can help."

Looking around the tidy drawing room, Evie complimented her, "All your lovely pieces look as though they've always belonged here."

"Most of these pieces were already here. Fortunately, there's an old carriage house and I've been able to store most of my furniture until I decide what to do with it all."

Evie took a quick sip of her tea for courage. "You know, everyone misses you so much, if you decided to change your mind and return, they'd all be overjoyed." For the briefest moment, Evie thought she saw a flicker of uncertainty in Glenda's eyes.

Drawing in a long breath, Glenda set her teacup down. "I suppose you sense something is not quite right."

Evie felt such relief she wanted to sink into her chair. Before she could even nod, Glenda looked at her and held her gaze for a moment while she weighed her words, a trait Evie was all too familiar with.

"Living here is different. It feels foreign to sit here in this lovely drawing room without someone from the village poised to enter it without any need of a formal invitation. I find myself thinking this will never feel like my home..."

"I'm sure it will be like that again," Evie assured her. "Soon enough, you'll be turning people away."

Glenda nodded. "Everyone is wonderful but... Well, yes... I do expect it all to be the same as before."

"The local villagers haven't had the opportunity to become better acquainted with you. It has only been a few weeks."

"Don't misunderstand me, my lady. I am determined to remain, if only out of sheer stubbornness. This is the first home I can truly claim for my own. You understand that."

Evie smiled. "I'm merely a caretaker at Halton House." Although, if she needed to or even wanted to, she could buy her own house. However, until Seth came of age, she had a job to do, making sure the estate ran smoothly for future generations.

Glenda appeared to cheer up. "Before I forget. I have a little something for you." She leaned over and, reaching beside her chair, she produced a parcel. "I think you can guess by the shape."

"May I open it now?"

Smiling, Glenda nodded.

Unwrapping the little parcel, Evie could barely contain her surprise. "Oh, Glenda. They're beautiful. How did you ever craft them?"

"I had some help, my lady. A local chap from the village of Woodridge carved the doves and I painted them."

"Two doves."

"They're turtle doves."

"Oh, they'll look splendid on the Christmas tree. Thank you." Once again, Evie felt Glenda had sidetracked her...

Meanwhile, back at Halton House

"We need a Scrooge."

Toodles and Sara looked anywhere but at Henrietta who tried to employ reason.

"That means one of you will have to give up the role of ghost. You can't be both a ghost and Scrooge."

"Why don't you volunteer?" Toodles asked.

Henrietta chuckled. "My dear, I am the best candidate to play the role of a ghost and I believe I could perform all three. Present, past and future…"

Toodles chortled. "Henrietta, if you play the role of the ghost of Christmas future we would all have to suspend our disbelief."

Sara agreed with a nod. "Although, I hear there are surgeons in Switzerland performing wonders with the revitalization of faces. I believe the procedure involves the insertion of wax."

Henrietta tilted her head back and produced her haughtiest expression. "I refuse to take offence. In any case, there's no reason to employ such drastic measures. I do believe there are theatrical tricks I can rely on to appear younger…"

Sara tapped her chin. "Oh, I remember now… It's paraffin wax, to be precise."

Henrietta pursed her lips. "Sara, I might be getting on in years, but my memory continues to serve me well. Gladys Deacon, the second Duchess of Marlborough, had that treatment performed on her nose. The wax slipped to her chin and she is now living with lumps on her face. I have no intention of deforming my face to appear more youthful. Some powder should suffice."

Toodles clapped. "Oh, yes. Let's try that now."

Henrietta's voice hitched, "We need a Scrooge. Can we please focus on that?"

"Not if it means giving up our designated roles," Toodles insisted. "We'll have to be more creative."

The door to the drawing room opened and Edgar walked in carrying a tray.

"Edgar," they all chorused. "Just the man we need…"

CHAPTER THREE

Three French Hens

The Village of Thornbridge

*E*vie hugged Holmes against her and turned to wave to Nanny Fulham thinking she probably wouldn't see her again until the following Christmas...

"You don't look happy about leaving Nanny Fulham," Tom said as Evie settled into the roadster.

"I'm not." Arranging a rug over her knees, she looked up and saw a man emerging from the side of the house. "I wonder who that is."

"That's William Brown. He lives across the lane in the farm. He brings in firewood and has been doing odd jobs for her."

"Oh, heavens. That's a relief. For a moment, I thought she had been living a totally isolated life."

"What about everything she told you in her letters?"

"I'm not sure I can believe any of it. Reading between the lines of everything she said to me while you were out here, I couldn't help feeling she wasn't being entirely honest with me." Evie's voice hitched. "Tom, I think she's hiding some sort of problem she doesn't wish to talk about."

"And you want to do something about it?"

"I feel I should. What if she's too proud to ask for help? It's possible she's entertaining some regrets about moving here."

"What if you imagined it all?" he asked.

Nanny Fulham had spent most of her adult life living at the Halton House estate. Had she known she would inherit a house? What if it had taken her by surprise and she had acted on impulse, moving away from everything she knew to establish herself in a new place? "Edmonds sensed something odd too."

"And if he hadn't said anything, would you have noticed something wrong with her?"

"Are you suggesting he instilled the idea in my head? If that's the case, I'm glad he did. However, I noticed something when we arrived. Her smile didn't quite reach her eyes."

"Countess, there's a nip in the air. At this time of year no one's smile quite reaches their eyes."

"You seem to forget you raised the matter after you went to the pub to ask for directions."

"True."

Evie knew there was a fine line between being

concerned about someone's welfare and meddling in someone's private affairs.

"Is it possible you imagined the odd reactions at the pub?" she asked.

He gave it some thought and then shook his head. "Perhaps you're right."

What could they do? Sighing, Evie gestured with her hand.

"Drive on?" he asked.

"Yes, I suppose so."

Tom got them on their way, driving at a sedate, pensive pace as he maneuvered his way along the narrow country lane.

The sky had turned a turbulent gray urging Evie to ignore her curiosity but she failed miserably. "Tom, when we reach the village, please stop."

"What's on your mind?"

"I want to satisfy my curiosity."

"Is this about that flyer? What are you going to do? Go into the store and express your interest in joining the choir to see what the response is?"

Evie shrugged. "I might."

"And why would someone who is clearly not from this village wish to participate in the choir?"

Evie glanced at him and drew her eyebrows down. "Well... I might be from the next village."

"And which village might that be? You'll have to know in case someone asks." He tapped his finger on the steering wheel. "It doesn't really matter because I'm not buying the idea of someone from another village wanting to join the Thornbridge choir."

"I could say I'm asking for a friend."

Tom groaned under his breath. "Do I happen to be that friend?"

"Maybe."

"That won't work."

"Why?"

"Because I might be asked to sing."

"Is that a problem? I've heard you sing. There's nothing wrong with your singing. In fact, you have a fine singing voice."

He stopped outside the pub and sat back. "Would you like me to come with you?"

"Tom, you didn't answer my question. Are you trying to change the subject? You know I'll only become more intrigued."

He murmured something under his breath.

"Worth a try? What was worth a try?"

Tom smiled at her.

"Oh, you were just pretending to be worried about singing. Why would you do that?"

He climbed out of the roadster and took his time walking to her side.

Evie huffed out a breath. "You think I'm sticking my nose in where it doesn't belong."

"I'm actually thinking our interest might make matters worse for Nanny Fulham." Tom leaned down. "What if Nanny Fulham is simply homesick? She's only lived here for a few weeks. That's not long enough for her to establish herself. It's obvious that you care about her wellbeing but sometimes it's best to leave things to sort themselves out…"

"You think I should mind my own business." Evie

agreed with him. However, she couldn't shake off the feeling there might be something going on here.

Tom held the door open for her. "Whatever you decide to do can't take too long."

She looked up at the sky. "Yes, it's not looking at all promising." She knew Tom didn't mind driving in the rain but she preferred to avoid it.

Giving a small nod, she said, "Let's go home."

Meanwhile, back at Halton House

Millicent hurried down the stairs and headed for the library. Her ladyship would be returning soon and she wanted to make sure the fire had been stoked.

Distracted by a loose button on her blouse, she looked up just as a footman appeared from out of nowhere and went to stand in front of the double doors leading to the library.

Steven stood with his back straight and his attention fixed on some point on the opposite wall.

When he didn't move, Millicent asked, "Is there something wrong?"

He glanced down at her and gave a small shake of his head.

"Steven, would you mind stepping aside. I'd like to go in."

"I'm… I'm afraid I can't do that, Miss Peters."

It took Millicent a moment to remember she was Miss Peters. "It's Millicent."

Steven cleared his throat. "Edgar has instructed us to call you Miss Peters."

"What? When... Why?"

"It's not our place to ask... Miss Peters."

Millicent rolled her eyes. "Anyway... What do you mean you can't let me through?"

"I have been instructed to stand here."

"But you weren't standing here a moment ago." Millicent frowned.

Steven glanced away. "That's because I was standing at the other door."

"Who asked you stand guard?"

He took a hard swallow and nudged his head to indicate the person or persons inside had given him instructions.

"Who's in there?"

"They're all in there."

"They?"

"Toodles and the Ladies Henrietta and Sara."

Millicent realized they were probably rehearsing their pantomime. "Well, I just want to go in and make sure everything is as it should be for her ladyship's arrival." She took a step forward but Steven stood his ground.

"They've given me strict instructions not to let anyone in."

Millicent wanted to protest but she realized it would only make the situation awkward. Then again...

The library had two doors and Steven couldn't possibly stand guard over both of them at the same time.

"All right. I'll leave you to it." She walked away and through a hallway door which led straight to the other door. Unfortunately, Steven read her intentions and rushed after her.

When he caught up to her, Millicent sidestepped him and rushed back to the other door.

"Miss Peters," he said in a harsh whisper. "Please don't make this more difficult than it already is."

Just as he reached her, the front door bell rang. They both froze. After a minute, they broke eye contact and looked toward the front door.

Stepping back, Steven straightened and gave his sleeve a firm tug. "We have to answer the front door."

"We?" Millicent smiled. Seeing his distraught expression, she huffed a breath and relented. "Oh, very well."

Steven walked briskly toward the front door, all the while looking over his shoulder. As much as Millicent wanted to enter the library, she couldn't make trouble for Steven.

He opened the door and, nodding, he stepped aside and Phillipa Brady entered.

"I know I'm not expected until tomorrow but I made good time driving up. Is everyone in the drawing room?" the young Australian playwright asked.

"Lady Woodridge hasn't returned yet, miss. However, Miss Peters is here…"

"Oh…" Phillipa turned and saw Millicent. "Who's Miss Peters?"

"That'll be me." Millicent walked up and welcomed her. "Miss Brady. Steven can bring in the luggage. I'll show you up to your room."

As they walked up the stairs, Phillipa said, "I hope I haven't walked in on something."

"Not at all." Millicent glanced over her shoulder in time to see Steven's look of relief.

Lowering her voice, Phillipa asked, "When did you become Miss Peters?"

Millicent grinned. "When her ladyship made me her secretary." She looked over her shoulder and then said, "But you can still call me Millicent."

"That's a relief. I have enough trouble remembering when to curtsey and when not to curtsey."

"This is your room." Millicent hurried inside and sent her gaze skating around the room to make sure everything was in its place.

Taking her hat off and easing out of her coat, Phillipa asked, "Where's Evie?"

"Her ladyship and Mr. Winchester should be arriving shortly. They've been to visit Nanny Fulham."

"And Toodles and the dowagers?"

Millicent firmed her lips before saying, "They are getting up to no good, I'm sure. Keep going."

Interpreting Millicent's worried expression, Phillipa nodded. "And Evie expects you to make sure they don't burn the house down."

Millicent's shoulders sagged as she wailed, "How can I when I can't even gain access to the library?"

Smiling, Phillipa assured her, "Where there's a will there is always a way."

Meanwhile... On the road to Halton House

. . .

Fifteen minutes into their drive Evie shot Tom a quick glance. She wished she hadn't changed her mind. Now she would spend the night tossing and turning and worrying about Glenda.

Settling back, she tried to take her mind off her regrets. Suddenly, she looked up and exclaimed, "Bisham."

Tom eased his foot off the accelerator. "What?"

"Bisham. That's the name of the village up ahead. I could have said I was from Bisham."

Shaking his head, he asked, "Countess, do you want me to turn back?"

Evie brightened only to realize how absurd it would be to return to Thornbridge. Sighing, she shook her head.

However, during the rest of the return journey, she occupied herself with a list. First, she would find out all she could about the village where Nanny Fulham had settled.

She spent a few minutes berating herself for not finding out before. Of course, Glenda had told her about it but Evie now realized she had painted a rosy picture and she had never mentioned her aunt. Evie searched her mind and tried to remember if she had ever asked Glenda about her family.

Over the years, they had met regularly at local events both in the village as well as at Halton House and Glenda had always been a regular guest at the Christmas parties. Then, there had been the afternoon teas attended by the local vicar and other villagers. She'd had many opportunities to delve...

Had Glenda ever spoken about her family?

Since she had inherited the house, Evie had to assume there was no other family.

That led her to imagine what she would do in Glenda's place. If she didn't have any family and she suddenly inherited a house, Evie thought she would think twice before venturing into the unknown.

Why had Glenda moved away from the place where she'd always been happy?

"Countess," Tom snapped.

Jolted from her thoughts, Evie demanded, "What?"

Holmes echoed her demand with a bark.

"I don't know what Holmes is doing but you are obsessing."

Evie gaped at him. She wanted to deny it but she found that she couldn't.

"You're quite right, I am. I can't help imagining the worst... I'm convinced Glenda is facing some sort of adversity..."

As the sound of the motor drowned out her words Tom leaned in and she had to repeat herself.

Nanny Fulham's life at Halton House had been easy. If she now faced some sort of difficulty, would she know how to deal with it?

When Tom slowed down Evie realized he was about to ask if she wished to turn back.

Pushing out a breath filled with resignation, she signaled for him to keep going. "Yes, I'm sure," she said even before he asked.

In any case, if Glenda needed them, Evie trusted her to be sensible enough to ask for their help as they were close enough to drive back at a moment's notice.

*a*s they drove through the Halton House gates and along the tree-lined avenue Evie turned her thoughts to the days ahead.

The Christmas tree would be brought in soon and that always generated an air of excitement from everyone. Then, there would be the round of luncheons, the annual gift giving for the local parish children which would include an afternoon tea for everyone, while the local choir always enjoyed providing a round of Christmas carols. All that would be followed by several dinners with some guests spending the weekend at Halton House and, finally, there would be the Christmas Eve dinner and luncheon the next day...

Evie almost felt exhausted thinking about it all.

"I think you have an early arrival," Tom said and pointed ahead to a roadster parked outside the porticoed entrance.

"Oh, it's Phillipa." Evie's spirits lifted as she welcomed

the distraction Phillipa would provide. Then she remembered there would be other distractions. Evie laughed. "You'll find this odd, but it's always a relief to see the house still standing. Although, I can't imagine what I think Henrietta and Toodles might do."

"Not Sara?" Tom asked.

Evie hummed under her breath. "I always like to imagine Sara as the voice of reason."

Tom laughed. "I'm sure Henrietta and Toodles would have no trouble leading her astray."

Evie wondered what Henrietta and Sara would say about her suspicions. They'd both known Glenda the longest. If Glenda had been trying to hide something, they would have picked up on it straightaway.

Being back at Halton House, she hoped to put all her concerns behind her. In a sense, she felt Tom had been right about leaving it all alone, even if he had noticed something odd himself.

Evie acknowledged the fact she had been worrying like a mother hen. Her visit to Nanny Fulham had been full of expectations. Glenda's move away from the Halton House estate had been felt by everyone, including the villagers, and they all wanted Glenda to be happy in her new life. Anything short of perfection would be perceived as a failure by those who would have preferred she stay right here where she belonged.

Giving a small nod, she silently agreed to step back and let time take care of everything.

Right on the tail of that thought, she had another one... "Oh, I've just had the most marvelous idea. I'll engage Phillipa's assistance in suggesting Millicent visit Mrs. Green for some new clothes."

Tom brought the roadster to a stop right beside Phillipa's motor car. He sat back and looked at Evie. "Are you sure that's a good idea?"

Heavens, whenever Tom questioned one of her ideas it seemed he had found some sort of hole in the plan.

Evie pictured the scene. She would take Phillipa into her confidence and then the young playwright would go forth and casually suggest to Millicent she could have some new dresses made to match her new position...

Liking the idea, Millicent would trot off to visit Mrs. Green and, in no time, she would have a new wardrobe. All achieved without the drama of being overwhelmed by the offer.

"I don't see anything wrong with my plan. Apparently, you do."

Tom nodded. "Millicent is trying to avoid setting a foot wrong. Once Phillipa makes the suggestion, Millicent will toss and turn and worry herself sick and then she will finally bring the subject to your attention and she will, no doubt, eventually figure out you were the instigator of the suggestion and she will be plunged into a week-long silence which will send the entire household into a state of panic when she makes one of her middle of the night announcements."

Evie rolled her eyes. "Tom Winchester, you take far too much pleasure in teasing me."

Laughing, he jumped out of the motor and walked around it to open her door.

Evie gathered Holmes against her and climbed out, saying, "As I've never cared to take myself too seriously, I hope to always be your source of amusement."

"I'll do my best, Countess."

A footman opened the front door and just before they walked in, Evie scooped in a breath, rolling her eyes as she heard Tom laughing under his breath.

"Yes, I'm bracing myself," she admitted. "Experience has taught me to tread with care."

"So far, so good," he said as they walked in and found the hall empty.

Evie wished they had timed the silence because she was sure it only lasted for a second.

Millicent and Phillipa came stampeding down the stairs at the same time as the doors to the library were flung open and Henrietta, Toodles and Sara rushed out.

Everyone talked at once, clamoring for Evie's attention.

When Millicent suddenly fell silent, Evie looked around the hall. Her gaze landed on the library doors and she saw Edgar emerging from the library. Without bothering to study the situation, she knew his appearance had caused Millicent's momentary silence.

Why had her new secretary been struck by the sight of him coming out of the library?

Evie didn't have time to answer the question because everyone's clamoring for her attention increased.

Tom leaned in and said, "Do you wish me to call for silence?"

It wouldn't be such a bad idea as she couldn't understand a word anyone was saying.

Putting Holmes down, she straightened and removed her gloves.

Edgar hurried toward her to take her coat.

"Edgar."

"My lady. I trust you had a pleasant journey."

The clamoring for her attention continued.

"Yes, thank you. Nanny Fulham sends her regards." Smiling at him, Evie noticed Edgar doing his best to avoid Millicent's glare.

Trouble in paradise? Evie wondered.

It wouldn't be the first or the last time, she thought.

Sighing, she turned her attention to her family and friends. Somehow, she managed to smile. Even as she noticed their attempt to grab her attention had switched and they were now squabbling amongst themselves. All except Millicent and Phillipa who took advantage of the opportunity.

"Milady, thank goodness you've arrived," Millicent said.

"Millicent. You all look so flustered. Has something happened?"

Millicent's cheeks colored. "Yes. Actually, no, not exactly, milady. I mean…" She glanced at the dowagers and Toodles and lowered her voice, "They refused me entry into the library and heaven only knows what they were doing behind closed doors and now I find Edgar has been there all along."

"Refused you entry?" Evie did her best to sound astonished.

"Yes, milady. Steven stood guard at the door and then he chased me along the hall."

"Chased you?"

Millicent gave a vigorous nod. "I planned on entering the library by the other door but he guessed my next move and gave chase."

"Oh, dear. Do you wish me to have a word with Steven?"

Millicent thought about it and then gave a reluctant shake of her head. "It might be best if I deal with the matter myself. I just felt you should know. It's dreadful that I should even bother you with such a trifling matter."

Evie bought herself some time by searching for Holmes, but she needn't have bothered as, instead of trotting off in search of a treat, Holmes had made himself comfortable by her feet and was looking at everyone with rapturous attention.

"You do what you think is best, Millicent."

"Evangeline," Henrietta burst out. "My apologies for interrupting, Millicent, but we have been waiting all afternoon."

Evie didn't dare look at Tom. Once again, she felt she didn't need to see his face to know he was smiling with amusement. "Henrietta, what can possibly be so urgent?"

"Well, since you ask…" Henrietta looked at a loss for words. "Actually… it's not really urgent. Although, when opinions vary so much, one does need to consult with a neutral party."

Toodles snorted. "All the varying opinions seem to be of your own making."

"Evangeline, they are ganging up on me. I have spent the entire afternoon trying my best to placate their increasing demands and criticisms and this is all the thanks I receive…"

The sound of the dinner gong drowned out Henrietta's voice. Caught by surprise, Henrietta looked around. "Heavens, is that the time?"

Instead of continuing with their grievances, Henrietta, Sara and Toodles all turned and headed for the stairs, followed by Millicent who hurried off saying, "I haven't even started to think about your evening outfit, milady..."

Bemused and puzzled by everyone's reaction, Evie turned to her butler. "Edgar?"

"Yes, my lady."

"Is your watch running fast? I could have sworn we still had an hour to go before you rang the dressing gong."

"Oh, yes... indeed, my lady. My apologies." He looked up and toward the stairs. "I suppose we can't call them back now."

"No, I don't suppose you can." She was about to turn when it occurred to say, "I assume the reason they are going upstairs is that they have moved in."

"Indeed, my lady. Lady Henrietta thought it best to spend a few days here while we..." Edgar cleared his throat. "Well, we are in the middle of..."

Sparing him the ordeal of breaching the code of secrecy, Evie said, "Yes, I suppose you are all rather busy and, sooner or later, we'll find out all about it."

A nudge from Tom drew her attention to the fact Phillipa stood nearby. "Phillipa! I haven't had the opportunity to welcome you."

"I made good time driving here. I hope you don't mind."

"Heavens, of course not. In fact, your timing is impeccable." Evie didn't explain but she felt she and Tom would need someone on their side to even the odds.

Turning to Edgar, Evie said, "As it is nowhere near the dressing hour, we will have some tea in the library, please."

Edgar stared at Evie without blinking. "Begging your

pardon, my lady. I think it might be more comfortable to have your afternoon tea in the drawing room."

Glancing toward the library, Evie wondered if she should ask for an explanation but, after the confusing welcoming party, she decided against it. "Very well."

She led them through to the drawing room with Holmes following at her heels. Settling down on a chair by the fireplace, Evie shook her head. "Tom and I were only gone for a few hours and now we've returned to a house in disarray. Do you know anything about it?" she asked Phillipa.

"I don't actually have all the details. Millicent and I have been upstairs unpacking but she mentioned something about having her authority undermined."

"Really? By whom?" Evie asked only to realize the answer had already been provided by Millicent.

"Well, it seems her presence was not wanted in the library."

"Oh, dear. The dowagers and Toodles have been working on a surprise pantomime. At least, that's what I think they're doing. They seem to be intent on being quite guarded about it all."

"Yes, I gathered as much." Brightening, Phillipa asked, "Did you enjoy your visit?"

"I wish I could say we did..." Evie's thoughts trailed off. Looking up at Tom who stood by the fireplace, she winced. "Tom, I'm afraid I'm regretting not stopping in the village."

"I thought you'd overcome that, Countess."

"Well, I can't seem to let it all go." She turned to Phillipa and explained about their suspicions.

"You think Nanny Fulham lied about being happy in her new home?" Phillipa asked.

Evie nodded. "It's possible she misled us to save face. Although, she's most likely to want to spare us the added concern, especially at this time of year. Also, I don't know her as well as the others do, but I know enough about Nanny Fulham. She's not the type of person to discuss personal issues."

"And you didn't snoop around the village," Phillipa said.

"I'm afraid I discouraged Evie," Tom offered.

Looking puzzled, Phillipa said, "But you noticed the odd behavior. Do you think you imagined it?"

"I'm afraid not," he admitted. "There might be something going on there but I suspect it might have to do with Nanny Fulham being new and the villagers not having had the opportunity to become better acquainted with her."

"Or it could be something really bad," Phillipa suggested.

Tom groaned. "Please don't encourage Evie."

"Tom seems to think Nanny Fulham should sort this out by herself. I happen to disagree." Evie sat back and folded her arms. "She's always avoided confrontations, that much I know."

Edgar walked in carrying a tray. Setting it down on a table, he stepped back.

"Edgar."

"My lady."

"Did my eyes deceive me or did I see you emerging from the library?" Evie teased.

Edgar glanced toward the door and was probably

wishing he had withdrawn when he'd had the opportunity instead of lingering.

"Edgar, I think the Countess wishes to know if you are in cahoots with the dowagers and Toodles," Tom said.

"In cahoots?" Edgar sounded offended. "That would suggest we were conspiring."

"Edgar, there's no need to fret. I'm sure whatever you're all up to is quite harmless." Evie stood up and walked to the table to help herself to some tea. "Edgar, do you remember Nanny Fulham ever mentioning her aunt?"

The question took him by surprise. He stood with his hands clasped behind his back and appeared to search his mind. "This is odd. I don't believe she ever mentioned her."

"Do you know if she actually expected to inherit or if it came as a surprise to her?"

"I'm afraid I couldn't really say. Come to think of it, she's never been known to talk about herself. I suppose that's because she lived here for most of her life and everyone knew her."

Except, Evie thought, they didn't...

Evie noticed Phillipa frowning. "Have you thought of something?"

Shrugging, Phillipa said, "I never met her. I assume she was your husband's nanny."

"Yes. Nicholas was very fond of her."

"Did she move on to another position?"

"No. She was given a cottage." Evie turned to Edgar. "Do you remember how that came about?"

"I'm afraid not, my lady. It all happened well before I arrived at Halton House."

Following Phillipa's train of thought, Evie realized

Nanny Fulham would have been quite young and nowhere near retirement age. "Perhaps Henrietta will know." Evie took a sip of her tea and sighed. Everything really did feel better after a cup of tea but if dinner turned out to be anything like the reception they'd received, she might end up needing more than a cup of tea to get through the evening.

CHAPTER FIVE

Dinner, Halton House

When Evie and Tom came down for drinks, they found Henrietta deep in conversation about the weather and the condition of the roads. Words flowed with ease and everyone appeared to be fully engaged.

Evie imagined they had all decided to behave and avoid whatever lingering issues they had argued over that day, each one taking turns to fill in the silence. When it was Toodles' turn, she chatted about her news from home saying Evie's three cousins had all asked if she ever intended returning home.

"They must miss you," Sara said.

"Nonsense," Henrietta muttered. "They've had her for a long time. Now it's our turn."

Henrietta's remark took everyone by surprise.

"It seems we're stuck with her," Tom whispered. "Henrietta doesn't want to relinquish her sparring partner."

At a signal from Edgar, Evie said, "Shall we go in now?"

During the entrée, Evie tried to find the best way to introduce the subject of Nanny Fulham without leaving herself open to further questions, but she had to compete with the others.

Henrietta and Sara spoke at length about the decorations in the village, something Evie hadn't noticed on their return, such had been her lingering preoccupation.

Finally, Evie found the perfect opportunity when Henrietta asked if the villagers of Thornbridge had decorated their village.

"I'm afraid we didn't notice. That probably means there weren't any decorations. Did you see any, Tom?"

"There might have been a wreath on a door... I can't say for sure."

Before anyone else could speak, the question erupted from her lips, "Henrietta, that reminds me about something Phillipa said. Did something happen to prevent Nanny Fulham seeking employment elsewhere?" Evie winced. A bull in a china shop would have been more sensitive.

Instead of a prompt response, Evie got silence. She thought she might have imagined an exchanged look between Henrietta and Sara.

If the question had taken them by surprise, they did not immediately show it. However, they seemed to be eager to avoid the subject.

"Is it my imagination or is this soup salty?" Sara asked.

Henrietta disagreed, saying, "If anything, it needs more

salt. Perhaps only a pinch. I wonder how that term came about?"

"Which term?" Sara asked.

"A pinch of salt. I don't actually pinch the salt. I simply pick up the salt shaker and… shake it over my food." Almost as an afterthought, Henrietta turned to Evie and said, "Nanny Fulham was provided for and then Nicholas offered her the cottage so she could remain at Halton House."

"Provided for? By whom?"

"I'm not quite sure. I only know she didn't have any financial concerns."

Edgar and the footmen began serving the next course, offering everyone a momentary diversion.

"What I don't understand is why she remained here instead of moving on to another position," Evie said.

Rearranging the vegetables on her plate, Henrietta said, "That's all I know. Indeed, that's all I cared to know."

"Do you think her aunt…"

Before Evie could finish her question, Sara interjected, "We liked Glenda enough to not ask questions."

What on earth did that mean?

Did Sara and Henrietta have questions about the arrangement? Questions they had never asked?

Evie reached for her wine glass. Instead of offering clarification, Henrietta and Sara had managed to make her more curious.

A young woman going into service to work as a nanny didn't suddenly retire after their charge grew too old to have a nanny. They generally moved on to another position.

Why hadn't it occurred to her before? Evie had never

given it any thought and then Phillipa had brought it to her attention...

As she continued to look at her wine glass, she tried to remember what she'd been about to ask Henrietta.

Then, she was sidetracked by another thought.

Taking a sip of her wine, she realized Nicholas would have been too young to make any decisions about Glenda's future.

She looked at Henrietta and Sara.

Suddenly, it looked as if they were hiding more than what went on behind closed library doors.

Henrietta must have noticed Evie's continuing mulling over the subject. "Evangeline, sometimes we must accept things as they are and leave them alone."

If only she could.

"Have you all sorted out your differences?" Tom's unexpected question distracted everyone, especially Henrietta who embraced the change of subject.

"Why, whatever do you mean?" Henrietta looked around the table but no one offered their support.

"When we arrived, you seemed to be at loggerheads over something or other," Tom offered.

"Nonsense. We only ever have lively discussions to spare ourselves the tedium of always agreeing about everything."

Tom's eyes twinkled. "So, you *were* arguing."

Henrietta brushed off his remark by saying, "We might have talked over each other, but we never expressed anger."

As Edgar and the footmen cleared the plates and served the next course, Henrietta brightened and began telling a tale about some gossip she'd received in a letter concerning a dance party given at Stafford House. The moment she exhausted the subject, she launched a thorough explanation of the history of the house.

Thinking it best to abandon the subject of Nanny Fulham, Evie said, "The second son of King George III."

Everyone looked at her.

"What about him, dear?" Sara asked.

"Earlier, Henrietta couldn't remember who had built Stafford House. It just came to me and I believe construction commenced in 1825. Unfortunately, the Duke died before the house was completed. I believe the house takes its name from the man who purchased it."

They all turned their attention to their meals again.

After only one bite, Sara said, "Is Nanny Fulham happy in her new home?"

Evie blinked and struggled to find a response. Luckily, Tom came to her rescue by answering, "Glenda is perfectly happy. She was eager to hear news about you all and she was particularly keen to learn what you were doing back here at Halton House." Tom looked at Evie. "We weren't sure what to say."

Henrietta took a quick sip of her wine and changed the subject. "Phillipa, that reminds me why I was telling everyone about the dance party. It was attended by an Australian."

"Really?"

"Oh, you shouldn't be so surprised, my dear. There are quite a few of your compatriots calling England home now. In fact, this person married a peer. She met him in Egypt during the Great War. You see, she came over on a tour with her mother and then war broke out and her brother was stationed in Egypt so she and her mother set off there and rolled up their sleeves, so to speak. In fact, their work nursing soldiers was highly commended. Anyhow, the Prince of Wales calls her a divine woman."

"Well, if I ever wondered how one married a peer, I now have my answer," Phillipa said.

To Evie, it seemed quite evident Henrietta had tried to divert the conversation away from the subject of their activities.

Just then, Tom drew Evie's attention by saying, "Evie, I'm trying to remember what lie we told Nanny Fulham about Henrietta."

Henrietta jumped in and, once again, diverted the conversation by saying to Phillipa, "You don't have the full story, my dear. You see, the peer I mentioned was injured and he ended up in hospital where your compatriot had been nursing her brother. They fell madly in love and refused all advice against the marriage. It is my understanding there had been a great deal of opposition as the man she fell in love with had a history of gambling."

Phillipa smiled. "Heavens, I wouldn't know what to say if someone introduced me to a peer I fancied on sight."

"As it happens, this lady married him and only a couple of years ago attended a dance party and met the Prince of Wales for the first time. Despite being married to a titled gentleman, she quivered with anxiety and asked her companion what she should say to the Prince of Wales. Her friend urged her to curtsey to the ground, call him sir and treat him like dirt."

Phillipa exploded with laughter. "Surely not."

"Indeed. I have it on good authority those were precisely the words of wisdom imparted to your fellow Antipodean."

This time, Phillipa snorted. "I've never taken to that reference. It makes us sound like strange little creatures which crawl out of the sea to feast on ants."

That remark prompted Henrietta to launch a discussion about the strange wildlife inhabiting Australia only to then resume her tale about the dance party.

Despite coming by the information secondhand, Henrietta left no detail out, most of which she would have known from her own experiences attending such grand events at said house. Indeed, she even noted the powdered footmen, yet another source of amusement for Phillipa prompting Henrietta to explain they only had their wigs powdered, not their entire bodies.

Sara steered the conversation away by saying, "You haven't said much about Nanny Fulham's new situation."

To Evie, it seemed odd that Sara should continue to pursue the subject since she had earlier tried her best to dismiss further discussions about Glenda's past. Was she now concerned about Nanny Fulham's welfare?

"What's there to say? She lives in a village much like ours and spends her time doing what she loves doing."

Their dinner turned into a battle of wits, with everyone intent on avoiding straight answers and changing the subject when confronted with direct questions. All this resulted in an amusing evening.

Every time Henrietta fell silent, either Tom or Evie taunted her with a question about their activities behind closed doors. That, in turn, prompted Henrietta to continue entertaining them with her convoluted stories, which seemed to have no point to them.

Later that evening, when Evie retired to her room, she walked in and collapsed onto her bed.

"Milady!"

"I'm exhausted, Millicent. And I can't remember why Tom and I decided we shouldn't tell…" Evie stopped and sat up. "Oh, never mind all that." She walked over to the dresser and removed her earrings. "Remind me tomorrow to sit down and discuss the lady's maid position. We really must decide where we are going to advertise it." When Millicent didn't respond, Evie turned. "Millicent? Is everything all right?"

"Yes, milady. It couldn't be better."

"So why are you pursing your lips?"

"Am I?"

"Yes, I believe you are."

Millicent shrugged. "Perhaps I'm still a little annoyed at the secret goings on around me. I don't see why the dowagers and Toodles think they need to work behind closed doors. I can be trusted."

"I shouldn't worry too much about that, Millicent. It has nothing to do with lack of trust and, I believe, it really has to do with Henrietta and the others not wishing us to see them in full swing of their creative process."

"It seems silly. We could help."

"Ah, yes, indeed. But they probably don't want our help."

"It's just the way they went about it, milady. I wouldn't be surprised if they put up a Do Not Disturb sign on the library door."

"We should actually be grateful they have something to keep them busy. Oh, before I forget, could you spend some time tomorrow asking around about Nanny Fulham? I want to know if anyone ever heard her talking about her aunt."

Henrietta and Sara did not wish to talk about the circumstances of Nanny Fulham's arrangement in staying on at Halton House even after she had concluded her duties as nanny. That much had become quite clear to Evie.

"I doubt anyone will know anything, milady. I only knew her from the times she attended the fêtes here at Halton House and I don't remember her ever talking about anything personal or asking anyone personal questions. I suppose that was her way of avoiding awkward questions."

Evie imagined everyone would have a similar opinion and the less people revealed about Glenda, the more curious she would become.

Someone had to know something.

"I'd still like you to try, Millicent. Perhaps someone will remember something."

"I'll do my best, milady." Millicent sighed. "I wouldn't be surprised if I'm told to mind my own business."

"Why would anyone say that to you?"

Millicent hesitated but Evie could see the need to unburden herself in the way she pursed her lips.

"Is this about your authority being undermined?"

"I have only been your secretary for a short while and it seems everything has changed."

"Are the others treating you differently?" Evie hoped that wasn't the case. She didn't want her household to be in discord.

"They're not. At least, not until today."

"Oh, Millicent. You know the circumstances were exceptional."

"Were they? How so, milady?"

"Henrietta was behind it all. In a sense, I fully understand her. Everyone always knows what everyone else is doing." With one exception, Evie thought, and insisted someone had to know something about Nanny Fulham's past.

She offered Millicent further reassurances and then bid her a good night.

As Evie drifted off to sleep, she remembered wondering if Henrietta and Sara knew more than they were letting on about Nanny Fulham. If they did, they were determined to keep the information to themselves.

What could she do to encourage them to talk?

And…

Could the secret be so bad they would continue to refuse to talk about it?

CHAPTER SIX

The next morning

*E*vie studied her reflection in the mirror and made sure she hadn't missed any buttons. "Millicent, will there be any surprises when I go downstairs for breakfast?"

She glanced over her shoulder and saw Millicent stop in mid-stride. Instead of providing a quick assurance, Millicent actually stopped to think about it.

"Well… I want to say everything is quite normal…"

"But?"

"As I came up, I noticed a couple of averted glances."

"And what did you make of that?" Evie asked.

"It could be nothing or it could mean the footmen couldn't bring themselves to look me in the eye in case they gave something away."

Intrigued, Evie asked, "What do you think they might be hiding?"

"I know Steven still feels awkward about yesterday's incident but he is also working on a Christmas gift and, of course, he wants it to be a surprise. I'm sure I'll love the little box."

"How do you know that's what he's making?"

Millicent grinned. "He loves working with his hands and I've seen him trek out to the stables every day and look over his shoulder before disappearing inside. Everyone knows he's set up a small woodworking area there. Nothing is so obvious than a man trying to keep a secret."

Evie smiled in agreement. "I'm as ready as I will ever be to face the day." She walked to the door. Before opening it, she stopped to entertain a stray thought.

Had Henrietta actually told them about the gossip she'd heard or had that tidbit been lost in her effort to divert their attention away from whatever she was hiding?

"Is something the matter, milady?" Millicent asked.

Sighing, Evie shook her head. "No, everything is perfect, Millicent."

Evie made her way downstairs and walked into the dining room in time to see Edgar casting a surreptitious glance at his watch. She guessed her butler needed to be someplace else...

"Good morning." Smiling, she walked to the sideboard and helped herself to some breakfast. Sitting down opposite Tom, she asked, "Tom, are we the only ones down for breakfast this morning or have the others already eaten?"

"You're the first one to come down, Countess. You might want to hurry."

"Why?"

Lowering his voice, Tom said, "Edgar has already tried to take my plate away twice. I think he's in a hurry to get going."

Taking her time to butter her toast, Evie said, "I am famished. Yes, I believe I could have a feast this morning. As the saying goes, breakfast like a king, lunch like a prince and dine like a pauper. I'm quite happy to tackle the first one, at least."

Out of the corner of her eye, she saw Edgar draw in a deep breath and release it as a sigh of resignation.

No one actually expected him to stand by just in case they needed a fresh pot of coffee. In that regard, Edgar imposed his own rules. A footman could just as easily do the job, but he preferred to do it himself.

Or so she thought...

The door to the dining room opened and a footman walked in. Edgar's relief registered in his bright eyes and smile. The footman took his place and, giving a small nod, Edgar made his exit.

"Surely they can't be rehearsing this early in the morning." Evie glanced at the footman. "I'd send Steven to investigate but I doubt he'll be pleased to leave his post. In many ways, Edgar's authority undermines mine and I do not wish to meddle with defining lines."

"I take it that means you will not be interfering with Millicent's dilemma."

Evie took a bite of her toast. As lady's maid, Millicent ranked high in the order of things below stairs. In fact, if she wished, she could have a maid bring her breakfast in bed and draw her a bath every morning. She knew of several titled ladies who extended that privilege to their lady's maids.

In any case, Millicent certainly received far more respect than a house maid. As her secretary, she had taken a step up the ladder, something which should afford her even more respect... Although, it seemed, that was yet to be determined.

The door opened and Phillipa walked in. As she greeted them, she exclaimed, "Something's different."

The footman cleared his throat, almost as if he wished to give her a hint.

"Edgar just stepped out," Evie explained.

"That's it. I always expect him to be standing by, ready to do your bidding."

Evie laughed. "Good heavens, you make me sound like a tyrant."

Phillipa raised a hand in apology. "I'm still getting used to the idea of people having butlers and an army of servants."

And yet Evie knew Phillipa hailed from a well-to-do family in Australia.

"All I can say is that we are living in interesting times." Any moment now Evie expected Henrietta and the others to burst in with... well, that would be a surprise. "Did you sleep well?"

"Well enough considering I stayed up half the night writing. I found last night quite entertaining."

"Marvelous. We inspired you. Will you be working on that today?"

Phillipa lifted a cover on one of the dishes and helped herself to some bacon and eggs. "I might but only if I can work out the next scene." Sitting down opposite Evie, she added, "The lady of the manor is having a conversation with her lady's maid. I know, that's rather close to home but I promise to change the names."

Evie remembered the conversation she'd had with Millicent the previous evening. She hadn't said anything in strict confidence. However, now that she thought about it, everything Millicent had talked about suggested she might be doing a great deal of soul searching.

Among her many grievances, Millicent had also been preoccupied with the many changes they'd all experienced over the last few years, starting with the Royal Family changing their name to Windsor and then accepting commoners as prospective wives for their sons. She'd also been fascinated by the fact thespians could now be presented at court. Mostly, Millicent had been trying to make sense of the changes brought about by the end of the war. Everyone had rejoiced and they had continued to rejoice. Life had become one great big party with no one taking anything seriously because there had been enough of that during the war.

Nodding, Evie decided Millicent had merely been trying to put everything into perspective. She'd hate to think her new secretary was unhappy with her lot in life.

"Millicent enjoys talking about anything and everything for no particular reason and I find her chatter quite soothing. What are you thinking of including in your play?"

"Maybe yesterday's episode. Apparently, it all happened just as I arrived but I missed witnessing it firsthand. I'll ask Millicent how she feels about it."

"She'll probably be thrilled to bits," Evie said. Or she

might decide it wasn't appropriate for the Countess of Woodridge's secretary to divulge detailed information and that could lead her straight into a week-long silence...

Dismissing the thought, she turned to Tom, "Is there anything of interest in today's newspapers?"

"I couldn't tell you. The newspapers haven't arrived yet."

"Oh, that's unusual." She turned to Steven. "Do you know anything about it?"

"No, milady. There's someone on the lookout for the delivery boy."

"I hope he hasn't met with an accident." She looked toward the windows. The skies looked quite drab and, by the looks of it, it had rained a little overnight. "The roads can become quite muddy and dangerous... Steven, go down and tell Cook to have a cup of hot chocolate ready for the boy, please."

When Steven hurried out, Phillipa leaned in and whispered, "That's very considerate of you. Not everyone would think of it."

"Perhaps not in town but it's a different story out in the country. Regardless of people's station in life, everyone knows everyone. At least, that's been my experience here."

After a few minutes of silence, the absence of conversation became almost uncomfortable. "Surely we don't need the morning's news to provide us with a subject for conversation."

"Speak for yourself, Countess. I usually wake up with a blank slate in my mind. If not for the newspapers, you'd hardly hear a word out of me. Actually, I'm surprised you don't have a new theory."

"About what?"

Tom studied his piece of toast. "Henrietta and Sara appear to be keeping more than one secret."

He'd noticed!

"There's no harm in that. I'm sure they know what they're doing. Anyway, I suppose we should enjoy the peace and quiet while it lasts. The next few weeks are going to be extraordinarily hectic."

"With more surprises along the way, no doubt," Tom said.

"Pleasant ones, I hope. I'm sure you're alluding to whatever Henrietta and the others are plotting and I trust they're putting their minds to something entertaining. I do enjoy a good pantomime."

When Steven returned carrying the morning's newspapers, Evie found herself breathing a sigh of relief.

He set the newspapers down on the table. "They've just been pressed, my lady."

"Do we know why they were late?"

He gave a small nod. "The lad ran into a delay in the village, my lady."

"Nothing serious, I hope."

"I'm afraid I didn't ask." Steven cleared his throat and looked toward the door. "Edmonds wishes to speak with you, my lady."

"Oh, do ask him to come in."

Her chauffeur walked in, his steps tentative, his expression uncertain.

"Good morning, Edmonds."

"My apologies for interrupting your breakfast, my lady."

"Is everything all right, Edmonds?"

"I'm afraid I've heard some news in the village this morning and…"

Evie put her hand up to interrupt him. "Edmonds, could you please find Millicent and tell her you wish to see me. Oh, and also tell her the news."

Looking confused, Edmonds said, "My lady?"

Evie avoided looking at Tom but she knew he was smiling.

Strictly speaking, Millicent's role as her secretary did not involve managing her social activities or day to day running of the estate. Rather, Millicent's focus would be on assisting her with her investigations but Evie felt this might go some way toward making up for the previous day's incident.

"Indulge me, Edmonds."

"Very well, my lady." He turned to Steven and whispered, "Do you know where I can find Millicent?"

Steven shrugged.

Nodding, Edmonds swung around and made his way out.

Sensing Tom looking at her, Evie shrugged. "I am trying to restore Millicent's confidence and… authority."

"You might have let Edmonds tell you the news first," he suggested.

"That would have been silly."

Ignoring Tom's lifted eyebrow, Evie took a sip of her coffee.

"What if Millicent decides you shouldn't be bothered with the news?" Phillipa asked.

Oh, dear. That hadn't occurred to her.

Nodding, Tom said, "The power might go to her head."

To her relief, Millicent appeared at the door to the

dining room. "Begging your pardon, milady. Edmonds has some news he thinks you'll be interested in." Signaling to Edmonds, who stood by the door, Millicent stepped aside.

Edmonds walked in and, with another prompt from Millicent, said, "It's about Nanny Fulham."

Evie gasped. "Nanny Fulham? Has something happened to her?"

Edmonds nodded.

Evie's voice hitched. "Why didn't you tell me... I mean... What's happened to her?"

"She's been accused of stealing three French hens."

CHAPTER SEVEN

*E*vie remained speechless for a full minute before exclaiming, "Three French hens? Where on earth did you hear that?"

Edmonds glanced at Millicent. When she gave him an encouraging nod, he continued, "When the newspapers didn't arrive this morning, I headed over to the village and found the postmistress in a state of distress. That's probably why the newspaper delivery was delayed." Edmonds shrugged. "She's in charge of organizing it."

Evie called for patience and hoped Edmonds would get to the news.

Edmonds stopped to gather his thoughts. "She was in a state of distress because she'd just received a worrying message. As you know, she manages the telegraphic communications. Anyhow, she received news from her counterpart in the village of Thornbridge about Nanny Fulham being in a pickle."

"What?"

Edmonds nodded. "That is how she described it."

"Can this be confirmed?" Evie asked. She knew rumors could spread with great ease and without any verification of their truthfulness. What if someone had set about spreading a malicious lie about Nanny Fulham?

Her fingers curled into a tight fist. If anything, this provided the proof she needed and an excuse to return to Thornbridge. Despite Glenda's assurances, her peace of mind was under attack.

"Did the postmistress have any other information?" Tom asked.

Edmonds shook his head. "That's as much as I could get out of her. She left her husband in charge and hurried out."

No doubt to share the news with everyone interested in Nanny Fulham's wellbeing, Evie thought.

By now, the entire village would know and, perhaps, even beyond.

"It can't possibly be true." Evie gave a fierce shake of her head. "Why would Glenda steal chickens?"

"Not chickens, Countess. French hens. I'm sure there's a difference. They were probably a special breed."

"No doubt about that," Edmonds said. "I happen to know they're *Faverolles*."

Evie puzzled over that. Before she could express her dismay, Millicent said, "Why would someone have French hens? What's wrong with our British hens?"

Everyone agreed, while Evie remained somewhat impartial. "We actually have some Rhode Island Red chickens. So I'm not entirely opposed to international breeds. However, this sounds like a lot of nonsense."

Everyone agreed.

"Edmonds, how do you know about their breed?" Evie asked.

Edmonds looked down at his shoes. "I'm sure it doesn't mean anything but... Nanny Fulham happened to mention the *Faverolles*... before you arrived, we were chatting... if you remember, I'd been having a cup of tea..."

Nanny Fulham had known about the hens? "Do you happen to remember how or why she came to mention them?"

"I'd been asking her about her neighbors and she mentioned one had a passion for collecting different breeds of chickens."

"What are you going to do?" Phillipa asked.

Evie felt everyone's attention turn to her as if she alone could provide a sensible course of action.

She definitely had to do something. Especially as the accusation of theft could be linked to the animosity Tom and Edmonds had sensed. Heavens, what if all this escalated to something really serious?

But what could she do?

"I'm sure the local constabulary will refuse to take the matter seriously."

"Are you really sure about that, Countess?"

"Tom. You seem to expect me to take immediate action." Only the day before he'd seen no reason to intervene by snooping around.

"You must admit there is now more reason to look into whatever this is," he said.

She wouldn't argue with that. In fact, Evie thought it almost felt as if the problem was reaching out to her and seeking her out, but how would she justify returning to Thornbridge?

Glenda hadn't asked for assistance. This suggested she wished to keep her troubles to herself.

"Thank you, Edmonds."

Evie sat back and drummed her fingers on the table. Could she have prevented this from happening? The question hovered unanswered for several minutes until she decided she had no way of knowing.

Drawing in a fortifying breath, she gave a small nod and stood up.

Everyone looked at her with hope in their eyes. She didn't need to explain herself but she could tell by the slight widening of their eyes they hoped she would share her thoughts with them.

Evie walked to the door. Sensing everyone's eyes still on her, she hesitated, stopped and turned to say, "I'm going to make a telephone call."

She walked out of the dining room, her brisk steps a testament to her determination. Crossing the hall, she headed straight for the library only to find the door closed.

In all the years she'd lived at Halton House she'd never known the door to be closed.

She turned the door handle and to her dismay, she found the door had been locked.

Locked?

Frowning, she bent down and looked through the keyhole. "That's odd." She couldn't see anything. It was almost as if something had been placed over it.

Still frowning, she walked around the corner and headed for the other entrance to the library. Before attempting to turn the door handle, she pressed her ear to the door and could have sworn she heard a panicked commotion inside.

Hurried steps approached the door. As the person reached the door, Evie turned the handle but met with resistance.

Not quite believing someone stood on the other side blocking her entrance, Evie turned the handle again. This time, she managed to push the door open a fraction.

There *was* someone on the other side preventing her from opening the door!

"Hello," she said.

"Yes?" came the soft reply.

She couldn't tell who had responded.

"Henrietta? Is that you?"

"No, dear."

"Sara. Please let me in."

"I'm afraid this is not a good time, dear."

"*Sara!*" Evie snapped.

She heard Toodles say, "You're all in trouble now. Birdie used her angry tone."

She didn't have an angry tone. How could Toodles say that about her? Clearing her throat and lifting her chin, Evie declared, "I need to use the telephone."

A whispered conversation followed. Then, Sara said, "Could you be a dear and use the telephone in Edgar's office downstairs?"

For the briefest moment, she considered going down to the butler's office only to dig her heels in. Evie drew in an exasperated breath. "I'm afraid that is not possible. This is an emergency."

Another hurried discussion followed before Sara said, "In that case, you'll have to give us one minute, please."

Frowning, Evie tapped her foot. "Very well, you have one minute."

She heard a scramble of footsteps headed toward the other door. Leaning back, she considered edging toward the hall to see if they had all made their swift exodus but she didn't need to as she heard their footsteps receding. A second later, someone yelped.

Not bothering to find out what that had been about, she eased the door open and, peering inside, she didn't see any trace of their activities. Whatever they had been doing here remained a secret.

Shaking her head, she headed for the desk and sat down to place the telephone call.

A short while later...

Evie returned to the dining room and sat down to finish her coffee. Mulling over the telephone conversation she'd just had, she didn't even notice her coffee had gone cold.

"Countess, are you going to keep us in suspense?" Tom finally asked.

Surprised, she lifted her gaze from the cup. "Oh, I didn't mean to." She set her cup down and smiled. "I telephoned Detective Inspector O'Neill." Distracted by another thought, she dropped her gaze to stare into her cup of coffee again.

"Yes?" Tom prompted.

Evie looked up but remained lost in thought.

"Your telephone conversation," Tom prompted again.

"Oh, I asked if he had a moment to contact the constabulary at Thornbridge. He said he would look into the matter and let me know as soon as he found out something."

"Did you tell him about our suspicions?"

"I gave him a brief explanation." She picked up her cup. Seeing it empty, she looked at Steven who promptly refilled it for her. "Thank you, Steven." Sensing Tom still looking at her, she said, "I suppose you want to know how the detective responded."

He nodded. "I am interested."

"Apparently, it's enough that we actually noticed something odd. It seems the detective now trusts our intuition."

"I'm surprised you're not rushing to Thornbridge," Tom said.

"And do what? We don't have all the details. I'm hoping this accusation will not be taken seriously. However, there is still the question of why someone made the accusation in the first place and therein lies the root of the problem."

"As you often say, it's all about asking the right questions," Tom suggested.

Evie looked confused. "Do I say that often?"

"I'm sure I've heard you say it at least once."

"That doesn't qualify it as a recurring trait," Evie murmured and nibbled the edge of a piece of toast.

They all fell silent, broken only when Evie asked, "By the way, did I imagine hearing someone yelp?"

The edge of Tom's lip kicked up. "No, you didn't imagine it. That was Millicent."

"Oh? What happened?"

"She thought she saw a ghost."

"A what? Where? How?"

Trying to keep a straight face, Tom said, "As she walked out of the dining room, she looked up and saw a specter floating up the stairs. She was wearing some sort of gossamer gown. She described the specter as having deadly white features and startled eyes."

"Henrietta? They must have been having a dress rehearsal." Expecting the day to become more demanding, Evie finished her breakfast.

Phillipa stood up, saying, "I have Millicent's permission to use a version of yesterday's incident so I should sit down and do some writing."

That took a load off Evie's mind as she felt too distracted to be good company. "There's nothing we can do about this matter until we receive some information from the detective so I'm going to attend to another task. What about you, Tom?"

"I'm sure the library is still out of bounds." Shrugging, he stood up. "I'll find something to keep myself occupied."

"You can actually use the library." Evie dug inside her pocket and produced a couple of keys. "I locked it so they can't go back in."

The drawing room

. . .

Evie looked at the clock on the mantle. It had only been five minutes since she'd last glanced at it.

Belatedly, she wondered if she should have spoken with more urgency. Then again, she didn't make a habit of disturbing the detective every day so he must surely know this was a matter of urgency.

Heavens!

What if her lapse in judgment put Glenda's life in danger?

Millicent cleared her throat.

That drew Evie out of her reverie. "My apologies. I've lost my train of thought. What were we talking about?"

"You wanted me to post an advertisement in *The Lady* and you were trying to work out the wording. Then, I suggested I should learn *Pitman's* shorthand and learn to use a typewriter and you agreed."

Evie gave her a bright smile. "Millicent. That is splendid. How can you possibly remember all my ramblings?"

"I have no idea, milady. There are so many thoughts floating around my mind and then there's everything you say... By the way, it was very kind of you to tell Edmonds to seek me out. When he found me, he looked thoroughly confused saying he didn't understand why he couldn't tell you the news directly. I told him to play along and not question your way of doing things."

The door to the drawing room opened and Steven walked in and set a tea tray down.

"Thank you, Steven."

When he left, it occurred to ask, "Do you know if Steven is happy being a footman?"

"I'm sure he is, but why do you ask, milady?"

"We don't have an under-butler."

"He's the head footman, milady. So it goes without saying."

"Well, I'd like to make it official. Perhaps you can convey the message to Edgar. Unless you think by doing so he will feel undermined and threatened."

"It would serve him right if he did feel that way, milady. If you don't mind me saying so, milady, he has taken full advantage of you, abandoning his post without even asking you for permission."

"It didn't even occur to me. But we can't lock horns with Henrietta. If she wants Edgar for her pantomime, then she will have him. Anyhow, what have we decided to do about the lady's maid?"

Millicent stared at her for a moment. "You decided to place an advertisement in *The Lady*."

"Did I? Oh, didn't you just say I did?" Not once, but twice, Evie thought. "What happened to trying something different?"

"You're still thinking about it."

She hadn't actually given it a moment's thought.

"We might need to abandon that idea or, rather, the lack of one. I'm sorry, Millicent. My mind is otherwise engaged."

"It's perfectly understandable, milady. You're concerned about Nanny Fulham. We all are. For what it's worth, I don't for a moment think she stole those French hens."

"Nor do I. But someone believes she did."

Did they have proof or was this a malicious rumor being spread about Nanny Fulham? Why would someone do that?

The door to the drawing room opened and the

footman walked in. "Begging your pardon, milady. Mr. Winchester asked me to tell you Detective Inspector O'Neill is on the telephone."

Evie shot to her feet and hurried out. When she reached the library, she almost skidded to a stop. There, she found Tom talking on the telephone, his tone jovial and quite chatty.

When he saw her, he said, "Here she is, detective."

Evie took the telephone. Hurrying through the pleasantries, she asked, "What did you learn, detective? Are the rumors true?"

"I'm afraid so, milady. Not only has a complaint been lodged but there are several witnesses."

"Witnesses? What do they say?"

"One says she saw Miss Glenda Fulham stealing the chickens."

"French hens," Evie murmured, her tone distracted.

"Pardon?"

"I doubt it's of any importance, detective, but they were actually French hens." Evie pressed her finger to her temple. "Is it a reliable witness? I mean, why do they think it was Glenda?"

"To quote the statement given by the witness, she looked guilty hurrying off carrying a large bundle."

Evie could hardly believe what she'd heard. "That could have been anyone and… anything. A bundle of… stale bread for cooking… or… or coal. She might have run out of coal or wood. Detective, please tell me you think this is all nonsense." Before he could answer, she said, "My apologies. I didn't mean to put you in the awkward position of taking sides."

"This is rather problematic, milady. The crime is as serious as poaching."

"They're saying the French hens were poached?"

"Actually, they were roasted."

"Pardon?" It was Evie's turn to sound confused.

"Bones were found buried in her garden."

"They could have been buried by anyone," Evie complained.

"Indeed."

Sounding exasperated, she said, "Were they French hens' bones? How could anyone possibly tell the difference?"

"The feathers, milady, were buried right alongside the bones. I'm afraid she will be charged with the theft of the French hens."

CHAPTER EIGHT

"**W**ell?" Tom asked.

Evie pressed her hands to her cheeks. She turned to look at the telephone she had just set down and considered contacting Lotte Mannering. The lady detective would surely know how to proceed.

"I cannot believe it. The police are taking the theft seriously. She will have to answer to the charges."

Tom nodded. "Shall I get the motor car ready?"

Evie looked at him as if he'd spoken in a foreign language.

Yes, of course, they needed to rush to Nanny Fulham's rescue but, first, they needed a strategy.

Frowning at the thought, she tried to determine what she meant by it.

A strategy required planning, but she didn't even really know what they were up against.

Prejudice against the newcomer?

Jealousy?

After all, Nanny Fulham had inherited a substantial property.

"I'm jumping to so many conclusions…"

"Do you believe Glenda stole those chickens?"

Evie shook her head. "No and now I'm obsessing about the reasons for the accusation." She looked up at the ceiling and growled. "We can't just ride in like the cavalry. I mean, I do want to go and give her our full support but what good will that do? We need to get to the bottom of whatever this is?" She looked at Tom and waited for him to say something. "You're supposed to ask how I think we should proceed. I'll spare you the trouble because I have no idea."

Tom stepped away and went to stand by the fireplace.

"If you're going to apologize for discouraging me earlier, please don't. I believe we now have good reason to return and we are quite justified in meddling, but I also think we need to find a way of doing it that will allow us to ask questions."

"Are you suggesting we should disguise ourselves?" Tom asked.

Evie nodded. "It's what Lotte Mannering would do." Swinging away, Evie walked around the library. "If we return, everyone will know we are there to offer Nanny Fulham our support. How do you think the villagers will react to our presence?" She didn't wait for Tom to answer. "They will resent us and clam up. I'm sure there are more than a couple of people involved in this accusation. So far, we know there is the owner of the chickens…"

"French hens," Tom corrected.

"The owner of the French hens and the person who

claims they saw Nanny Fulham hurrying away with a bundle." Evie's arms lifted and fell. "What sort of proof is that? Anyhow, let's not forget the people Edmonds heard talking about the choir and the ones you saw at the pub. They are likely to side with the owner of the French hens and support everyone who claims to be a witness."

"Are you suggesting the villagers are colluding?"

"I honestly don't know what to think. Also…"

"What?"

Evie went to stand by the window. "We do need to ask the right questions and I believe Henrietta and Sara will have some answers." There had been something curious about the way they had both behaved the previous evening during dinner, Evie thought.

"Do you think Nanny Fulham's past has something to do with this?" Tom asked.

Evie shuddered. Earlier, she hadn't wanted to jump to any conclusions or even think about taking any action until they had more information. Now they knew the police were proceeding with charges. Now they needed to act.

She turned to face Tom. "Why? Why would anyone accuse Nanny Fulham of theft?"

The door to the library opened and Phillipa and Millicent peered in.

"I hope we're not interrupting," Phillipa said and stepped inside. "Only… we were eager to know if you'd received good news."

"I'm afraid not." Evie turned to Millicent. "Please find Edmonds and get him to drive you to the village. I need you to talk with absolutely everyone and try to find out what they know about Nanny Fulham. If anyone is reluctant to speak, don't take no for an answer. Keep prodding until you get something out of someone."

Millicent gave a vigorous nod and rushed off.

Evie brushed her hands across her face. "And suddenly I'm jumping into action and acting with urgency. I hope this doesn't make matters worse for Nanny Fulham."

"Perhaps you should contact Lotte Mannering and ask if she has any suggestions," Tom turned to Phillipa and explained, "Evie thinks we'll need to disguise ourselves."

Phillipa smiled. "That shouldn't be too difficult."

Evie sighed. "I'm not so sure about that. Quite a few people saw us yesterday and, of course, they'll recognize the roadster."

Phillipa shrugged. "Find another vehicle. Tom's very good at doing that. Oh, and take me along with you. You say people have already seen you but they haven't seen me."

Evie didn't feel at all convinced this would work. "How will that help?"

Phillipa sat on the edge of the sofa. "You're right in thinking you should disguise yourselves."

"We might be able to change our appearances and avoid recognition but I'm sure they'll remember Tom's accent."

"That's not a problem. There are lots of Americans here. The trick will be to divert everyone's attention from what they know and assume about you and show them something else."

Tom nodded. "You sound confident. I think I should go procure a vehicle and leave you to work out the details."

"Good idea. We'll have everything plotted out and scripted when you return."

Managing to produce a smile, Evie said, "First, you might need to explain what you just said about showing people something else."

"Oh, it's simple. Think of a thespian… a well-known stage actor. Everyone sees photographs of him so they know what he looks like. Then, he goes on the stage and puts on a performance which mesmerizes everyone into accepting an entirely different character. He is no longer the actor. Instead, he is whatever role he is playing. In real life, the man is debonair and quite handsome but, on the stage, with the right make-up, clothes and acting abilities, he can turn into an indigent person…"

"Oh, Lotte did that once. In fact, she had no trouble making us all believe she was quite mad."

Phillipa laughed. "I don't doubt that for a moment."

Easing into a chair, Evie leaned forward. "We need people to feel comfortable enough with us to open up and answer our questions. We can't pretend to be mad."

"Let me think about it for a moment."

Evie didn't want to discourage Phillipa. However, she had no experience disguising herself. She assumed it would take a great deal of talent and imagination. She knew Lotte completely embraced her roles, even going as far as changing her speech pattern and the way she walked.

Phillipa straightened. "I know what we can do."

Oh dear…

"You look worried. You shouldn't be."

"I think I'll reserve judgment until after I've heard your idea."

"We could pretend we are from a film studio in Hollywood. That's where all the studios are."

"What?"

Phillipa nodded. "It's perfect. Most photoplays are filmed in studios but some intrepid directors are moving away from that and want to film their photoplays in realistic settings. We could say we are looking for a perfect English village to use for a movie." Phillipa looked up in thought. "That's actually a really good idea. Perhaps I'll try my luck in the moviemaking industry."

Evie shifted to the edge of her seat. "I'm all ears."

"What was I saying?" Nodding, Phillipa continued, "Oh, yes, people are enthralled by the idea of being on the large screen. We could entice them further by saying we are looking to use locals in the photoplay."

"But we won't have any equipment."

Phillipa grinned. "We don't need any. We are in the early stages of production and merely looking around."

"What role do you think I could play?"

"You could be a director or... a producer."

"What about Tom?"

"He could be our chauffeur or another producer."

"But if we disguise ourselves as Hollywood people, how are we going to approach Nanny Fulham?"

Phillipa sat back. After a moment, she smiled. "We could let it be known we are driving around looking for an ideal house. Does she live in a cottage?"

"No, it's more like a small manor house."

"Perfect. If anyone asks, we could say we think the house is ideal. Of course, we'd need to speak with the owner. That will justify our visit to Nanny Fulham."

Evie looked up at the clock. Tom had only been gone for a few minutes. She had no idea how long it would take him to procure another motor car. Meanwhile, Millicent and Edmonds would probably spend the rest of the morning in the village...

"I suppose we should find suitable clothing. What does a photoplay producer wear? Should I be flamboyant or businesslike?"

"Do you have a beret?"

"Yes, I'm sure I do." Rising to her feet, Evie scooped in a big breath. "Dark spectacles. I have a couple of pairs."

"Perfect."

They both made their way upstairs to Evie's bedroom and rummaged through her wardrobe looking for suitable clothing.

"I've just realized, we don't know how long this will take." Should they pack for several days or could she resolve this matter in one day? "Oh, if we stay longer than a day, we'll have to think about accommodation."

"I assume there's a pub," Phillipa said.

"Yes."

"We could telephone ahead and ask if they have any rooms available. While we're at it, we could ask if anyone else with American accents have come by that way recently. If they say yes, I could then sound worried about our competition sniffing around the village. I'm sure that will intrigue them and I'll have the opportunity to hint at our reason for visiting the village."

"Have you done this before?" Evie asked.

"Lied my way into a house? I believe I have. In fact, I'm sure that's how I ended up here the first time."

SONIA PARIN

Evie dug around her wardrobe and emerged with a beret and a velvet cloche hat. "Try these on." Handing the hats over, she resumed her search through her wardrobe. "What do artistic types wear?"

"Play it safe and wear black."

"Won't we look somber?"

"Nondescript," Phillipa suggested. "It will help our disguise."

Opening a drawer, Evie declared, "I found the spectacles. One is tinted gray/black, the other is greenish."

"Do you have bright red lipstick?" Phillipa asked.

"I'll have a look around. There might be one given as a gift by one of the cosmetic girls a while back. Millicent doesn't like throwing anything away because, in her opinion, you never know when it might come in handy." As she searched for it, she asked, "How do you think we should act? When Lotte disguises herself she appears to change her entire personality."

"I'm inclined to say we should be reserved, but if we all act in a reserved manner we will end up looking rather somber." Phillipa hummed in thought. "I'll create a couple of characters. I could be the type with a will of iron but lively and chatty in a businesslike way, tempered by humor."

"That sounds convincing."

Phillipa drummed her fingers against her chin. "As for you... Can you be languorous?"

"You'll have to give me some clear directions."

"Make your gestures dreamlike." Phillipa swept her hand out. "Like a reed swaying in a pleasant breeze or the gentle lapping of waves against the shore. You walk as if

86

in a dreamlike state. Your voice is a diaphanous whisper... Think of yourself as a lazy lady."

Diaphanous whisper? Lazy lady?

Holding up the lipstick, Evie stretched her hand out, her gesture slow like a ballerina's. "Is that what you want?"

Phillipa nodded. "Perfect."

"They'll think I'm drunk."

Grinning, Phillipa nodded again. "And they won't suspect you of prying into their business."

"Oh, you are a genius."

"Thank you. I try my best. Now, say it again but let your words waft out."

"*Oooohhhh, you arrre a geeeenius.*"

"*Bravissima!*"

"Oh, dear... drawing out the vowels made me lose my train of thought."

Phillipa tried on the tinted spectacles. "They sit comfortably."

Taking the other pair, Evie put them on. "I purchased them in Paris one summer and can't remember ever wearing them. We spent a few weeks in St. Tropez and didn't see anyone else wearing them." She turned to look at her reflection. "How do I look?"

"You definitely look the part. Like someone who's spent time in an opium den."

"Will that work in my favor?"

"Anything that distracts people from the real you will work in your favor."

"I'll have to practice stretching my vowels and sounding impervious." Looking at the clothes she'd pulled out of the wardrobe, she said, "I suppose I should hunt down some luggage."

An hour later, they made their way to the library, both dressed in their black clothes, hats, and tinted spectacles.

"Am I walking right?" Evie asked. "Or should I try to look more bored."

"It can't hurt. Before I forget, I should telephone the pub in Thornbridge," Phillipa said.

"While you do that, I'll sit and practice being languorous."

In the middle of making a swaying gesture with her hand, Tom walked in.

Evie raised her arm and waved... languorously.

"Hello," he said, his tone cautious.

"Helloooo."

Tom's eyebrows lifted slightly. It took him a moment to recognize Evie. "Countess?"

"Noooo."

"No?"

"I am... Estelle Buchanan."

Turning, Tom spotted Phillipa sitting at the desk talking on the telephone.

He turned back to Evie who lowered her tinted spectacles, and said, "Yes, it is me."

"What's... going on?"

"I am in disguise and being languorous. Did I really fool you?"

"As a matter of fact, yes, you did. What else have you done to yourself?"

"Oh, nothing much. These are my clothes, but I'm posing as a creative, nonchalant person."

"You're slumping and waving your hands about."

"I'm reclining." Smiling, she nodded. "And it's working. Also, I'm wearing a beret and these tinted spectacles."

"Dare I ask?"

"The spectacles? Oh, I suppose they are meant to make me look mysterious or impervious. Perhaps even a person of dubious character who indulges in illicit substances."

"Is that why you're slurring your speech?"

"I'm a creative." Evie waved her hand. "My mind is filled with... creative ideas."

"I see. And will Phillipa be slurring her words too?"

"No, she will be my opposite... Oh, Phillipa hasn't come up with a disguise for you. What would you like to be?"

"I don't mind just so long as I don't have to slur my speech."

"We are all in the film industry." Realizing Tom hadn't been there to hear Phillipa's idea, she filled him in on the rest.

Tom frowned. "I don't know anything about that."

"You have a Brownie camera. That's all you need to look the part. Anyhow, did you manage to find a motor car?"

He nodded. "It's an Austin saloon. We should be quite comfortable."

"Maaaarvellous. We have some luuuggage."

"We do?"

Sitting up, Evie pushed back her tinted spectacles. "Yes, we decided we should play it safe. Although, I'm hoping this won't take too long as Seth will be arriving in a few days' time. Oh, dear. I just remembered. Seth is coming for Christmas."

"Are you going to start worrying about setting a bad

example? I should think you'd be more worried about being chased out of Thornbridge."

"Oh, Phillipa is sure we'll have the villagers wrapped around our little fingers. She thinks everyone wants to be in motion pictures."

Phillipa finished her telephone conversation and joined them. "They have rooms available so I made tentative bookings for the three of us."

"Did they ask any questions?"

Phillipa nodded. "The man I spoke with was curious about my Australian accent but then lost interest in that when I told him I'd be arriving with a couple of Americans in tow eager to find the perfect location for their next photoplay."

"Fabulous. You paved the way for us." Smiling at Tom, Evie explained, "Phillipa believes we can create our own scenario."

"A mirage?"

"Yes. People will believe what they see in front of them."

"Well, then... You seem to have everything under control. I suppose I should go throw some clothes together." He turned only to stop. "So... Am I expected to change?"

"Oh, no. Everyone needs a straight man," Phillipa said. "You can come as yourself. Although, you might want to be suave and perhaps a little abrupt."

"Suave *and* abrupt?"

Evie agreed. "Oh, yes. We are going to dazzle and distract the villagers."

"Yes, but are we still on a rescue mission to clear Nanny Fulham's name?"

"That, my dear Tom, is the whole purpose of this charade." Evie jumped to her feet.

"Countess, you forgot to be languorous."

"Yes, I became distracted. I just remembered, before we leave I need to have a word with Henrietta and Sara. I need to be quite alert for that encounter."

CHAPTER NINE

*All the world's a stage, and all the men and women merely
players*

William Shakespeare

As Evie made her way up to the attic, she warned
herself to proceed with caution. Both Henrietta
and Sara had already shown their reluctance to talk about
Nanny Fulham's past. While they had been disinclined to
reveal what they knew, Evie hoped this latest development would change their minds.

She reached the attic doors and, not surprisingly,
found them locked. "This is only a minor hurdle. First, I
have to get them to open the door." When her knock on
the door went unanswered, she tried knocking harder
and pressed her ear to the door.

What if they were in the far corner of the attic and couldn't hear her knocking?

They were definitely inside. The locked door confirmed that.

She called out their names. When that failed to produce the desired result, she tried calling out Edgar's name. As her butler, he would feel duty-bound to respond.

Unless, of course, the others pulled rank.

"Evangeline!"

Caught by surprise, Evie jumped back. She couldn't help looking over her shoulder thinking the voice could have come from anywhere.

However, to her relief, the door eased open a fraction. She leaned in and saw an eye peering back at her. "Henrietta. I need to have a word with you."

"This is not a good time, Evangeline."

"I'm afraid it's an emergency."

"Another one?" Henrietta sighed. "Very well."

"It's about Nanny Fulham." Evie told her about the theft of the three French hens.

"What nonsense," Henrietta declared.

"I agree. Unfortunately, the local police have decided to take the matter seriously."

"How can we help?" Henrietta asked.

Evie took a gamble and said, "You and Sara seem to know something about Nanny Fulham's past."

The door edged close. Before Henrietta could completely close it, Evie pressed against it and as the door opened wider, she came face to face with a ghost.

Unprepared and caught by surprise, she yelped. "Good

heavens!" It took a moment for Evie to remember Henrietta had dressed up as a ghost but she hadn't expected her to look so convincing. Not that she'd ever seen a ghost before...

"Evangeline, there is nothing to be gained by exposing Nanny Fulham's past. I know she wouldn't be happy about it."

"What if this incident is somehow related to her past?"

"I don't doubt it," Henrietta murmured.

Evie frowned at the remark. "Then, tell me what you know."

"It's not my tale to tell, Evangeline. We must respect Nanny Fulham's privacy and that is all I'll say on the matter. You will have to sort this out some other way." The door shut and the key turned.

For the second time, Henrietta had refused to tell her what she knew.

While dismayed by Henrietta's stubbornness, Evie realized the information she withheld had to be quite significant.

She didn't have time to engage in a battle of wills. Right now, they needed to return to Thornbridge.

As she made her way downstairs, she tried to think of reasons why someone would keep a secret. As Henrietta had said, it wasn't her tale to tell. Loyalty and empathy came to mind. "It must be a sensitive matter."

She reached the hall and found Tom and Phillipa had already loaded the suitcases into the motor car and were waiting for her.

"Countess, you don't look happy. Does that mean Henrietta refused to talk to you?"

"She talked to me. She just didn't tell me what I wanted to know. Now I'm worried because she said it's not her tale to tell." Henrietta had sown the seeds of curiosity the first time she had alluded to it. Now, Evie's curiosity had sprouted.

"That confirms it," Phillipa said. "There is something in the nanny's past and it might be related to what is happening now."

Evie's nose crinkled. "I'm hoping that is not the case. If it is, we'll have to pressure Nanny Fulham into revealing her secret and I wish to spare her further embarrassment."

"Shall we go?" Tom asked.

Surprised by Tom's sudden eagerness, Evie nodded. "Yes, please. Oh…" She looked around the hall but didn't see Holmes. "We can't take Holmes with us. Someone might have seen me in the car with him and they'll make the connection..."

Just as she was about to go searching of him, Steven appeared and she charged him with the task of looking after Holmes.

As they set off with Tom doing the driving and Evie and Phillipa sitting in the back seat, Evie dug around her mind trying to remember if she'd ever heard whispers about a scandal in Glenda's past but her thoughts were interrupted when Phillipa asked, "Is that Millicent?"

Looking out the passenger window Evie saw Millicent and Edmonds standing outside one of the village stores.

When Tom stopped the vehicle, Evie waved and called out Millicent's name. Her secretary and chauffeur looked in their direction. After a brief exchange, they approached them, their steps tentative.

"I don't think they recognize us, Countess."

"You might be right." Waving, Evie called out again, "It's us, Millicent."

Despite hurrying her step, Millicent's eyebrows were drawn down into a look of suspicion. When she finally recognized them, she ran toward them, exclaiming, "Milady! I thought you might be white slave traders."

Phillipa whispered, "Did she say slave traders?"

"Best not to ask," Evie murmured. "It probably has something to do with a newspaper article she read."

"Milady!" Millicent leaned in and peered inside the motor. "Why are you all dressed in black and... why are you wearing those dark spectacles?"

"We are in disguise, Millicent." Evie told her about their plans to entice the local villagers to talk. "Have you been able to find out anything?"

Millicent shook her head. "Edmonds and I were just on our way to visit Mrs. Leeds. She's very fond of *Flake* chocolate so we went to the store to get some. Personally, I don't care for the way the chocolate breaks off. Anyhow, we hope the sweet will soften Mrs. Leeds into confiding in us. You see, she knew Nanny Fulham the longest." Millicent dug inside her handbag. "I also picked up a bar of *Mr. York's Motoring Chocolate*. You should take this with you in case something happens along the way and you get hungry. Did Cook pack you a basket?"

"I'm afraid I didn't think of it. In any case, the village isn't far and Tom can manage any problems we might encounter."

Millicent didn't look convinced. Nodding, she said, "We should hurry. Mrs. Leeds enjoys a bit of chocolate with her cup of tea."

With a wave goodbye, Tom got them on their way. Once they cleared the village, he asked, "Are you eating that chocolate now?"

Evie looked down at the bar of chocolate, only then realizing she'd peeled off the wrapper and had eaten half of it. Swallowing her mouthful of chocolate, she asked, "Would you like some?"

"No, thank you. I'm too busy trying to avoid an incident on the road which would require us to stop and rely on our one and only *Mr. York's Motoring Chocolate*."

Apologizing, she said, "It only goes to show how preoccupied I am." She turned to Phillipa and offered her some chocolate.

Declining, Phillipa said, "You'll probably be surprised to learn I don't have a sweet tooth."

Evie slipped the remaining bar of chocolate inside her handbag. "I wonder if it would have been easier to pretend to break down near the village."

"Would you have given people your real name?" Phillipa asked.

"No, and I see your point. Regardless of how we arrive at the village, we can't do so as ourselves. And, yes, I am experiencing a few doubts. Mostly, I'm afraid I won't be able to keep up the charade. Lotte Mannering is quite a natural at it. Within a short time, she can go from being one character to another."

"I'm sure she's had years of experience," Phillipa offered.

In reality, Evie couldn't stop worrying about their meddling. Had she remembered to assure Nanny Fulham they were only a short distance away and ready to assist with anything?

"In case anyone is wondering, I will take full responsibility for dragging us into this."

Phillipa smiled. "It's kind of you to offer, Evie, but I'm

used to barging in where I'm either not welcomed or expected."

During the remainder of the journey, Evie puzzled over Henrietta's behavior. She hadn't been overly concerned by the news of the theft. In fact, she'd been more preoccupied with keeping her rehearsal a secret. It seemed unusual, especially as she was so fond of Nanny Fulham.

"We've arrived. Are we ready?" Tom asked.

Remembering to employ a languid tone, Evie said, "Oh, I suppose it's time to mesmerize everyone into telling us the absolute truth of the matter." If only it could be as easy as that, she thought. With any luck, Phillipa's ploy would work a treat, with everyone eager to ingratiate themselves. "Tom, did you remember to bring your little Brownie camera along?"

"Of course."

"Wonderful. I'm glad you thought of it. At least, you will look the part."

"We've been noticed," Phillipa said and gestured ahead.

A woman walking along the main street stopped to look at them. She carried a large bag, quite possibly full of groceries. As Tom continued on, the woman set the bag down and turned to follow their progress.

"She's intent on having a tale to tell when she arrives home," Evie mused. "There's no point in arriving home and saying you saw an unfamiliar motor car unless you can also say if it stopped in the village."

Approaching the pub, Tom slowed down.

Evie glanced over her shoulder and saw the woman still watching them. "She will want to know if we are going inside the pub. Once we do, I imagine she'll hurry home and send her husband to investigate. We should take note of the number of people in the pub. Within a short time of our arrival, I believe the number will have increased."

Phillipa said, "We've already made our bookings so at least one person knows of our arrival and he has my name. He will most likely have told everyone present."

"Oh, that reminds me. What names are we using? They'll have to be easy to remember. I think I'd like to be Marjorie Dubois."

"That's not the name you gave me earlier," Tom said.

"Well, I can't remember what it was. Marjorie is much easier and I had an aunt named Dubois. She married a Frenchman."

"Wasn't Glenda's aunt named Marjorie?" Tom asked.

"You're right. Should I stick with Marjorie? It might trigger a response." As the motor car continued on, Evie leaned forward. "Tom, you've just driven past the pub."

"Indeed, I have, and now I'm turning."

"May I ask why?"

"We are on a scouting mission," he explained. "Despite our long journey... I assume we have journeyed far, we are eager to take in the sights." As he spoke, he continued driving and heading toward Nanny Fulham's house.

When they reached it, he slowed down. The drapes in the windows in the front room were drawn open. Belatedly, Evie wished she had asked the detective about the process of accusation. Would the local constabulary take Glenda into custody? Or would they merely issue her with some sort of order to appear before the magistrate to answer to the charges?

Tom continued driving at a sedate pace, slowing down even further when they approached a farm.

Relieved he hadn't stopped outside Nanny Fulham's house, Evie said, "As much as I wish to know how Glenda is, we need to remember we are here to gather information from the villagers without giving away our identity."

Pointing ahead, Tom said, "That looks like a large estate. I wonder if it's owned by a titled gentleman."

They tried to see as much of it as they could before a copse of trees blocked it from view.

"It actually looks like a larger version of Nanny Fulham's house," Tom observed.

Evie dug around inside her handbag and produced a little black book in which she wrote, "Find out who owns the large house."

Phillipa chirped, "I've just realized I'll get to watch your methods of investigation in action."

"Some people would say there is method in my madness. Most of the time, I think there is madness in my method."

"So... what are you doing right now?" Phillipa asked.

"Observing. I haven't seen a single farmhouse in disrepair. That's always a good sign of prosperity and a good landlord." She looked toward the large manor house but it was now well and truly hidden by trees.

When Tom turned and headed back to the village, Evie made a point of keeping an eye out for the large manor house. As they neared Nanny Fulham's house, it finally came into view again.

Even from a distance, she could see the similarities in architecture. Had Glenda's house once belonged to the large manor house?

Reaching the village, he turned into the road leading away from the pub and meandered along all the little streets, obviously still pretending to show an interest in the idyllic setting.

By now, Evie thought the entire population of Thornbridge would know about the unfamiliar motor car driving around.

Finally, he brought the motor car to a stop outside the pub and they all took a moment to prepare themselves for the charade.

"Let me do the talking," Phillipa suggested. "I'll distract them with my ditzy blonde routine."

"You have a routine?"

Nodding, Phillipa said, "It comes in handy when I need to get myself out of a tight spot. Oh, and Tom… You could do something I've seen directors do."

"What's that?"

"You hold out your hands and form a square with your fingers and look through the square. It's like forming a frame for a picture. It's how directors decide on positions for their actors and the scenery behind them."

"It sounds simple enough and I'm sure everyone will think I've lost my marbles."

Drawing in a deep breath, Evie said, "I'm ready to sound disinterested and… languorous. Oh, I know… I could be against the idea of making the photoplay in this village and you could be all for it while Tom will remain neutral and quite busy taking his photographs. Make sure to capture anyone who looks suspicious, please."

As she climbed out of the motor, she looked up and was surprised to see the woman who'd witnessed their arrival still there. She had been joined by two other women.

"We must have driven around for half an hour. She's been standing there all this time. That shows a great deal of determination, especially as she had no idea we'd be coming back this way," Evie mused.

"Maybe the pub owner has already spread the word about our arrival," Phillipa suggested.

"I hope that's the case because I'd hate to think we've already been recognized."

CHAPTER TEN

he pub, like most of the other buildings in the village, had diamond shaped glass on their windows. Evie couldn't tell for sure but she thought she saw someone just stepping away from the window, suggesting their arrival had been witnessed.

Tom walked in first and Evie and Phillipa followed.

As weary travelers, they had decided to walk in and head straight over to a table, if they could find one. There, they could spend some time merely observing and perhaps having a drink while deciding what they would do next.

Giving her watch a glance, Evie saw that it was well after midday. With any luck, they shouldn't have any trouble finding a place to sit.

The chill of the day followed them inside and they all looked toward the large stone fireplace. Unfortunately, the tables near it were all occupied by a group of men dressed in their warm tweed coats.

Evie didn't see a single woman which made her

wonder about the men. Were they married and avoiding going home for their luncheon or were they attending to business in the strange way men usually did by visiting a club?

As expected, they all expressed their curiosity by turning to look at the new arrivals. A tall, brawny looking man with broad shoulders, cropped hair and his shirt-sleeves rolled up to his elbows walked past them carrying a tray stacked with plates and glasses.

He acknowledged them with a nod but continued walking.

While Tom and Phillipa made their way to a table, Evie followed several steps behind trying her best to look disinterested. She still wore her spectacles so she assumed the pub wasn't as dark as it seemed to be.

Instead of joining Tom and Phillipa at the table, she veered toward the fireplace and stood in front of it with her hands stretched out to capture the warmth.

The men at the nearest table didn't bother to hide their curiosity with the two men who had their back to her making a point of turning to look at Evie.

Ordinarily, Evie would have offered a polite smile. Not today, she thought. Remaining in character, she ignored them and looked thoroughly disinterested.

As soon as she sat down with Tom and Phillipa, Evie lowered her voice and asked, "Tom, is there anyone here you remember seeing yesterday?"

He gave a small nod.

As she had her back to the men, she asked, "Are they still looking at us?"

Again, Tom nodded.

Raising her voice, Phillipa exclaimed, "I think it's a

perfect setting. It's just the sort of village I imagined using as a backdrop for our photoplay."

Taking that as a cue, Evie gave a shrug of insouciance and, remembering to emphasize her vowels, she said, "I'm not so sure it's right. A film studio would be perfectly adequate."

At a nudge from Phillipa, Tom stretched his hands out, formed a square shape and pretended to look through it as he moved his hands across. "It has a nice atmosphere and there's enough natural light."

Just then, they were all startled by a hard thump. Evie signaled toward the window. "A black bird just smashed against the window. I do hope it's all right." She leaned forward and nodded. "Oh, yes. Look, it's unsteady but rejoining the three black birds on the building opposite. Is that an omen?"

"Four black birds? I'm sure that is a good omen," Phillipa said.

"No, I rather think not. Maybe the next village will offer something better." Evie heard a low murmur coming from the group sitting at the next table.

The barkeeper approached them to take their orders. The limited menu offered game pie or stew, which suited them perfectly. He did not ask if they were the ones who'd made the bookings for rooms. For the time being, at least, he just wanted to take their orders. With a small nod, he turned and walked away.

After a moment, Tom leaned in and whispered, "One of the men followed the barkeeper and now they're having a private conversation at the bar. They're both taking turns to look this way."

At least they had met with success and were generating interest. That's all that mattered. With any luck, someone would finally break the silence and approach them. If that didn't happen, they would simply have to think of a way to broach the subject.

Evie couldn't sit still and this made looking languorous difficult. She needed to speak with Glenda and make sure she was all right. For all they knew, she could have been hauled to prison. She had to be beside herself with worry. Evie simply couldn't understand why she hadn't contacted them to ask for help.

"We'll have to tell them," Tom murmured.

"What?" Evie asked.

He nudged his head in the direction of the barkeeper. "That's what he just said."

"How do you know?"

Tom shrugged. "I just know."

Evie frowned. "You guessed?"

Tom pushed out a breath and revealed, "I can read lips."

Evie forgot to be languorous. "You what?" She had a vague memory of once asking him if he could read lips and she didn't remember him owning up to it.

He shrugged. "It's a skill I developed during the war. When you're in the trenches, you can't always make yourself heard."

Astonished by the news, Evie looked over her shoulder. The man who had approached the barkeeper nodded and made his way to the door.

"I wonder whom they need to inform and what they need to let them know."

Was news of their arrival about to be shared with someone significant? Could they jump to conclusions?

Them...

Evie drummed her fingers on the table only to be stopped by Phillipa who reached across and put her hand on hers, mouthing, "Languid."

Evie switched to nibbling the inside of her lip as she thought every village had at least one large manor house owned by someone who had the greatest stake in land ownership in the area.

They had already seen such a house.

Did the barkeeper wish to inform the owners of the large house of their arrival? Or, did *them* refer to the people responsible for accusing Glenda of theft? In Evie's mind, she imagined several people coming together and organizing themselves to gang up on Glenda. *Them* didn't necessarily have to be the owners of the largest estate in the area, it could be a couple of villagers or... the entire village.

Their meals arrived. The barkeeper set a large tray down on the table and distributed the various dishes. Evie poured herself a cup of tea and both Phillipa and Tom enjoyed a glass of beer. As she sipped her tea, a leaflet on the tray caught her attention.

A glass of good beer is better than a pint of tea.

Tom must have seen it too because he smiled at Evie and raised his glass of beer in a mock salute.

When the barkeeper walked away, Phillipa asked, "What's that about?"

Tom explained, "I read an article about it in the newspaper. Brewing companies are taking a stand against the possible introduction of prohibition."

Puzzled, Phillipa said, "And what's the point of having that flyer in a pub? We hardly need to be convinced."

Evie set her cup of tea down. "I was focused on my tea. Did anyone notice anything about the barkeeper? Did he look at us with curiosity?"

Both Phillipa and Tom shook their heads.

"I was enjoying my beer so I didn't notice anything," Tom said. Lowering his voice, he added, "The fellow who walked out has been gone for about ten minutes. We'll have to wait a while longer to see what that was all about."

Evie tasted her stew and decided to suspend all her concerns so she could enjoy the meal. However, halfway through it, her worries returned and she wished she'd had more time to work on a better strategy.

Tom and Phillipa could have come here disguised as movie makers while she could have driven here with Edmonds and headed straight to Glenda's house. As she considered the idea, she realized there would have been issues of communication to deal with. Although... Edmonds could have acted as a messenger. She had no idea how Lotte Mannering managed to put her plans into action or, indeed, how long it took her to come up with a feasible plan.

Admittedly, she had acted on impulse. As soon as they'd heard the news about the accusation, she'd known they would have to do something.

Phillipa nudged Tom. "I think Marjorie is having a conversation with herself."

Resuming her role of Marjorie, Evie said, "I'm entertaining my doubts about this village. I do think the one we saw earlier has greater appeal and potential."

As she spoke, Tom's attention shifted to the men sitting at the next table. Evie interpreted the small nod he gave as confirmation they had heard her remark.

Continuing with the fictional tale, Phillipa suggested, "We should have another look around and then put it to the vote. Although, even before we do that, we should perhaps move on to the next village. You might be right..."

The edge of Tom's lip lifted and Evie assumed this meant he'd seen the men at the other table react to Phillipa's statement.

Evie finished her stew and sat back to sip her tea. At some point, they might need to go along with the idea of taking their search for the perfect village further afield so they could use the time to contact Millicent at Halton House. She knew they couldn't try to contact her from this village.

Evie imagined they could drive to the next village and use the post office there but what if the post office person became suspicious and conveyed the information back to the post office in Thornbridge? If she sent a telegram, they would see the contents of the message and if they had a telephone and she asked to use it, they would most likely overhear the conversation.

As she wondered what Lotte Mannering would do, the door to the pub burst open and a woman rushed inside. She looked about until she located the barkeeper. Approaching him, she had a frantic conversation with him.

"Five gold rings?" the barkeeper exclaimed.

The woman gave a vigorous nod and her voice hitched, "Mrs. Hardfellows said she stepped out of the house for only a few minutes and when she returned she just knew something was wrong. Sure enough, after a search through the house she found the gold rings missing from her jewelry box."

The men at the next table huddled together to exchange their opinions.

Hearing the murmurs, the woman looked over her shoulder and gave a firm nod. "Yes, there's a thief among us and we all know who it is."

Another incident?

And what did she mean they all knew who it was?

CHAPTER ELEVEN

Five golden rings?

*a*fter sharing the news, the woman rushed out of the pub and continued on her way, no doubt determined to reach everyone in the village.

The barkeeper was joined by a couple of people who walked in off the street, clearly eager to discuss the matter, which they'd obviously already heard about.

The woman hadn't actually named Glenda but, of course, she must have meant to implicate her.

Looking at the men sitting at the next table, Tom took the initiative and asked, "What was that all about?"

Before they could answer, the barkeeper walked up and cleared some plates, saying, "It's a small local matter. Nothing serious."

Why would he try to dismiss the incident and sweep it under the carpet?

Frowning, the barkeeper looked at Tom and said, "If you don't mind me saying so, you look familiar."

They all stilled.

Had they been found out?

They hadn't actually discussed what they would do in such a case. While they hadn't broken any laws, they had gone to the trouble of disguising themselves so they could engage with the locals and get the information they needed to understand why the accusation had been made against Glenda.

When they'd walked in, they hadn't introduced themselves as the people who'd booked rooms at the pub. However, the barkeeper must have made the connection.

If he recognized them as the people who had visited the village the previous day, they'd have to explain why they were now pretending to be someone else...

The villagers wouldn't take kindly to being duped and, with their disguises exposed, they wouldn't get any answers...

As had become her habit, Evie found herself wondering what Lotte Mannering would do if faced with such a predicament. She would soldier on, Evie thought. Yes, Lotte would definitely continue on with her charade or provide a reasonable, credible justification for her ruse.

The barkeeper crossed his arms and nodded. "Are you one of those movie people... an actor?"

Tom put on a great performance looking quite surprised. "Me? Oh, no. I'm strictly a behind the scenes man." He pointed to his camera and then stretched his hands out and formed a square through which he viewed the barkeeper. "You could be up on a big screen. Have you ever thought about it?"

The barkeeper leaned in slightly and appeared to be looking through Tom's square.

Straightening, he shook his head. "I wouldn't know what to do, I'm sure."

"Oh, it's easy," Phillipa chirped. "You just follow the director's instructions."

"I'd look like an old fool."

"You wouldn't," Phillipa assured him.

Brushing his hand across his chin, he studied Phillipa. While Evie couldn't tell how he would respond to the encouragement, for the first time since arriving in the village, Evie felt they were making some sort of progress. Phillipa had been right. The idea of appearing in a photoplay had him mesmerized. The men at the other table had fallen silent and were most likely picturing themselves appearing in a photoplay. She saw one running a finger along his moustache while another tried to flatten a wayward strand of hair.

"And you want to make one of those motion pictures in this village?" the barkeeper asked.

Phillipa nodded.

As they had already decided they would each take opposing sides, Evie saw her opportunity and gave a lazy shake of her head.

Seeing her, the barkeeper frowned.

"We're looking for a village with character," Evie said in her best languorous tone.

He looked startled and spread his hands out. "We have that in droves here."

Sitting back, Evie shrugged. "Perhaps but it might not be what we want."

Now he looked annoyed. "This is a perfectly fine village."

Struck by inspiration, Evie drawled, "Oh, dear. We are not exactly looking for perfect. You see, the camera captures absolutely everything. The story we're filming is dark in sentiment, very dark. So, a perfect village wouldn't suit at all."

His dark eyebrows drew down. "Like I said, this village has character."

Evie tipped her head to the side. "Mystery. That's what I'm looking for." She gestured with her hand, making a sweeping motion. "Something under the surface. You can't quite see it but it's there lurking in the corners."

Now the barkeeper looked puzzled.

"Layers," Evie continued her cryptic explanation. "On the surface everything looks perfectly fine, almost ideal, but underneath it all..." she sat back and, smiling, she lowered her voice, "there is something wrong. That's what I want to see."

He gave a stiff nod and said in a gruff tone, "We have plenty wrong here too."

Evie made a point of looking around. Humming, she said, "Really? Everything looks perfectly lovely."

He nodded again. "Trust me. We're not as ideal as we appear to be."

Evie shrugged and looked as though she'd lost interest.

Leaning forward, Phillipa lowered her voice, "Has there been a robbery in the village?"

"I'm afraid so," he said.

"Is this unusual?"

"We're a strong community. Nothing like this has ever happened here."

"Do you have a suspect in mind?" Phillipa asked.

The men at the other table must have overheard her because they all leaned forward and murmured their opinions.

"The police are handling it all," the barkeeper said. "When will you decide if you're going to make your movie here?"

Phillipa looked at Evie who shrugged and said, "I still think we should look at another village with more character and... more people. We haven't seen many people out on the streets."

The barkeeper reasoned, "It's winter. No one likes to venture out unless they absolutely have to."

"Do you have Christmas services at the church?" Tom asked.

"Of course." The barkeeper sounded offended. "And a choir. A very good one at that."

"I love a good choir," Phillipa exclaimed. "Do they practice often?"

Giving a distracted nod, the barkeeper continued to look at Evie, his eyebrows drawn down into a dark scowl. "Every other day."

Phillipa leaned in and whispered something to Tom.

"My friend here," Evie said and gestured toward Phillipa, "loves to sing in the choir and being so far from home..."

"She's welcome to join in. The more the merrier," he said.

And there it was again. Proof they were still welcoming people to join the choir, but not Glenda.

Why had Glenda been excluded?

Looking at Phillipa, Evie said, "Did you hear that? You

can join the choir here. Or, we could set off to the next village."

"We have rooms booked here. I say we stay for a while. We can always drive around..." Phillipa looked up at the barkeeper. "I should have said, I telephoned earlier to make a booking."

He nodded. "I'll make sure your rooms are ready."

Before Phillipa could confirm their booking or decide they would move on, he walked away.

So far, they had only managed to clarify one question. They were still welcoming people to join the choir. That only reinforced their suspicions. Nanny Fulham had been excluded on purpose and that meant she had been targeted. Why? Because she had only recently arrived? Surely that couldn't be the reason.

Tom once again turned to the men sitting at the next table. "Who owns the large manor house?"

One of the men provided the information with a sense of cheerfulness they hadn't seen since their arrival. "The Grahams."

There had only been a hint of deference toward the name. If the man had spat out his reply, Evie might have assumed the family didn't have his respect.

"And what about the smaller manor house near it?" Tom asked.

The men conferred with each other before one of them answered, "A newcomer."

This time, the information was delivered with less enthusiasm.

"Does *he* have a name?" Tom asked.

"It's a woman," the same man offered.

In Evie's opinion, his response hadn't answered the

question. Evie glanced over her shoulder and saw the men all looking askance as if trying to avoid eye contact with Tom.

Pressing for more information, Tom asked, "Does she have a name?"

Picking up his mug of beer, one of the men said, "She calls herself Fulham."

The man who spoke didn't express any disdain toward Glenda. In fact, his voice had been devoid of any expression. However, he'd answered at his leisure which might have given him enough time to reel in his true feelings and speak without any emotions giving away how he really felt.

Making sure the others heard him, Tom looked at Evie and Phillipa, and said, "That's the house we liked the look of."

Better and better, Evie thought. They now knew the name of the person who owned the large estate and Tom had just revealed they had an interest in Glenda's house so that would pave the way for a future visit without inviting suspicion.

With only a few hours of good daylight left and their meals finished, they each nodded and stood up. Evie couldn't see what more they could gain by remaining at the pub.

The men at the table followed their exit, each one making a small gesture by tipping their heads slightly.

Had they made new friends? Evie couldn't help smiling at the thought. After the way Glenda had been treated, it seemed unlikely that anyone living here would welcome an outsider.

Unless…

Unless the outsider had something to offer.

Stepping out of the pub and making sure they were well out of earshot, Evie said, "Well done, Tom and Phillipa. By the time the sun sets, everyone will know we're considering making a movie here."

"You played your role extremely well, Countess."

"Thank you. I'm becoming rather fond of being languorous. Although, it does take some effort. I keep having to think of those oppressively hot days in summer when everything slows down. I just hope it doesn't become a habit with me. Henrietta will do more than raise her eyebrows, I'm sure."

"What do we do now?" Phillipa asked.

Evie was about to answer when she saw Tom hunch his shoulders and look away. "What's the matter with you?"

"William," he whispered.

"Who?"

Looking over his shoulder, he straightened and repeated, "William. The farmer who lives across the road from Glenda's house. I didn't want him to recognize me."

Evie turned and saw the farmer walking into the pub. "Do you think he saw you?"

Tom shook his head. "He glanced our way as he crossed the street. I don't think he had a good look. Just in case, we should hurry."

The day looked thoroughly gray and the air had a chill that would eventually work its way to the bones. They still had a few hours before the sun set and they couldn't afford to waste them.

Evie hugged herself and turned toward the main street. She wanted to see Glenda and now they had the perfect alibi. However, curiosity compelled her to suggest they visit the church.

Making their way there, Tom pointed to a flyer on a store window.

Evie didn't bother to wonder if it had been left there as an oversight. They already knew the choir had room for more.

As the barkeeper had pointed out, they met every other day. Unfortunately, this happened to be the wrong day.

"Should we proceed?" Phillipa asked.

If they happened to find the vicar at the church, would he know anything about excluding Glenda from the choir? And, if he had some insight into the matter, would he share the information with them? Evie didn't think so.

"How can we justify going to see him?" Evie asked. "What will the vicar think if a group of strangers question him about the choir and about Glenda not being allowed to join?"

"He'll think he's been found out and realize he will face eternal damnation," Phillipa suggested.

"Good heavens, are we actually going to suspect a member of the clergy of... what? Malicious behavior toward one of his flock?" Evie shook her head. "We'll have to tread with care and come up with a better plan."

As Evie tapped her chin in thought, Tom suggested, "We could call on Nanny Fulham. It's what you've been wanting to do since we arrived."

Evie agreed. "Perhaps this time she'll be more prepared to open up to us." She tried to dismiss her first attempt to get Glenda to confide in her and did her best to focus on a better outcome." Oh, there's an idea. Once we establish that we've met her, and I'm sure people will notice us going to her house, we can then visit the vicar, bring up the subject and say we'd recently met someone with a beautiful singing voice who would be ideal for the choir."

Just then, she turned and saw a curtain shift in one of the windows. When she mentioned this, Tom stretched his arms out and made a square with his hands.

Belatedly, he remembered his Brownie camera. "A picture tells a thousand words. I saw that in an advertisement." He prepared the camera and took a couple of photographs.

It suited their purposes, Evie thought as she and Phillipa posed for Tom. "Take a photograph of us." Evie saw another curtain shift. "We are definitely drawing attention."

After taking several photographs of the village, they returned to the motor car and headed to Glenda's manor house.

During the time it took to travel the short distance, Evie worried about the encounter.

On their first visit, everyone had noticed something wrong. Evie had employed her utmost diplomacy, giving Glenda the opportunity to confide in her, but she hadn't.

Now, she had more questions to address. Questions about Glenda's past. Henrietta knew all about it but she'd said it wasn't her tale to tell, so they would have to rely on Glenda's common sense.

By the sounds of it, Glenda had been financially independent and she'd chosen to stay on at Halton House. Indeed, she had been given a cottage on the estate. That was quite a significant gesture. Over the years, there had been several servants retiring and being given a cottage in which to live in. Then, there had been a married couple. This had been before Evie's time but she knew the woman had been Henrietta's lady's maid and she had wanted to marry. Her husband had worked in London at a printer's office and, instead of facing the prospect of the maid leaving her and moving away from Halton House, Henrietta had made a cottage available to them and had found the husband a position in a nearby village.

Why had Glenda been given a cottage when she hadn't been anywhere near retirement age?

Evie wished it could be a simple matter of no one wanting to say goodbye to Nanny Fulham, but she knew there had to be more to the story.

All too soon, Tom said, "Here we are."

CHAPTER TWELVE

Old Salter Lane, Glenda Fulham's house

"How do we do this?" Evie considered several scenarios, each one resulting in Glenda looking surprised yet relieved to see them. Precisely what she wished to avoid. What if someone saw them?

It seemed like a simple task. Walk up to the door, knock, smile and... She turned to Phillipa. "How would you feel about leading the way and Tom and I will stand behind you. Or, better still, we'll remain out of sight. When Glenda invites you in, we'll slip in. I don't see anyone around but I don't want to risk her seeing us and asking us in straightaway. We don't know who might be watching."

A curtain shifted in, prompting them to decide.

"Sounds like a perfect plan." Phillipa nodded. "Although, it might be best if you both stay here."

"Are you sure?"

"She might recognize you but she doesn't know me."

Agreeing, Evie and Tom watched Phillipa walk up to the front door. She knocked on the door, stepped back and stood in sight of the front parlor window.

"I do hope Glenda is not startled by the visit." Evie realized this might not have been such a bright idea.

The police might have called on Glenda and, no doubt, left her in a jittery state. She could be feeling apprehensive about answering the door to strangers. "I hope this works." She'd hate to be responsible for causing her unnecessary distress.

Finally, they saw the front door open. However, Phillipa blocked their view of Glenda so they couldn't see her reaction.

"I wonder what Phillipa is saying to Glenda. Can you see her face?"

"I can see Glenda's expression," Tom said. "She looks stern."

"Impossible. Glenda is incapable of looking stern," Evie complained. Closing her eyes Evie groaned as she recalled Henrietta's dire warning.

There's nothing to be gained by exposing Glenda's past.

"If we persevere, that's precisely what we'll be doing, but what if it's the key to her present predicament?"

"What are you talking about?" Tom asked.

"I'm just thinking aloud."

Tom gestured ahead. "Phillipa's coming back."

"Does she look pleased? I can't tell. She looks almost distracted... No, more like disinterested."

Tom snorted. "She looks cold."

"I'm worried. If Glenda invited her in, surely Phillipa would have beckoned us."

Tom studied her for a moment. "Countess, I'm beginning to think patience is not one of your virtues."

"I've never made that claim about myself." And yet she'd been quite patient with Henrietta and her antics.

Lost in her thoughts, Evie had a delayed reaction to the tap on the passenger window.

"What's happened?" Evie asked.

"Glenda has agreed to see us."

That sounded odd. "Did it take a lot of convincing?"

Phillipa nodded. "At first, I tried to keep up the pretense but she didn't seem keen on the idea of allowancing strangers inside her house. Then, I had to tell her you were in the car. She actually found that hard to believe."

"Did you explain the reasons for us being here?"

Phillipa nodded. "Not in great detail. Is she usually so reserved?"

"Why do you ask?"

"She gave it a great deal of thought before finally relenting."

"Oh, did you explain about our disguise?"

"Briefly. I told her enough but left the details up to you."

"So she knows Tom and I are here but she is suspicious about our reasons for coming."

Phillipa nodded.

Evie didn't understand why Glenda had hesitated.

Tom and Evie scrambled out of the vehicle. For the sake of anyone watching, Evie paced her steps and focused on being blasé. A small garden surrounded Glenda's house, but the house next door was close enough for the neighbors to be able to see into her front garden.

The front door stood ajar. Evie called out a greeting. When she didn't hear a response, she eased the door open and walked in.

Glenda stood with her hands clasped in front of her. Her expression gave nothing away, not even surprise at seeing them. However, the fact she hadn't answered or offered a welcoming smile told Evie the nanny did not appreciate this unexpected visit.

Evie smiled. "Glenda, I'm glad to see you are all right." She didn't detect any signs of distress. However, she could tell Glenda was trying to gauge the situation.

Finally, she inclined her head slightly. "My lady. Do come in. It's quite chilly today." She led them through to the front parlor and while they sat down, she remained standing.

Evie knew Glenda was talking about the weather and not the accusation of theft. However, Evie was inclined to read between the lines.

Deciding to get straight to the point, Evie said, "I'm not sure how much Phillipa has told you. We heard about..."

Glenda raised her hand and waved it. "Nothing to worry about, my lady. It's really all just a prank."

"*A prank?* Involving the police?"

"They have a job to do and must appear to be doing their duty. It's really nothing serious."

"You've spoken with them?"

Glenda nodded.

Evie studied her expression. Glenda remained calm and relaxed. Evie hoped that meant there had been a positive outcome. "Did the police dismiss the accusation?"

"They were satisfied with my response."

"So they're not taking the matter further?"

"As I said, they must appear to be doing their duty."

Evie didn't like the sound of that. If the police were not going to take the matter further, they would have said the matter was closed. In her place, Evie would have demanded assurances.

"Glenda, I don't mean to worry you, but while we were at the pub, we heard about another incident concerning five gold rings. A certain Mrs. Hardfellows claims her rings were stolen when she stepped out of her house. Have you heard about it?"

Glenda eased down onto a chair and made herself comfortable. "No, I haven't heard anything. It's very odd because news tends to travel quickly here. I'm sure I'll hear about it all in the morning."

"Do you know Mrs. Hardfellows?"

"I think I met her the first day I arrived. I'm afraid the weather hasn't been that inviting so people tend to stay indoors and when they need to go out they tend to hurry." Glenda tilted her head and, for the first time, smiled. "I understand you are all in disguise."

"Yes, we wanted to avoid biases. We thought people would be more inclined to speak to us rather than..."

Glenda's eyebrow hitched up. "Yes?"

"Well, I'm sure everyone knows I visited yesterday."

Glenda looked from one to the other. "You want people to speak with you but you don't want them to make the connection between us?"

Evie nodded. "For the time being, at least. They might speak more freely."

Despite Glenda's belief, according to Detective Inspector O'Neill, the police were indeed taking the matter seriously, but Evie didn't want to worry her.

"There is something going on here, Glenda. We don't for a moment believe you stole those French hens. Either someone else stole them or someone is deliberately spreading false rumors about you."

"Why would anyone do that?" Glenda asked.

"We don't know. Perhaps it has something to do with you inheriting this house. Or… it's possible someone has merely taken a dislike to you. Some people thrive on making others miserable."

Glenda relaxed and sat back. Smiling, she assured Evie, "Lady Woodridge, there really is no need for you to concern yourself with this matter."

Evie straightened. Glenda's blithe attempt to dismiss the seriousness of the accusation had the opposite effect.

"Glenda, is there any truth to the theft of those chickens?"

"I couldn't really say for sure. I understand the owner has won ribbons at the fair. It could be a case of his rival stealing them." Glenda looked down at her hands. When she looked up, she smiled. "My lady, I really do appreciate your concern. Please believe me when I say there is no reason to worry."

Tom and Phillipa had remained standing and Evie saw them inching away. She sensed their discomfort and she didn't blame them.

No matter how much she pushed for information, Glenda would not confide in her.

"If you don't mind, Glenda, we will remain in the village for another day or so." Before Glenda could object, Evie added, "Just in case this nonsense turns serious. I could not live with myself if I thought you were being forced to deal with it all by yourself."

Glenda sighed. "Very well, if you insist, my lady."

Evie declined the offer of tea and, saying she could be reached at the pub, they left.

"I don't think Glenda approves of you calling yourself Marjorie Dubois," Phillipa said as they settled into the motor car.

That wasn't all she disapproved of, Evie thought. Glenda had been less than enthusiastic to see them and now Evie worried she had well and truly stepped over the line.

"I'm more concerned about this second accusation." Had the theft been reported to the police? "How can we find out the identity of the owner of the chickens Glenda is accused of stealing? We also need to get someone to point out Mrs. Hardfellows. I'd like to speak with her."

"French hens, not chickens, Countess" Tom said, his smile suggesting he wanted to lighten the mood.

Evie huffed out a breath. "French hens. Gold rings. What next?"

They returned to the pub just as a blustery wind swept through the village. The skies were a dark gray and Evie thought she caught sight of flashes of lightning streaking across the horizon but she couldn't tell if that was a sign of a storm approaching or heading in the opposite direction.

Walking in, all three headed straight for the large fireplace to warm themselves and get the lay of the land.

"It's odd. Standing in front of the fire, I only now realize I've been cold," Phillipa remarked.

"I agree." Also, Evie had been too preoccupied about Glenda to notice the cold. Shaking her head, she murmured, "I'm entertaining the strangest impulse."

Hearing her, Phillipa asked, "And what's that?"

"I want to give Glenda a good shake. I have no idea what's happened to the common sense she's known for."

There were more people in the pub, including some women and they were all doing a splendid job of pretending to ignore them but Evie could see them taking turns to glance their way.

"Is it official? Are we staying on?" Phillipa asked.

"Yes, please. We can't abandon Glenda now."

"Even if she doesn't want us here?"

Evie drew in a breath. "Right or wrong, we are staying. I'm not going to allow something as trivial as pride to stand in the way."

"Countess, it's not your pride that's at stake here."

Evie stood firm. "I hear prisons can be quite damp. I'd prefer it if Glenda didn't find out for herself."

Rubbing his hands together, Tom nodded. "I'll go get the luggage."

Phillipa and Evie remained by the fireplace, both casting covetous glances at the table next to it currently occupied by a group of farmers.

Evie told herself they had probably toiled in the fields

since before dawn and deserved to be seated near the warmth of the fireplace. Then she remembered there was little work done on the land during winter. Even Glenda had said the locals didn't venture out much during this weather. Had curiosity about the Hollywood movie makers compelled them to leave their warm homes?

As they continued to warm up, Evie tried to avoid fixating on Glenda's reasons for taking such a light-hearted approach to the accusation and allowed her mind to wander.

A woman inherits a house, she then moves in, Evie thought.

What if someone else had entertained hopes of inheriting the house?

She remembered Glenda saying her aunt's husband had been a local. Did he have family living in the area?

If they knew his full name, they might be able to ask around. Evie knew better than to expect Glenda to provide that information. She had no doubt in her mind Glenda would continue to shut her out.

The barrage of questions assailing her were scattered when Phillipa nudged her and drew her attention to a couple sitting nearby.

"They're definitely talking about us," Phillipa whispered.

The man and woman were engaged in a murmured conversation but then the woman's voice rose.

"They never found out who did it," the woman said. "She had her throat cut from ear to ear. I swear every time I walk by that house, I have to hurry my step because I think I can hear her moaning."

The man nodded in agreement, saying, "I cross the street."

The people at the next table all joined in the conversation and, in no time, the entire pub was buzzing with the murmured conversations about a woman who'd had her throat slit from ear to ear and could be heard moaning in the dead of night.

While transfixed by the spectacle, Evie noticed glances being cast their way. She suspected everyone was eager to catch their reactions and to make sure they were listening to their tale.

The barkeeper must have made a point of letting everyone know she wanted an extra layer of *something* to make the village more appealing for their movie.

She imagined the villagers thinking a woman being murdered in the dead of night would shroud the village with an air of mystery and intrigue.

Doing her best to look disinterested, Evie turned her attention to the flames.

Tom returned and joined them by the fireplace. "Our rooms face the street and the doors have locks."

Evie's eyebrows curved up. "Locks? Are we concerned about our safety?"

"It never hurts to be on guard. We don't really know what's what." He looked around and lowered his voice. "What's everyone so excited about?"

"A woman had her throat slit," Evie said.

"What?"

"Don't be alarmed if you hear moaning in the dead of night," she warned.

"When did this happen?"

Evie shrugged. "We don't know."

"But I was only gone for a few minutes."

Phillipa and Evie exchanged a look of amusement.

"We first heard about it from the couple over here at this table," Evie whispered. "Then, everyone started talking about it."

"I suppose the police will be asking everyone questions." He looked around. "These are all the same people who were here when we arrived. I wonder how long they've been at the pub."

"Why are you curious about that?" Evie asked.

"I'd hate to be the one to say it, but one of them could be the killer."

Evie hid her smile and Phillipa had to look away.

"Has anyone mentioned Glenda?" Tom asked.

"Oh, heavens. Why would they?"

"Because they'll probably try to blame her for the death." Tom frowned. "It's strange. When we came in, I didn't hear any talk of the death and, while I was getting the luggage, I didn't see anyone come in. How did everyone hear the news?"

"News?" Evie looked puzzled. "What news?"

Tom scowled at Evie. "About the woman who had her throat slit."

"Oh, that…"

Tom growled, "There is no dead woman."

"Probably not but everyone seems to be desperate for us to believe it."

"I swallowed that hook, line and sinker."

"My apologies. You just walked right into it. I must admit, it's rather a curious story and it's difficult to tell if it's true or not."

Phillipa shook her head. "I'm inclined to think it isn't."

Had the villagers made it all up for their benefit?

If they could organize themselves at a moment's notice to fabricate a tale and spread the tale of a woman being murdered just to impress them, could they also conspire to steal three French hens?

CHAPTER THIRTEEN

The pub

As it was still early for dinner, they each went to their respective rooms to freshen up. Tom had said their rooms faced the little main street so it seemed they were the only guests staying at the pub.

Evie walked in and was pleasantly surprised. The room offered all the comforts she might need for a brief stay, with a large bed, a comfortable chair and a dressing table and stool.

Evie sat down and removed her hat and earrings, while her reflection fired a thousand questions and observations at her. One in particular caught her attention.

"Everyone is pretending."

She looked out the window and pondered the thought. Sheer necessity had driven them to hide behind a façade and pretend to be movie makers. That had worked in their favor. Now all the villagers wanted to impress them with the notion their village would be the ideal setting for their movie.

Giving the barkeeper the impression she opposed the idea and Phillipa favored it, had set something in motion. They would have to wait until the next day to see what they could do with that. Although, they'd already had a taste of the villagers concocting a story about a murdered woman.

She changed out of her travel clothes and found something that didn't need pressing. Freshened up and dressed, she decided to spend a few minutes clearing her mind, but her thoughts refused to disperse.

Everyone wanted something and it seemed they would go to any lengths to get it.

Puzzled by the stray thought, Evie wondered if their plans to make a movie had disrupted the assaults on Glenda. Evie knew that was a strange way to refer to the accusations but that was precisely how she perceived them.

Would everyone forget about their targeted victim and focus on impressing the Hollywood trio or would they juggle the tasks of trying to impress them while making Glenda's life difficult and what did they stand to gain by doing that?

A knock at the door to her room had her swinging round. Before she could answer it, Phillipa called out, "It's me, Phillipa. Can I come in?"

"Yes, the door is unlocked."

"Is that wise?" Phillipa asked as she walked in and closed the door behind her.

Evie smiled. "Do you really believe our lives are in danger?"

"You heard what Tom said." Phillipa sat down on the edge of the bed. She too had changed out of her day clothes, choosing black wide legged trousers and a blue blouse.

Evie laughed. "I think we're quite safe. Remember, they want us to make our movie here."

"Speaking of which… Did you find the conversation odd? How do you think they came up with that idea of a woman being murdered? I'm sure I would not have been able to think of something so macabre in such a short time."

"However it came about, I hope everyone remains enthusiastic. It will make our task of engaging them in conversation that much easier…" Evie's thoughts trailed away and another took its place. "She calls herself Fulham."

"What about it?" Phillipa asked.

Shaking her head, Evie murmured, "One of the men sitting near the fireplace said that earlier. He was referring to Nanny Fulham. What do you think he meant by that?"

"Isn't that her name?"

"I've always thought so. What if it's not her real name? The remark seemed to suggest it."

"If she's not Glenda Fulham then who is she?" Phillipa asked.

Had they nudged a door open? When Glenda had worked at Halton House as a nanny, she had been quite young. Had she sought to start afresh with a new identity?

"I seem to be asking myself one question after another and getting absolutely no answers."

Phillipa snorted. "That's not a fair exchange."

Glenda had referred to the accusation as a prank. Evie couldn't accept that. Standing up, she walked the length of the room. "Let's assume this… whatever this is, all started with Glenda inheriting her house."

Phillipa nodded. "I'm happy to go along with that."

"Her aunt had been married to a local man. We know she was a widow. Did he have any family?"

Phillipa gave it some thought. "Yes, it's possible there's a disgruntled relative. Perhaps someone who had pinned their hopes on inheriting. Now he's taking out his revenge on Glenda by making her life difficult."

Evie nodded. "I'd like to find out his name. We know the church keeps records, so that might be a good place to start." She had hired Millicent as her secretary for precisely this type of work, but it wouldn't be easy to contact her without risking exposure. Making a telephone call would be the most expedient way of contacting her but Evie didn't dare chance it. "We might need to return to Halton House." Even a telephone call to Lotte Mannering would ring alarm bells with the post office mistress.

"Or, we could be creative," Phillipa suggested.

"What do you have in mind?"

"Give me a minute, I'll come up with something."

Evie sat down and counted to sixty. "Anything?"

"What?" Phillipa laughed. "I think I'll need more than a minute."

"Oh, my apologies. You're usually quick to come up with ideas." Standing up, she suggested going downstairs.

As they walked out of the room, they met Tom in the hallway.

"I was about to knock on your door," he said and looked at Phillipa and then back at Evie. "Did I miss anything?"

"Only more questions," Evie grumbled.

"Evie wonders why Glenda might be going by the name of Fulham."

"Isn't that her name?" he asked.

"That's what we're not sure about."

He nodded. "I foresee a visit to the church. Do you even know where she was born?"

"I have no idea but I assume her aunt married here. In any case, the church records might include her maiden name. What about you? Did you come up with any new ideas?"

Tom laughed. "Unlike you, I have no difficulties in clearing my mind."

"Oh, I forgot my tinted spectacles." Evie rushed back to her room. When she caught up with Tom and Phillipa, they both studied her as if she'd suddenly grown another head. "I must remain in character."

Downstairs, they were surprised to find the pub full. To their even greater surprise, a table had been reserved for them.

The animated conversations flowed. Absolutely no one turned to look at them. This made Evie wonder if they had all been instructed to carry on as if they were not there. This, in her opinion, would only make the villagers' efforts to impress the Hollywood trio more obvious.

The barkeeper saw them arrive and walked over to the

table ahead of them, removing the reserved sign he had put there with a flourish.

"I thought it might be best to save you a table. We get crowds every other day, but I never know on which days."

"Has something happened in the village to bring everyone out?" Tom asked as he sat down.

The quick-thinking barkeeper said, "Everyone had a good harvest this year. Of course, everyone in the village benefits. Anyhow, they are still celebrating. I think it will continue on until next year." He looked over his shoulder toward the bar and then said, "There's someone who wishes to meet you. Mr. Graham came in for a drink and I took the liberty of telling him about your plans."

How convenient, Evie thought.

The name sounded familiar. As the man approached, she remembered someone had mentioned the name when identifying the owner of the large estate near Glenda's house.

The barkeeper made the introductions. "This is Mr. Albert Graham."

Evie realized he wasn't just the owner of the large manor house. He would also most likely be the villagers' landlord.

The man wore a heavy coat suggesting he had only dropped in for a few moments. Perhaps long enough to catch sight of the enterprising trio who promised to use the village as the setting for their movie.

He looked to be about forty. Evie didn't notice a single gray hair on him but there were a few lines bracketing his mouth and spearing out from the edges of his eyes. He looked tall but not as tall as Tom.

While his eyes sparkled with friendliness, Evie noted

something hard and calculating beneath the look. When he turned away, she imagined his expression would change. His smile would fade and his eyes would harden.

"I've only just returned from London and now I'm glad I stopped by the pub. I hope you've been made welcome."

Tom and Phillipa nodded while Evie assumed her bored expression and only committed to a confounding shrug and a nod.

"We would be very pleased if you would join us for dinner tomorrow night. Jon here will tell you how to find us."

Evie looked at the barkeeper and tried to commit the name to memory. Not such a simple task when she'd been referring to him as the barkeeper.

"We'd love to," Phillipa said.

"Well..." Albert Graham hesitated and then nodded. "Do enjoy the evening." He turned, walked back to the bar and stood there for a moment drumming his fingers and glancing over his shoulder, almost as if he regretted cutting the conversation short.

"That was odd," Tom whispered.

The barkeeper, stepped forward and gave the table a wipe.

Clearing her throat, Phillipa asked, "Shall we order some drinks?"

Evie spent some time asking about the wines available while Tom and Phillipa settled for beer again.

When the barkeeper walked away, Phillipa smiled. "You are determined to stay in character."

"Absolutely." Leaning forward and lowering her voice, Evie asked, "Is Mr. Graham still at the bar?"

Phillipa nodded. "He's having a word with the barkeeper and glancing this way."

"Did he strike you as being less than confident?" Evie thought she had sensed something awkward about him.

"Yes," Phillipa agreed. "It's odd. We know he's the owner of the largest property in the area. Aren't they usually quite sure of themselves? Lord of the manor and whatnot."

"Perhaps he's not sure about us," Evie mused. "After all, he doesn't know anything about us except whatever the barkeeper told him and he only knows what we told him."

"Which isn't much," Phillipa said. After a moment, she asked, "Have you given any thought to what might happen once everyone discovers we won't be making a movie here?"

"We'll cross that bridge when we come to it. Before that happens, I'm hoping we'll have discovered the truth about the accusations of theft. Meanwhile, we can enjoy our deferential treatment. Look, we have the best table by the fireplace."

Their drinks were served and the barkeeper took their orders for dinner.

"I don't believe I have ever had fish and chips." Evie and Phillipa chose the same dish while Tom opted for a hearty pie.

"Are you ever going to take those spectacles off?" Tom asked.

"I don't know the first thing about looking artistic. I'm sure they help." Sipping her wine, Evie made a mental list, prioritizing their needs. Or, at least, trying to. She still had too many questions and each one required her equal attention.

Who owned the French hens and where did he live? Had Albert Graham extended the invitation to dinner so he could learn more about their endeavors and their interest in the village? They assumed he was the largest landowner in the area so he would obviously have a vested interest.

Also…

The location of his manor house so close to Glenda's house raised questions. Had the house belonged to the estate at some point?

That reminded her they also needed to find out the identity of the previous owners. Glenda's aunt had inherited the house from her husband. It seemed incredible that he wouldn't have any family, but, of course, not impossible.

Their meals were served. While satisfied with her choice, Evie couldn't help casting a covetous eye at Tom's hearty pie.

Noticing this, he smiled and edged his plate closer to him.

"Should we say something amusing?" Phillipa whispered. "Everyone else seems to be enjoying a good laugh."

Tom burst out laughing and Evie produced a chuckle.

A few heads turned and Evie saw a couple of people smiling their way. Seeing their joviality had met with approval, they continued enjoying their meals and bursting into occasional laughter, taking turns to lean in and pretend to say something incredibly witty.

During one of their outbursts, Evie noticed everyone's attention drawn to the front door.

She turned and saw a couple had entered. A man and a woman. They walked up to the bar and approached the barkeeper. The woman turned to look toward the fireplace. Evie thought she appeared to be in the family way. She had her hands wrapped around her front and looked quite pleased with herself.

If Evie had to guess, she'd say they were not from the village. As the woman's gaze skated over the tables, she met several gazes looking back at her with curiosity. Evie didn't see anyone acknowledging her, which could only mean they didn't know her.

The conversation between the barkeeper and the man ended. The man had a brief word with the woman and then exited the pub, no doubt going out to retrieve their luggage.

The woman stood at the bar for a moment and then approached the fireplace.

When she reached it, she looked toward their table, inclined her head and said, "Good evening."

Evie gave her a small smile and turned back to her meal.

As she took a bite of her fish, she frowned. The voice had sounded familiar.

She glanced over her shoulder and studied the woman's profile.

She wore a hat tipped down over her forehead that almost hid her eyes. A light brown ribbon edged the rim of the hat and met on the side to form a large bow which partially hid her face.

Evie turned back and leaned forward. Before she could say anything, Phillipa took that as her cue and laughed.

Waiting for the laughter to subside, Evie then whispered, "There's something familiar about that woman."

Phillipa's eyes widened. "Oh... Oh, I think she's about to faint."

Evie swung around and saw the woman's hand flying up to her forehead. When she swayed, Tom shot to his feet and rushed toward her, catching her before she fell.

"Ma'am, you should sit down," he said.

"Oh, oh... dear. I think I stood too close to the fire."

Tom drew out a chair for her.

Keeping her head lowered, the woman said, "I'm sure I'll be perfectly fine in a moment. I really don't wish to disrupt your dinner..." Regardless, the woman sat down. Smiling, she thanked Tom. "You are much too kind."

Evie frowned. Leaning in, she studied what she could see of the woman's face. There really was something oddly familiar about her.

Surprised, she whispered, "Millicent?"

CHAPTER FOURTEEN

The pub

"Millicent? Is that you?"

The woman who bore a remarkable resemblance to Millicent exclaimed, "Oh, do we know each other? That is my name... I'm Mrs. Fletcher. Mrs. Millicent Fletcher." She tugged her cloche, pushing it down further over her eyes.

Sitting back, Evie continued to study what she could see of the woman's face.

Evie looked at Millicent every day but she did not scrutinize her. Regardless, she would recognize her anywhere. Although, she'd never put it to the test. What if she saw Millicent in a place where she didn't expect to see her?

She accepted the possibility of there being someone else in the world who shared physical similarities with

Millicent but what would be the chances of that person also sharing the same Christian name?

The barkeeper rushed toward their table and set a cup of tea down. "Is there anything else I might bring you?"

Millicent smiled up at him. "Oh, no. Thank you."

As the barkeeper walked away, Evie thought she heard the woman say a drop of brandy might have been more appreciated.

"Brandy?" Evie asked.

"What?"

"Brandy? In your condition?"

The woman picked up the cup of tea and took a quick sip. "My condition?"

Evie dropped her gaze to the woman's robust looking waistline. "*Enceinte.*"

"Oh..." Mrs. Fletcher patted her stomach. "I'm afraid I have a weakness for teacakes."

She wasn't pregnant? "My apologies..."

Mrs. Fletcher looked toward the door. "What could be keeping Ed...ward. Our motor car started acting up and we couldn't go any further. For a moment there, I worried there might not be any room at the inn." She leaned in and whispered, "The barkeeper said there are people from Hollywood making a movie. Isn't that exciting? If we stay here long enough, we might appear in it."

A sudden draft of cold air signaled the door opening. Evie turned but the man who'd entered had already hurried across the bar. Evie assumed it had been Mr. Fletcher as she managed to catch sight of him carrying a suitcase in each hand before he disappeared through a door.

"Oh, my heavens, it is a chilly night. I'm so glad we were able to secure a room," Mrs. Fletcher exclaimed.

"And how long do you think you'll stay?" Evie asked.

Instead of looking at Evie, Mrs. Fletcher lowered her head. "I suppose for as long as it takes... to fix the motor car."

"Where are my manners," Evie said. "I should introduce you. These are my colleagues, Phillipa and Tom." She decided to leave out their surnames because she couldn't remember if they had changed them.

"Lovely to meet you and... once again, thank you for rescuing me. I am feeling much better. Perhaps I should go up to our room."

"Oh, no. Do please join us for dinner," Phillipa invited. "As you can see, there are no other tables available."

"I really shouldn't impose."

"We insist."

Mrs. Fletcher looked away. "Oh, there's Mr. Fletcher and he's beckoning me."

"Ask him to join us," Phillipa encouraged.

The man approached the table and that's when the jig was up. Evie's eyes narrowed.

Edmonds.

She looked at Mrs. Fletcher who peered at her from beneath the rim of her hat.

It *was* Millicent. Just as she'd suspected.

"Hello," Edmonds said.

"Edward," the so-called Mrs. Fletcher said. "These kind people have asked us to join them for dinner." She made the introductions.

"You look remarkably familiar," Evie drawled.

Edmonds cheeks colored. "Yes, well... I've heard say

everyone has a double somewhere in the world. Do I detect an American accent? Perhaps my double is in America and that's where you think you've seen me before."

Belatedly, Evie groaned under her breath. Something had compelled Millicent to travel here. Had she discovered something significant about Glenda Fulham? If so, they would have to find a way to talk away from prying eyes and ears.

She looked at Millicent who sat back smiling and sipping her tea. The cloche remained in place, as low as it could be, but Evie now saw beyond the flimsy disguise.

How could she not have noticed? Before she could berate herself, Evie told herself Millicent had averted her gaze and had kept her head down and, at first, she thought she had recognized her.

"Did you get a nice room?" Evie asked.

Edmonds gave a vigorous nod. "Oh, yes my... I mean... I'm sorry, I didn't catch your name."

"Marjorie Dubois."

The barkeeper brought fresh glasses of beer for Phillipa and Tom and poured more wine for Evie, a service she hadn't actually expected so she assumed he wished to try to overhear something of interest.

"You should order something to eat before it's too late and the kitchen closes," Phillipa said.

"I recommend the game pie," Tom offered. "It's truly the best I've had in a long while."

"That sounds good," Edmonds nodded. "And... a beer for me, please."

"More tea for you, Mrs. Fletcher?" the barkeeper asked.

"Oh, I believe I will indulge and have a beer too, thank you."

The barkeeper raised an eyebrow. Clearly, he too had assumed Millicent had been in the family way.

"Then again... Yes, tea will do nicely."

Edmonds gave them a nervous smile. "Don't mind us. Do please continue with your meals."

"Is it very cold outside now?" Phillipa asked.

"Moderately so, yes." Rubbing his hands, Edmonds looked about and added, "This must be a nice pub."

"Apparently," Evie said in her bored tone, "everyone comes here on every other day." Tilting her head, she looked at Millicent. She still couldn't believe she hadn't fully recognized her. Heavens, while she'd sounded familiar, she hadn't even recognized her voice, not with any certainty. Evie would swear she hadn't sounded at all like herself. Millicent's speech pattern was always dramatic and full of exclamations, but she had sounded demure...

The barkeeper returned and served Millicent and Edmonds their meals.

"Did you travel far?" Phillipa asked.

"Oh, yes," Millicent said. "We have been traveling since this morning. At one point, we lost our way and had to retrace our steps."

It seemed Millicent had a knack for telling tales.

Glancing beyond their table at the next table, Evie could see the people there leaning back, almost as if trying to catch what Millicent was saying.

"Are you traveling anywhere in particular?" Phillipa asked.

Millicent looked at Edmonds and smiled. "We are

looking for our new home and hope to settle in before Christmas."

"Will you have enough time?"

"We've been told the house has enough furniture to get us started. However, first, we have to see it and the village as well. I need to know I'll enjoy living in the area. I only hope we are not delayed too long as we might miss out on the house. Edward will telephone tomorrow and let them know we have been delayed."

Seeing Edmonds or, rather, Edward, nodding, Evie imagined Millicent had spent the entire journey here admonishing him and making sure he remained in character because, of course, they would need to pretend they didn't know anyone.

"I suspect everyone is curious about us," Millicent said, adding, "We told the barkeeper enough about ourselves so he should be able to spread the word about us. We are quite harmless." She leaned in and whispered, "He said there have been some thefts in the area but he assured us we shouldn't worry because the culprit will be apprehended soon. At least we know we can lock the door to our room."

They were sharing a room?

Tom finished his pie and said to Edward, "I know a little about motor cars. Would you like me to take a look at yours?"

Edmonds nodded. "I'd appreciate that."

Excusing themselves, Tom and Edmonds went outside.

Since there wouldn't be enough light to see what they were looking at, Evie knew the offer had been Tom's way of having a private word with Edmonds.

At least someone would be getting some answers tonight.

"I wonder who the Hollywood people are," Millicent said.

Phillipa gave her a bright smile and, keeping up with the farce, told her it was them.

"Oh, heavens. How thrilling. Will you be making a movie here? Do you know many stars? Oh, do you know Rudolph Valentino? I cannot wait to see him in *The Sheik*." Millicent swooned. "I'm sure I will make Edward take me three times, if not more, to see it. I have a cousin who lives in America and she wrote me the longest letter telling me all about it."

"So what happens if you miss out on the house you're going to see?" Phillipa asked.

Millicent shrugged. "Then we'll have to keep looking."

"You might have some luck here. From what we've seen, this is a nice enough village."

"My Edward knows a lot about motor cars. He'll have it up and running in no time but perhaps we can stay for the morning. Do you think that should be enough time for me to look around?"

As Millicent and Phillipa talked about the village and houses in general, Evie tried to work out a plan. She hoped they'd be able to talk later when everyone went upstairs. She hadn't noticed any floorboards creaking and the door hinges hadn't made any noise so it should be safe enough to sneak around in the middle of the night.

When they'd set off earlier that day, Millicent and Edmonds had been on their way to speak with someone and had planned on sweetening the deal with some chocolate. She hoped Millicent had met with success.

Otherwise, they would have to spend the better part of the day trying to engage people in conversation without giving themselves away. And if they couldn't find a lead… Well, Evie hadn't considered giving up nor leaving. Certainly not until they knew the persecution wouldn't continue.

Tom and Edmonds returned and sat down.

"Were you able to fix it?" Phillipa asked.

"No, Mr. Fletcher will have to call away for a part. He's already asked the barkeeper if there is anyone in the village who fixes motors. Unfortunately, there isn't."

Phillipa exclaimed, "Oh, dear. How long will it take for the part to come? Mrs. Fletcher said you are keen to move on and go and see that house you want."

"We'll know more in the morning," Edmonds explained. "I'll telephone them. I know a fellow. He should be able to help me out."

At least, Evie thought, they had managed to keep up the ruse, keeping everyone trying to listen to their conversation entertained.

As they placed an order for coffee, Evie looked at her watch. They only had another half an hour before the pub closed.

So far, no one had made a move to leave and they remained everyone's center of attention. Evie had no idea what people expected to see or hear.

When the coffee arrived, Evie sipped it at leisure, all the while trying to work out a plan. When they all made their way upstairs, she would need to let Millicent know her door would be open. Evie didn't know if sound traveled on the narrow staircase, so she didn't want to risk being too obvious. She'd have to find some way to convey the message.

Would Millicent understand hand signals?

She certainly understood the importance of remaining discreet, hence her disguise, but would she know to keep it up even as they moved away from anyone who might eavesdrop?

Glancing at Tom, she wondered if he had acquired any other skills in the trenches. He'd said he could read lips. She imagined he could do a better job than she ever would of making himself understood by using hand signals.

Millicent put her hand over her mouth and yawned. "Oh, you'll have to excuse me. All that driving has made me weary. Not that I did any of the driving. Although, Edward thinks I do since I'm always giving him instructions. Anyhow, I'm surprised I've managed to stay awake this long." She finished her coffee and set the cup down. "Thank you for inviting us to share your table. It's been lovely chatting with you. Will we see you at breakfast tomorrow?"

Phillipa answered for everyone, "We do hope so."

"Well then… Good night." Millicent stood up.

Evie tried to catch her attention but Millicent seemed intent on following through and bidding them a goodnight.

She couldn't very well hurry after her, not when she had a languorous act to keep up.

As Millicent and Edmonds made their way out of the pub and up the stairs, Phillipa asked, "Where is that barkeeper? I wouldn't mind a brandy before going up."

Phillipa looked around and, spotting him, drew his attention.

"I think I'll go up now," Evie said.

Tom looked at his watch and nodded. "I'll be going up shortly."

Evie forced herself to take her time. When she finally reached the stairs, she glanced up but Millicent and Edmonds had already disappeared. How would she find Millicent's room?

Making sure there was no one about, Evie hurried up the stairs. Reaching the next floor, she studied the doors opposite the rooms at the front of the building. She looked down at the gap between the floor and the door but didn't see the lights on. She walked past Tom's room and then Phillipa's room and came up to her room. That's when she noticed another room, right next to hers. She walked up to the door but again didn't see a light shining through the gap.

Abandoning the idea of talking to Millicent, she went into her room. Closing the door, she leaned against it.

Millicent had come here for a reason and she had to trust she'd find a way to speak with her. Pushing off the door, she took a step and noticed a piece of paper on the floor.

"Smart girl, Millicent." She picked it up. As hoped, it was a note from Millicent!

She was in the room next door and they had a connecting door which Evie hadn't noticed because a screen hid it from view.

Moving the screen, Evie pressed her ear to the door.

The note said to tap twice, wait a moment and then tap once.

Evie followed the instructions to the letter.

After a moment, the key turned and the door opened.

Seeing nothing but darkness, Evie stepped back.

"Oh, thank goodness, it's you," Millicent said as she emerged from the dark room.

"Who did you think it would be? I tapped just the way you asked me to."

"I'm so sorry, I forgot how many times I asked you to tap." Millicent walked in, followed by Edmonds. "My heavens, what a day we've had." Millicent sat on a chair only to spring back up again. "Begging your pardon, milady."

"Oh, do sit down, Millicent. Now, tell me, what brought you here?"

Easing down on the chair again, she said, "We spent most of the day trying to decide how best to contact you and in the end we decided we had no choice and had to come here ourselves, but knowing you'd all come in disguise, we then had to decide how we would disguise ourselves, never mind that no one here would know us but you never know. Someone from this village might have visited our village and they might have seen me and somehow found out I was Lady Woodridge's maid and then your story would lose credibility because they would then put two and two together and figure out you were not the person you said you were…"

"Millicent."

"Yes, milady?"

"While we're here, it's Marjorie," Evie reminded her.

"Oh, yes. I'm sorry, I didn't think. Someone could have their ear pressed to the door as we speak and then the ruse would be discovered and, as they say, the jig would be up... I suppose you're wondering about my voluptuous figure. Edmonds said no one ever notices the chauffeur so he didn't need to try to look different and I told Edmonds I didn't want to spoil all your hard work so I needed to make sure no one would recognize me easily." She smiled. "I used some padding but it shifted. I'm supposed to have wide hips and instead I've ended up with a huge stomach. I don't know how Lotte Mannering manages to keep her disguises in place—"

"Millicent!"

"Right, yes... well, remember how Edmonds and I were going to talk to Mrs. Leeds and had purchased some *Flake* chocolate because she enjoys it with her cup of tea?"

Evie nodded.

"She kept us talking for an hour. A full hour," Millicent complained. "And, after all that time, we walked away with nothing."

CHAPTER FIFTEEN

*M*illicent fumed, "You can't imagine how cross I felt and Mrs. Leeds is the one who is always going around saying she's known Nanny Fulham the longest."

Evie called for patience.

"Anyhow, not all is lost because, after we left her, we called on Mrs. Patterson."

Evie encouraged her with a nod.

"Mrs. Patterson wanted to impress me. You see, word had spread about me asking questions and she wanted to let everyone know she knows Nanny Fulham better than anyone else. Anyhow, she remembered Nanny Fulham going on a trip. She didn't tell anyone but Mrs. Patterson did some investigating. She happened to visit—"

Evie held her hand up. "Let's call her Glenda. After all, that is her name."

"Oh... is it? Yes, of course..." Millicent shrugged. "Where was I?"

"Mrs. Patterson visited Glenda."

"Oh, yes," Millicent nodded. "And she found Glenda quite busy although she wouldn't say what she was doing, something Mrs. Patterson finds irksome because if you ask what someone is doing and they say they're not doing anything, well… they're obviously lying because you just found them in the middle of doing something. Determined, Mrs. Patterson sat down. Usually, she would have left the person to whatever they were doing but, in this instance, she wanted to know. If you ask me, Mrs. Patterson always wants to know what people are getting up to."

"Millicent!" Evie urged.

"Glenda went to make a pot of tea and Mrs. Patterson happened to glance at a piece of paper sitting on a table. Of course, if you ask me, she snooped around until she found something worthy of her attention. Anyhow, the piece of paper had the name of this village underlined right alongside a date, which was the day after Mrs. Patterson went to visit her. As in, the next day. Mrs. Patterson decided Glenda was planning a trip somewhere. Well, as it happened, the next day Glenda left. Only, no one saw her leaving. Mrs. Patterson had planned on, in her words, bid her farewell, but she set her alarm clock wrong and missed Glenda's departure by an hour. In any case, Mrs. Patterson is friendly with the fellow at the train station so she asked him and, to her surprise, he said Nanny Ful… I mean, Glenda, had taken the train that morning to Thornbridge and she'd carried a small suitcase."

Evie sat on the edge of her bed and fought the temptation to cup her chin in her hand. She knew Millicent would eventually get to the point. Hopefully, she would lose track and just blurt out the news.

"Mrs. Patterson spent the day trying to join the dots. It made no sense because Glenda never went anywhere and suddenly there she was packing a suitcase and leaving. She scoured the local newspapers looking for news about Thornbridge and a possible reason for Glenda to visit. But she found nothing. Then, later in the day, her sister came visiting with her husband. They found Mrs. Patterson quite flustered by something so they asked her about it and she told them about Thornbridge." Millicent smiled. "She was overjoyed to hear the day before her sister and brother-in-law had driven out somewhere... I can't remember where and, along the way, they'd stopped to have luncheon and the husband picked up a newspaper and he remembered reading something about the village of Thornbridge. It turned out to be an obituary. I've never understood how some people pick up the newspaper to find out who has died and then they read the news."

"Whose obituary was it?" Evie asked.

"Marjorie Evans' obituary."

"Evans."

Millicent nodded. "Mrs. Patterson decided this had to be Glenda's aunt."

Finally, they had a surname. Now they could try to find information about her husband.

"So Mrs. Patterson concluded that Glenda had come to Thornbridge to attend the funeral," Millicent continued. "Two days later, Glenda returned but, of course, she didn't talk about her trip. Although, a short while later, we all heard about Glenda inheriting the house in Thornbridge."

"Millicent, when we return to Halton House, you will have to point out Mrs. Patterson. She is a gem."

"Yes, of course. Although, given enough time, I'm sure I would have unearthed the same information."

"I have no doubt about it, Millicent."

Evie sprung to her feet and walked around in a tight circle. Now they could find out if there were any disgruntled relatives. Stopping, she tapped her chin.

She goes by the name of Fulham...

Were they on the brink of discovering something else about Glenda?

"Now, what's this about a thief?" Millicent asked. "Was the barkeeper referring to Glenda? He didn't mention the French hens."

Distracted, Evie nodded. "Five gold rings have been stolen."

Millicent's eyes widened. Her voice hitched with disbelief, "And Glenda is being accused of the theft?"

"I believe she will be." Evie told them about their visit that afternoon and how Glenda had remained annoyingly stalwart in her commitment to not making a fuss.

Evie's back teeth clenched.

She didn't understand Glenda's reason for being so secretive. What if she was actually hiding something?

"Well, there's no what ifs about it," she said aloud. If Henrietta had shared what she knew with her, it might have saved everyone a lot of trouble.

Millicent looked at Edmonds and shrugged.

Evie stopped her pacing and looked at Millicent and Edmonds. "We need to find a way to keep you here. The more eyes and ears the better."

Millicent grinned. "Edmonds has already thought of a

way. Tomorrow, he will contact his friend who will tell him it will take more than a week to get the spare part. He will then place another call to another friend who will tell him we have missed out on the house."

"Perfect."

Millicent's smile crumbled.

"Millicent? What's wrong?"

Her secretary's lower lip wobbled. "We missed out on our house. It was going to be our dream home…"

Oh, dear.

Grinning, Millicent said, "Was I convincing?"

"Heavens, yes."

"When Edmonds breaks the news tomorrow, I must remember to show my disappointment."

"Rest assure, no one will suspect a thing, Millicent."

Millicent nodded. "We spent the entire afternoon trying to come up with a solid plan. We couldn't move past the idea of us looking for a house and Edmonds said we needed the story to be believable so he suggested we use a friend of his as a contact. He arranged it all. We needed a real person and a real telephone number. Otherwise, if the post office person is anything like the woman in our village, they would have known we were up to no good."

Evie felt she didn't always come up with the brightest ideas. However, she was blessed with people around her who could step up and prop her up. "Good thinking. Both of you, well done."

After Millicent and Edmonds returned to their room, Evie sat and waited for Tom and Phillipa to knock on her door. At some point, she must have dozed off. When she woke up, she was startled to discover it was the middle of the night.

Whatever Tom had discussed with Edmonds would have to wait until the next day.

Evie crawled into bed managing to put her jumble of thoughts to sleep only by focusing on their dinner invitation.

Could Mr. Albert Graham and his wife be the people the barkeeper had been referring to when he'd said they needed to let *them* know?

The next morning...

The knock at her door stirred Evie fully awake. When the door opened and Phillipa peered inside, Evie groaned and put the pillow over her head.

"I take it you didn't sleep well last night?" Phillipa asked.

"I did just fine until the moaning and groaning woke me up and kept me awake for most of the night. I fear that story about the woman who had her throat slit might be true."

Phillipa laughed. "And you think she's haunting the entire village?"

"At this point, I'm willing to believe anything to justify the moaning and groaning." She sat up and brushed her hands across her face. "Give me ten minutes, please."

Phillipa nodded. "I can smell the enticing aroma of sausages and bacon. I'll meet you downstairs."

Evie rolled out of bed and splashed some cold water on her face.

The moaning and groaning she'd heard had been quite real. While she'd read about the power of suggestion, she could not have imagined hearing the noises. Had the villagers put on a performance especially for her?

A short while later, she went down to breakfast and found everyone except Edmonds had already settled down to a hearty breakfast.

Millicent gave her a cheery greeting. "Did you sleep well... Marjorie?"

"I fear the ghost of the murdered woman kept me awake," Evie grumbled.

Seeing Millicent's puzzled expression, Phillipa told her about the story they'd heard the previous day.

"Oh, oh, dear. I'm afraid there is a perfectly good explanation for that," Millicent said.

Evie's eyebrows curved up. "Do tell."

"Well..." Millicent's cheeks colored. She lowered her voice to a whisper. "Edmonds and I had to share a room because the barkeeper thought we were a couple which, of course, we're not. So we had to find a compromise and that meant... Edmonds had to sleep on the floor. That's why he hasn't come down to breakfast yet. He's upstairs trying to straighten his back. As good natured as he is, when I suggested a flat surface like the floor would do the trick, I'm sure he wanted to throw a shoe at me. I've never seen such a dark expression on him."

While relieved the moaning and groaning hadn't come from a murdered woman, Evie expressed her concern for Edmonds' crooked back.

"He's young and strong. He'll manage well enough." Tom poured Evie a cup of coffee. "You should start with this. It's nice and strong."

The pub hadn't opened its doors to the public yet so they were the only ones sitting down to breakfast and, with the barkeeper busy in the kitchen, they could speak freely.

"What do you have planned for us this morning?" Tom asked.

Evie rubbed her fingers along her temples. "Evans. Thanks to Millicent's tenacity, we have a name to investigate. It will hopefully lead us to a next of kin, if there is one."

"How did Millicent discover that?" Phillipa asked.

"She spoke with…" Evie looked at Millicent.

"Mrs. Patterson." Millicent adjusted her padding. "It keeps shifting."

Phillipa put her finger to her lips and a moment later, the barkeeper appeared with a platter full of bacon, eggs and sausages and a fresh pot of coffee.

Thanking him, Millicent gave him a bright smile. "Last night I heard the most incredible story about three French hens being stolen. Is that true?"

The barkeeper nodded.

"Oh, dear. Who would do such a thing?"

"The police are looking into it," the barkeeper said.

"The owner must be beside himself," Millicent continued.

The barkeeper nodded. "That he is. They had dozens

of ribbons between them. To think they ended up in someone's cooking pot."

"My Edward was wondering if they belonged to someone he'd read about in the newspapers but he couldn't remember his name. You see, my Edward is very fond of chickens and he insists on attending every village fair around, trekking from one village to the next to see the displays."

He nodded. "Last year's winners were announced in the newspaper. That' where he might have seen the name Duncan Miller," the barkeeper offered. "He's been spending his nights armed with his gun and keeping an eye on his other hens."

"Oh, I'm glad you told us. My Edward and I enjoy taking walks in the evening, especially when we visit villages. There's something quite charming about small villages at night. Just as well we didn't go out because we might have been mistaken for thieves."

"The village is safe enough, Mrs. Fletcher. Just make sure you don't wander along Old Salter Lane at night."

"Is that where he lives?"

He nodded.

"Thank you. We'll keep that in mind. Although, I'm sure my Edward will be able to sort out this business with the motor car today. We really are keen to continue on our way and see our house." Millicent laughed. "Just listen to me. I'm already referring to it as ours."

Once again, Millicent had come to the rescue, putting on a magnificent performance and discovering new information.

They now had a name and address and it happened to

be Duncan Miller who lived on Old Salter Lane where, as it happened, Glenda lived.

The barkeeper wiped the table and returned to the kitchen.

Tom whispered, "Countess, we have our work cut out for us."

Evie nodded and looked toward the window. The day looked gray and quite uninviting but they would have to trek out and explore Old Salter Lane. "We could go for a walk." That way, she thought, they could poke around and pretend to be looking for an ideal backdrop for their movie. She turned to Millicent. "And what will you be doing this fine morning?"

Keeping her eye on the bar, Millicent said, "Once my Edward recovers from his trials and tribulations, I suppose he will look into fixing our motor car..." Nodding, she continued, "The coast is clear now. While Edmonds makes his telephone calls, I could investigate the local church and locate Marjorie Evans' grave. I could talk with the vicar."

"Yes, please. That's a perfect plan, Millicent. Although, I'd prefer it if you and Edward... I mean, Edmonds stayed together." During their travels, Evie hoped they would encounter something else, something unexpected. Anything that would appease her concerns. Then, they could return to Halton House. Evie sighed and told herself to prepare for yet another surprise. She looked at Tom and Phillipa. "Did anything interesting happen last night after I retired?"

Tom shook his head. "Everyone stayed until the last possible moment. Then, Phillipa and I had the pub to ourselves but we didn't want to force the barkeeper to stay up on our account."

"Here's Edmonds," Millicent whispered.

Freshly shaved with only a minor nick on his chin, he greeted them and sat down, his back ramrod straight. "I trust everyone had a good night's sleep."

Phillipa nodded, "Everyone except Evie. She believes she heard the ghost of the woman who had her throat slit moaning and groaning during the night."

"A woman was killed? When? How?"

Evie remembered Edmonds hadn't heard the tale.

As it seemed to take his mind off his sore back, they all nodded and proceeded to tell him the tale.

CHAPTER SIXTEEN

Old Salter Lane

*R*ugged up against the morning chill, they set off to explore the village on foot. Turning into Old Salter Lane, it didn't take them long to notice their progress was followed by villagers casting discreet glances their way from the comfort of their warm homes.

While they were all confident everyone knew what they were up to, Tom had his Brownie camera and made sure to periodically stretch his hands out and form a square.

When they came across the first semi-detached building, they knew they were getting closer to Duncan Miller's house.

They imagined the owner of the French hens lived further out and perhaps closer to Glenda where the houses were detached and surrounded by small parcels of land.

"I keep seeing curtains shifting," Phillipa whispered. "Any minutes now, I expect to see someone coming out to follow us. In fact, they're probably trying to come up with a reason for doing so."

Being under constant surveillance meant they needed to remain on guard as every step they took would be scrutinized and questioned.

"Interesting," Evie said. "I haven't given Henrietta a single moment of my time. I'm probably too cross with her."

"You haven't mentioned anything about being cross," Tom said.

"It goes without saying. Henrietta could have spared us this trip. I haven't even spent time trying to understand the reasons for such secrecy. What could Glenda be hiding?"

"Illegitimacy," Phillipa said.

"What?" Evie could not have sounded more astonished.

"Glenda might be illegitimate."

The thought hadn't occurred to Evie and it didn't make sense. Glenda hadn't had any financial worries. Where did the money come from?

Evie looked at Phillipa.

"What?" Phillipa asked.

"It's actually a genius idea. I'm not sure why but, sometimes, thinking about the impossible or even the absurd clears the way for other ideas."

They continued walking along the lane pretending to take in the scenery. Smoke from the chimneys swirled into the air, the elegant plumes thinning out before drifting away and disappearing. Frost blanketed the land. Evie followed the flight of six birds emerging from a bank of fog and thought they looked like geese.

"I have a growing feeling of apprehension I simply can't shake off," Phillipa said. "It's almost as if I expect something to happen. I wouldn't be surprised if a woman runs out of one of the houses screaming."

Evie shivered and hugged herself. "Now I'm feeling it too."

Tom pointed ahead. "This must be Duncan Miller's house."

Evie was about to ask how he could tell when she saw a post standing beside the gate. It had a sign with a picture of a colorful hen. To Evie it just looked like a hen but she knew it had to be a French hen.

"Do we barge in?" Phillipa asked. "Everyone seems so keen on the idea of a movie being made here, I'm sure no one will think of complaining if they see us wandering into the yard to look at the French hens. Duncan Miller probably has a chicken coop somewhere out the back."

As she talked, Phillipa veered off the road and onto the garden path. Evie and Tom had no choice but to follow.

Stopping, Evie looked down the lane. Glenda's house sat three doors down. She glanced at the two houses next door and wondered if one of the owners had witnessed the theft. A silent witness, she thought—unbiased and unwilling to come forward.

"Are we risking life and limb?" Evie thought to ask. "Remember what the barkeeper said about Duncan Miller standing watch over his remaining French hens. He is most likely armed."

They heard the crunch of footsteps approaching. A man appeared around the corner of the house and stood with his hands in the pockets of his large coat.

He studied them for a moment and then called out in a gruff tone, "Can I help you?"

As they drew nearer, Evie thought she recognized him from the pub.

Tom said, "My apologies. We became caught up in our conversation."

"You're those movie people," Duncan Miller said, his tone not revealing his feelings on the matter.

"We were talking about a scene in the movie," Phillipa explained. "There's a chase scene through the village and one of the characters runs into a property and we wondered if there might be a way out the back."

Duncan Miller held her gaze for a moment and then nodded. "The properties along the lane all back into the Grahams' land."

Evie wondered if he had just unintentionally pointed the finger at the real culprit. Or, at least, at the possibility of the real culprit being someone from the neighboring estate.

That would definitely widen the field. Evie assumed the Grahams lived on a large estate and that meant they employed dozens of people.

"We heard something about the theft of some chickens," Phillipa said. "Are you the owner?"

He gave a stiff nod.

"Heavens. Did it happen at night or during the day?"

Even before he answered, a stray thought lodged in Evie's mind...

"Middle of the day," Duncan Miller responded.

"So there was a witness. It's good to know you can rely on your neighbors."

"We're a strong community of like-minded people."

That was the second time Evie had heard someone make the claim. Reading between the lines, she interpreted the remark to mean the community excluded outsiders. Newcomers were always perceived as outsiders until and if they were made to feel welcome. Therefore, it stood to reason, there could only be one suspect. Glenda Fulham.

Testing the waters, Phillipa said, "Well, at least the police are taking the matter seriously."

Evie held her breath. How would he answer that?

The detective had assured her the police would indeed take the matter seriously and, in fact, he'd compared the theft to the grievous act of poaching.

"That seems to be the case," he said.

His answer struck Evie as odd. She'd expected him to express a certain degree of determination in making sure the matter would be taken seriously.

Looking over his shoulder, he appeared to be impatient to get on with the business of looking after his remaining French hens so they thanked him for his time and headed back toward the road.

Before resuming their walk, Tom stopped to stretch his hands out and form a square. After which he took a photograph with his Brownie.

They walked on, slowing down when they approached the next house. No one spoke until Tom said, "Countess?"

Evie glanced at Tom. He always seemed to know when something bothered her or when she had a moment of clarity and was entertaining an idea. "Just before, I had a stray thought... According to Detective Inspector O'Neil, the bones and feathers were discovered in Glenda's yard. If you see someone stealing chickens, how long would it take you to report the crime? Long enough for the culprit to arrive home, cook the chickens, eat them, and then bury the bones?" Evie shook her head. "The story didn't make sense before because I couldn't picture Glenda doing something so silly. Now, the story has lost even more credibility."

What did the inconsistencies mean?

Evie couldn't see any other way of reading the situation. Someone had decided to lie.

Worse.

From the start, she'd suspected more than one person could be involved in this false accusation. The entire village had banded together to impress them with the suitability of the little village for their movie. Could they also join forces to make trouble for one of the newest arrivals?

"And for the umpteenth time, I ask myself... Why?"

Tom and Phillipa did not ask her to explain.

"In all the time Glenda lived at the Halton House cottage, she never visited her aunt, Marjorie. At least, not that I know of. I'm sure Millicent would be able to confirm this by asking around. Does that strike anyone as odd? She had a close relative but she never visited her. It didn't stop her from attending the funeral and, by the sounds of it, spending some time at Thornbridge. According to Mrs. Patterson, she had packed a suitcase for her journey." Had she kept in touch with her aunt? Had they corresponded? How had she heard about the death? Had a solicitor been in touch with her?

"There might have been animosity between them," Phillipa suggested.

"And yet, Glenda accepted her inheritance," Tom said.

"Where inheritances are concerned, people are prepared to put aside their differences," Phillipa argued.

Evie shook her head. "This is Glenda. She is a highly principled woman." Falling silent, she shook her head again. "Perhaps you're right." She looked toward Glenda's house. Visiting her again in order to force Glenda to reveal the secrets she was no doubt hiding and determined to keep hidden would be a waste of time. Evie would prefer to avoid a confrontation, at least until they had more information, something solid they could use to encourage Glenda to confide in them. "Let's head back. With any luck, Millicent and Edmonds will have discovered something significant."

"Are you still hoping there'll be a disgruntled relative biding their time?" Tom asked.

"That's an interesting choice of words." Someone biding their time is usually waiting for something to happen. Perhaps a favorable conclusion."

"Oh," Phillipa exclaimed.

She had their full attention but Phillipa seemed to take her time to gather her thoughts, something Evie was all too familiar with.

"I'm entertaining your theory of another relative. What if there is a caveat in the will?"

"That's an interesting idea. What are you suggesting?" Evie could think of a couple of examples.

"Assuming there was some sort of animosity between Glenda and Marjorie Evans, there might have been a special clause requiring the beneficiary to behave in a certain manner."

"Such as staying on the right side of the law?" Evie glanced at Tom. She knew he preferred hard facts to speculative ideas.

He surprised her by nodding. "I like that. It fits in nicely with the ridiculous accusation."

The more Evie thought about the idea, the more she found herself willing to accept it.

"We should head back to the village. I doubt there's anything more to see here."

Another thought occurred to Evie. Looking over her shoulder toward Glenda's house, she wondered if she had misread Glenda.

If they continued on to her house, would they find Glenda at home, wringing her hands with worry or would she be sitting back, feeling rather pleased with herself? Perhaps even smug?

Glenda had been calm and accepting of the situation, almost as if she believed she held the upper hand. "She knows something we don't know and if I go anywhere near her, I'm afraid I will take her by the shoulders and shake some sense into her," Evie whispered.

"Threatening physical violence, Countess? You must be at the end of your tether. Do please reserve some for Henrietta as I'm sure she will require it."

"No need," Evie said. "I suspect we'll find her locked up in the attic while Toodles and Sara prance around as ghosts. Their squabbling is sure to end badly."

When they reached the main street, they looked toward the pub and then toward the church.

Evie found herself thinking she wouldn't mind

retrieving their luggage and heading back to Halton House. Glenda did not welcome her help. Why persevere?

Nudging his head toward the pub, Tom asked, "Left, toward warmth and sustenance, or right, toward the unknown and possible disappointment?"

"I've lost track of time. By now, Millicent and Edmonds must have scoured through the graveyard and returned to the pub." And, she thought, if they hadn't found anything then... she really couldn't justify pursuing the matter.

Phillipa pointed ahead. "I see them. They've just come out of the church."

Evie looked toward the church and saw them. Instead of heading toward the main street, they turned and headed in the opposite direction. She assumed they were going to the churchyard.

Feeling discouraged, Evie said, "If they'd found something, they would have headed for the pub." As she spoke, Evie noticed a man standing in the corner looking toward the church. He had a newspaper tucked under his arm and was leaning against the wall.

Was he spying on Millicent and Edmonds?

He turned around and walked off in the direction of the pub. Evie thought he had either seen enough or he'd seen Millicent and Edmonds heading his way.

They crossed the street and when they reached the other side, Tom said, "You two go on ahead. I'm going to follow this fellow."

Evie and Phillipa headed for the church, with Evie looking over her shoulder. Tom walked several paces behind the man who, as expected, went straight to the pub. She guessed Tom wanted to see if he was merely going to the pub or if he had been charged with the task of reporting on Millicent's activities. She wondered what someone looking out the window would make of the scene. They were probably rushing to put their coats on so they could run over to the pub to report on Tom following the other fellow…

Evie and Phillipa decided to be strategic. Instead of heading straight for the church, they walked right past it and stopped to look at the house next door. After appearing to have a conversation about it, they turned back and were about to walk past the church again when Phillipa made a point of giving Evie a tug, appearing to talk her into going to the churchyard. If anyone saw them, they would think they'd been doing their survey of the village and Evie or, rather, Marjorie, hadn't been interested in the church.

"You respond well to directions," Phillipa said.

They saw Millicent and Edmonds meandering their way around the graves, every now and then stopping to read the headstones. They already knew Marjorie Evans had been buried here and Evie assumed they wouldn't have any difficulty finding the grave. In fact, she thought Millicent would have done that first. She couldn't imagine why she'd returned to the graveyard.

Hearing someone approaching, they both turned.

"Tom." His steps were hurried, suggesting he'd been eager to catch up with them. "Has something happened?"

He shook his head. "Just as we suspected. The fellow saw Millicent and Edmonds and stopped to see where they were going. When he saw them coming out of the church, he went to the pub to report. I lingered near the entrance long enough to hear him tell the barkeeper. It seems Millicent and Edmonds led him to believe they wanted to look around the village as a possible place to live in."

"Heavens, Millicent is turning into a woman of mystery with hidden talents."

They continued on until they came up to Millicent.

Edmonds tipped his hat back and smiled at them. "Millicent spun such a tale, I'm sure the vicar's head is still spinning. She's catching her breath now."

"I'm collecting my thoughts," Millicent said. "I've been telling so many tales, I don't want to lose track of them." She pointed to a grave. "This is Marjorie Evans' grave and the one next to it is her husband's grave, Anthony Evans."

"Was the vicar helpful?" Evie asked.

Millicent nodded. "I baited him by mentioning the French hens then I told him I'd heard a tale about a woman named Glenda being responsible."

Edmonds laughed. "Then, Millicent started talking about our fictional house and our problem with the motor car. Suddenly, she slipped in a question about Glenda, asking how long she'd lived here. When the vicar mentioned she'd only recently moved here, Millicent asked him a few unrelated questions and, in no time, she had him eating out of her hands. He's quite a chatty fellow."

Millicent nodded. "We found out Mr. Evans was an orphan."

An orphan? "How on earth had they managed to buy such a property?"

"That's what I wondered." Millicent grinned. "I actually wondered aloud. The vicar said Mr. Evans worked as a clerk in a law office."

Evie thought about Glenda's little manor house. Would a clerk earn enough to purchase such a house? She didn't think so.

"Did they marry here?" Evie asked.

"Oh, yes. The vicar showed us the registry entry. They married in 1885."

Evie looked at Marjorie Evans' gravestone. "She married late in life." Marjorie Evans had been born in 1845 and by 1885, she had been forty years old.

Something about that year rang a bell but Evie couldn't think why it sounded familiar.

Millicent grinned.

"What?" Evie asked. "There's more?"

Nodding, Millicent said, "Marriage records state the residences at the time of marriage."

Marjorie Evans had been living in Bath. How on earth had she met Mr. Evans?

Millicent continued to grin. Without being prompted, she said, "There was no special license."

Looking puzzled, Evie said, "That obviously means something but I'm afraid you'll have to spell it out for me."

"A license allows a couple to marry outside their parish in another church. As Marjorie had lived in Bath, we assume she wasn't from this parish."

"And... are we wrong to assume that?"

"We must be because they didn't need to obtain a special license. Banns is listed in the registry and that means Marjorie belonged to this parish. When I saw that, I asked myself how that could be." Millicent became quite excited. "So I then asked the vicar who scratched his head and then told me Marjorie had been born here and, before marrying, she had been living here for a number of months."

"Where?"

"At the pub. Apparently, she'd worked there in the kitchen."

"What brought Marjorie back? Why did she move away? Actually, when did she move away?" Evie drew in a breath and put her hand up. "It seems the moment we find some answers, we are inundated with more questions."

"Perhaps we should focus on the one burning question," Tom suggested. "How did they come to live in such a house?"

They decided to part ways, with Millicent and Edmonds leaving first and returning to the pub.

"We need to prioritize our questions. Otherwise, I won't be able to think straight," Evie said.

"It seems the ownership of the house is essential to our quest."

Tom's wording could not have been more appropriate.

They were indeed on a long and arduous search for... something.

CHAPTER SEVENTEEN

"It looks like the entire village is at the pub," Tom said as they walked in.

The man they'd seen hovering near the corner of the street watching Millicent and Edmonds stood at the bar nursing a glass of beer; perhaps his reward for spying and reporting back.

Seeing them, the barkeeper walked up to the table next to the fireplace and had a word with the customers who all nodded and stood up to leave.

"It seems we are about to receive preferential treatment," Evie mused.

Phillipa grinned. "This is the life."

Evie saw the customers who'd given up their table squeeze into another table, as if unwilling to leave the pub for fear they might miss out on a new development.

"Do you see Millicent and Edmonds?" Evie searched the other tables, half expecting them to be trying to blend in with the locals. In fact, it really wouldn't surprise her if Millicent ended up becoming acquainted with every single villager. Impressed with Millicent's display of casual bravado and resourcefulness, Evie felt confident no task would be too great for her new secretary.

"Is that the farmer who helps Glenda?" Evie asked as she signaled toward a corner table.

"Looks like him," Tom said.

Phillipa, who had a view of the door leading upstairs, said, "Here she comes."

Glancing over her shoulder, Evie saw Millicent stop for a moment to scan all the tables. She walked toward a corner to peer around it, almost as if she wanted to see if she could find a free table. Turning back, she stopped by their table.

"It looks like I'll need to wait for someone to leave," she said.

"There's no need for that, Mrs. Fletcher. Join us," Phillipa invited.

"Thank you."

"Where's Mr. Fletcher?"

"He's resting." Millicent winked and lowered her voice to say, "Edmonds wants to catch a nap to make up for his sleepless night. Have I missed anything?"

"No," Evie said. "And I'm happy to simply sit and eat luncheon." If she stopped thinking about the reasons for being at Thornbridge, at least for half an hour, she might refresh her mind and gain a better perspective on the information they already had.

"Oh, I nearly forgot to say we asked the vicar about the choir. It seems he's happy to welcome anyone who wishes to join. As we might be spending a few days here," Millicent said, "I thought we might join." Raising her voice, she added, "I'm afraid we have missed out on the house."

Playing along with the ruse, Phillipa commiserated with her. "Oh, that's a shame. Do you know if there are any houses available here? You seem to be quite taken with the village."

Millicent nodded. "We've heard about a cottage but it's quite rustic and in need of repairs."

As Millicent continued talking about the possibility of finding a house here, Evie found herself frowning.

Millicent had said Marjorie Evans had married in 1885.

The year had triggered something in Evie but, at the time, she hadn't known what.

Drumming her fingers on the table, she watched the barkeeper clearing a nearby table. When he finished, he took the tray back to the bar and returned to take their orders.

The options were limited to game pie and stew. This time, Evie had some game pie. Not that she noticed placing the order as her mind remained fixated on the date.

It taunted her and refused all attempts to be shelved.

Evie listened to the conversation around her but didn't hear a word. She cast her gaze around her and noticed everyone looking their way. Again, she could see them, but her awareness was faint as her mind continued to fixate on the date.

It seemed oddly coincidental for Millicent to mention it, almost as if it was meant to mean something.

Evie remembered looking at Marjorie Evans' gravestone and calculating Marjorie's age when she'd married in 1885. She'd been forty years old.

In a moment of clarity, Evie knew the reason why the date sounded familiar and it left her speechless.

Her husband, Nicholas, had been born that year.

Marjorie Evans had married the same year her husband, Nicholas, had been born.

Was it a mere coincidence or had she just made a significant connection?

She looked at the others but couldn't think of a way to communicate with them. There were too many people intent on listening to their conversation so Evie had to bide her time.

"Of course," Evie exclaimed.

Tom's eyebrows shot up. "Countess?" he mouthed.

Remembering Tom's talent for reading lips, Evie mouthed back, "Nicholas was born in 1885." She watched him trying to digest the information and waited for understanding to dawn. When it didn't, she went on to explain the rest but, in her excitement, her words collided and she only succeeded in confusing Tom.

Thinking she would explain later, Evie dug inside her handbag and produced a fountain pen and her notebook. She scribbled down some notes, making her writing as legible as possible so she could refer to her notes later.

Excitement coursed through her. She wanted to hug Millicent but knew the action would be out of character and raise suspicion.

By the time their meals arrived, she had filled several pages with notes, every sentence ending with an exclamation mark.

"Is Marjorie writing the movie script now?" Millicent asked.

"She likes to set down her thoughts before she forgets them," Tom explained.

As Phillipa didn't possess his ability to reads lips, she didn't know Evie had stumbled upon a thread and she was now intent on pursuing that thread until it connected to something.

It had to be significant. Otherwise, why had she noticed?

Happy with the small step she had taken, Evie put her pen and notebook away and settled down to eat her pie.

"I almost forgot we are having dinner with the Grahams tonight." Evie hadn't packed any evening gowns because she hadn't expected to dress for dinner. "I suppose they'll have to take us as we are."

Halfway through their meal, Millicent caught the attention of the barkeeper and asked him to prepare a tray for Mr. Fletcher saying she would take it up.

"He should be awake by now. Choir practice is in an hour," Millicent said and lowered her voice to add, "it'll be interesting to see how many people attend."

Moments later, the barkeeper brought the tray of food. Thanking him, Millicent made her way upstairs.

Having finished her meal, Evie sat back and played with the salt shaker. A few minutes after Millicent had left, she set the saltshaker down and stretched and yawned. "I think I might take a nap. I wouldn't want to fall asleep halfway through dinner."

Trying to avoid drawing attention to herself, Evie took her time going upstairs. Inside her room, she was about to knock lightly on the connecting door when it opened and Millicent walked in.

"I thought you might have missed my message, milady."

"Message?"

"Yes, bringing the tray up myself." Millicent snorted. "I have no experience being a wife, but I'm sure that if my husband wanted a nap because he'd slept poorly, I wouldn't be waking him up to force him to eat in order to then drag him to choir practice."

"Oh, yes, of course."

"I'm ever so curious about all that writing you did, milady."

"Marjorie."

"What about her?"

"I mean, you must call me Marjorie."

Millicent blushed. "I forgot."

"Anyhow, yes, it is partly about Glenda's aunt, Marjorie. When you mentioned she'd married in 1885, I thought there was something familiar, even significant, about the date."

"And did you find something significant?"

Evie nodded. "My husband was born that year."

"That could be a coincidence," Millicent reasoned.

"It also happens to be the year Glenda Fulham came to Halton House."

"Oh."

Evie paced around the small room. "That's as far as I got. At first, I only fixated about the coincidence of Marjorie Evans marrying the same year Nicholas was born. Then, I wondered what else might have happened that year and that's when I realized it was the year Glenda came to work as a nanny." Evie stopped and looked at Millicent.

"What?" Millicent asked.

"I'm... I'm thinking."

"Could you do it aloud?"

"You said Marjorie was born here."

Millicent nodded. A second later, she frowned. "Did I say that?"

"I think you did. I'm sure you did. Anyhow, that must mean her sister was also born here."

"Her sister?"

"Yes, Glenda's mother."

"Oh, I see." Millicent stepped back and sat on the chair.

"You saw Marjorie's name in the marriage registry."

Millicent nodded.

"I assume there must be an entry for her birth."

"There might be. This is dreadful. I can't remember..." Millicent looked up at the ceiling.

"What?" Evie asked.

"I'm trying to remember something I heard once... about registering births. I know the law changed..."

"How so?"

Millicent straightened. "Churches used to register births, marriages, deaths and, yes, even divorces. Then there was some sort of legislation and a national registry set up. I just can't remember in which year this happened. I only mention it because I don't want you to get your hopes up. The birth might or might not have been registered at the church."

"Millicent, do you think you could ask the vicar about it?"

"About the year?"

"No, about Marjorie's birth entry in the registry."

"Oh... How do I do that? Is this really important?"

"I'm hoping you'll then be able to ask him about her sister and… maybe even Glenda."

"How do I explain my interest? Oh, dear… I've suddenly lost my confidence. I'm so sorry, milady… I mean, Marjorie."

"That's perfectly fine, Millicent."

"Why do you want that information?"

"I'm not sure. Perhaps because we know next to nothing about Glenda and all this started because… well, because we know next to nothing about her." Evie sat on the edge of the bed. Glenda had stayed on at Halton House and she hadn't had any financial concerns. Had her parents left her money? Was that why she'd been able to retire early? It seemed like a perfectly simply explanation. One she hadn't considered before.

"When I obsess about something, I seem to turn a blind eye to the most obvious answer or explanation." Standing up, Evie sighed. "Nothing bad has really happened. Glenda hasn't been hauled away to prison and, best of all, no one's been murdered." If everything continued to be relatively normal, then they could stop worrying and asking questions and return to Halton House.

A light knock at the door was followed by Phillipa's swift entrance. "My apologies. I thought I heard someone coming up the stairs and I didn't want to be caught in the act of knocking on your door. Has something happened? And… What was all that writing about?"

Evie had to retell the tale about the significance of 1885. When she finished, she heard another light knock at the door. Easing it open, she saw Tom looking down the hall. Taking hold of his arm, she pulled him inside.

"1885," he said. "Did you write about that or something else?"

For the third time, Evie explained the connection she'd made.

"What does it mean?" Tom asked.

Evie lifted her shoulders and huffed as she lowered them. "Your guess is as good as mine but it has to mean something."

"Oh," Millicent exclaimed.

Thinking she had made a connection, Evie's eyes brightened. "What is it, Millicent?"

Millicent held up a finger calling for time and paced around in a tight circle.

"Countess, your condition is contagious."

Finally, Millicent stopped. "Not all births are registered in churches. There was some sort of law passed in the 1800s. Until a certain year, churches registered all births, marriages and deaths, but then it was decided to keep better records and the government..." Millicent waved her hand. "I don't remember the details. Oh... Oh... I remember the year. 1837. It was the year Victoria became Queen Victoria."

Frowning, Tom asked, "And what does all that mean?"

Millicent's eyes widened and she wailed, "I don't know." Turning to Evie, she asked, "Am I about to lose my position as your private secretary?"

"No, Millicent. How could you think that?" Evie went to stand by the window. "I think Millicent is concerned that even if she gains access to the birth registry she might not find the information because Marjorie Evans was born in 1845 and in 1837 births began to be registered... in some sort of central registry office."

Looking relieved, Millicent nodded. "Yes, I think that's what I meant."

"I see." Tom looked confused. "At least, I think I do."

Evie hugged herself as she remembered Henrietta saying sometimes it was best to leave things alone.

In a moment of frustration, she found herself thinking she should heed Henrietta's advice, reasoning that no action had been taken against Glenda for the theft of the French hens. Yes, indeed, it might be time for everyone to return to Halton House.

Edmonds cleared his throat. Turning, Evie saw him standing at the door connecting their rooms.

"Has something happened?" he asked.

"Marjorie has made a connection but we don't really know what it all means," Millicent said.

"Who's Marjorie?" Edmonds asked.

"Edward," Millicent stomped her foot.

Looking thoroughly confused, Edmonds asked, "Who's Edward?"

"It's obvious you're still half asleep. But there's no time to dwell on that," Millicent said. "We must go to choir practice and somehow try to gain access to the registry. Come along, I'll explain it all along the way."

CHAPTER EIGHTEEN

Several hours later

When Millicent and Edmonds failed to return from choir practice, Evie worried something might have happened to them. Just then, there was a knock at her door. She recognized the single rap as Tom's.

Evie let him in and was surprised to find he'd changed into his formal attire. "You came prepared."

"Are you suggesting you didn't?"

"It goes without saying. I didn't expect to be invited to dinner."

"Countess, herein lies a lesson. When attending to an investigation, always come prepared."

Evie's eyebrow curved up. "Are you being smug?"

"Smug? No, never. I'm just crowing."

"With any luck, the Grahams won't make a fuss."

"I somehow doubt it," Tom said. "Mr. Graham looked the type."

"Really? He struck me as lacking confidence. He certainly didn't have much to say to us. I'm thinking he might have been concerned about extending the invitation without first consulting with Mrs. Graham. In any case, they are expecting us for dinner soon, and Millicent and Edmonds haven't returned. We can't just leave without knowing they are all right."

Setting her at ease, Tom suggested they should investigate. "We'll drive up to the church and I'll go in."

"On what pretext?"

"I'll say we were driving by and I saw someone skulking about. Worst-case scenario, they'll think I've fallen for that story about the woman who had her throat slit. I already did once but my ego can take another hit."

Evie slipped on her dark spectacles. "Attending a dinner party in my day dress will be a novelty but I'm as ready as I'll ever be."

They stepped out of her room just as Phillipa was coming out of her room.

When Phillipa saw her, she frowned. "You can do better than that." She wore a black velvet evening jacket with a long black satin dress and a sparkly headband, her hair gleaming gold and her general demeanor looking quite glamorous.

"I'm suddenly feeling drab," Evie declared.

Phillipa took hold of her arm and guided Evie to her room. A short while later, they emerged with Evie now wearing an elegant velvet evening coat in a dark green and a dress to match.

"You both look smashing," Tom declared.

"Thank you. Although, now I'm feeling quite inade-
quate. Phillipa actually traveled with two evening outfits."

If they drew attention from the customers in the pub,
they didn't notice. Evie's thoughts were fixed on the night
ahead. They all needed to remain in character and find
out if Albert Graham had anything to do with the accusation made against Glenda.

For all she knew, Albert Graham stood to benefit from
Glenda's woes. He might even gain something significant.

They'd find out soon enough but, first, they needed to
make sure Millicent and Edmonds had not come to any
harm.

With that purpose in mind, they made their way to the
motor car and drove the short distance to the church.

When they arrived, they leaned out the windows and
stared at the church.

"I don't hear singing or music," Evie said. "And the
church looks dark."

Phillipa pointed toward the corner of the church.
"There's a light in the building next to it. It might be the
vicarage."

Tom stepped out of the motor and walked with
purpose toward the vicarage.

Remaining in the car, Evie and Phillipa followed his
progress, leaning to one side to see the moment he slowed
down. When he was a few steps away from the window
with the light, he crouched.

"I see Tom came prepared with formal dinner wear,"
Phillipa murmured.

Evie rolled her eyes. "Yes, I should know better next
time. In fact, when we return to Halton House, I'll ask
Millicent to give me instructions on packing a suitable

suitcase for any occasion that might arise, including the need to dress as an indigent person or a farm laborer."

As they waited, Evie talked about Lotte Mannering's many talents. "I'm sure she's worn other disguises but Tom and I didn't notice. That goes to show how good she is."

They saw a shape moving in the shadows and hurrying toward the motor car.

A few seconds later, the door opened and Tom climbed in.

"Well? Does the vicar have them tied up?" Evie asked.

"Countess, you have a vivid imagination. They're dining with the vicar and his wife and appear to be having a jolly good time."

"Oh, I see. That's a relief." In the next breath, she said, "What do you think she's doing?"

Tom drummed his fingers on the steering wheel. "She's probably employing her cunning." Looking over his shoulder at Evie, he added, "I hope you realize your lady's maid or, rather, your secretary, is quite cunning and resourceful."

"Yes, Tom. I have come to learn that firsthand. I believe Caro taught her well." Her previous lady's maid had been quite talented, and she continued to impress, stepping into the role of Lady Evans without any problems.

They left the village and drove along a road running parallel with Old Salter Lane. According to the barkeeper, it would lead them straight to Graham House.

"I wonder if the house is also accessible along Old Salter Lane," Evie mused. "The architecture looks too similar to Glenda's house for it to be a coincidence."

Phillipa nudged Evie and pointed to the right. "Is that the back of Glenda's house?"

The light was fading fast but the house, sitting in the near distance, was well lit. In fact, Glenda probably had all the lights on in the house.

That worried Evie.

In her mind, she entertained the worst scenario she could imagine, picturing the police arriving to make an arrest. They were probably searching through her house looking for evidence to convict her.

Would they find the five gold rings in her possession?

"Countess," Tom used his warning tone. "Whatever you're thinking, you should stop right now."

Heavens, he hadn't even turned to look at her. "You're right. However, I was just picturing the police knocking on Glenda's door to make an arrest. At worst, she'll spend a night in prison and, in my opinion, that might not be such a bad idea. Maybe then she'll come to her senses and accept our help." She could only hope all those lights on in her house didn't mean anything.

Tom slowed down and drove through a set of gates flanked by stone pillars. Torches lit the way along a straight road leading to the house. A considerate touch, she thought.

"They've practically rolled out the red carpet for us," Evie said.

"I suppose making a movie in Thornbridge would be quite lucrative for the village," Phillipa said. "Mr. Graham might want to have us as guests for the duration of filming."

Evie grinned. "You seem to forget we are not really here to make a movie."

"They don't know that."

At some point, they'd have to start thinking about the moment when everyone discovered they were not movie makers from Hollywood.

Phillipa expressed the same thought, suggesting they might need to steal away in the dead of night. "At least Millicent and Edmonds will remain free of suspicion. They're both quite good at playing their roles."

As the sun set, Evie had difficulty making out the landscape but she thought she could see a lake directly opposite the house.

"There's a lake," Tom pointed out.

"Yes, I noticed and... I think I see something in there." Evie squinted and tried to make out the shapes. "They look like fairly large birds."

"Swans," Tom suggested. "There's six of them. No... wait... I see one just landing. There's seven. They're probably settling in for the night."

"Do they sleep on water?" Evie asked. "I suppose they do but I've never noticed."

As soon as Tom brought the motor car to a stop, the front door opened and a man they assumed was the butler stepped out.

"You're right, Phillipa, they are giving us the royal treatment. I fear there might be a lot of questions about our activities."

"Don't worry, I'll make sure to answer all the awkward questions."

The butler rushed to open the door for them and was surprised to find Tom was not the chauffeur.

Tom muttered, "I think he was about to direct me to the service entrance."

They followed the butler into the hall where Evie took in the black and white square marble tiles and high beamed ceiling. A large tapestry covered one wall while paintings she assumed were of ancestors covered the other walls. A log shifted in the large stone fireplace at one end sending sparks flying up the chimney. While the owner of the house had no title, she imagined the house had been in the family for a long time; a product of the family's illustriousness.

The butler took their coats. "Mr. Graham—"

Whatever he was about to say was cut off by the sound of angry shouting, followed by a door slamming.

Flinching, the butler cleared his throat. "Mr. Graham will be with you shortly."

A door opened and Albert Graham walked out, his attention on the floor as he raked his fingers through his hair. Looking up, he saw them and, dismissing whatever had taken place moments before, he plastered a smile on his face.

"Welcome to Graham House." Turning to the butler, he said, "Drinks? Yes, drinks."

As Albert Graham led them to a grouping of chairs and sofas near the fireplace, Evie realized the drinks were going to be served in the hall. At one time, she thought, the hall had been the center of activity in such houses. Indeed, the hall at Halton House was always used for their balls and Christmas festivities. So it didn't seem to be that odd. However, Evie had expected to be shown through to a drawing room where they would find other guests. She supposed it meant they were actually the only guests dining at Graham House.

"I'm afraid my wife, Elizabeth, has been delayed. She

should be down momentarily." He looked up and toward the butler. Giving a nod, he said, "Martinis?"

Everyone nodded in agreement.

Evie looked toward the carved staircase and imagined another staircase connecting to it. They'd just heard Albert Graham arguing with someone and, jumping to conclusions, she assumed that someone had been his wife, Elizabeth. She also imagined Elizabeth Graham had found some way, other than the main stairs, to make her way upstairs so she could then make her entrance.

She hoped they hadn't been the source of the argument. It seemed rather odd to clash right before guests were due to arrive. Surely they were mature enough to put their differences aside until their guests had left.

The butler served the drinks. As Evie took a glass, she saw him casting his gaze toward the stairs.

"Jones only knows how to make Martinis one way. I hope you won't mind." Albert Graham took a long sip from his glass. Lowering it, he suddenly brightened. "I say, this news I've heard is marvelous. Are you all really making a movie here?"

"We're still deciding," Phillipa offered.

"It's all very exciting. The entire village is talking about it." He leaned forward and lowered his voice as if about to impart a secret. "You know they've asked me to put in a good word. If there's anything I can do or say to make this happen... of course, you can all stay here. That should be very exciting. For us, at least."

It struck Evie as odd that he should suddenly have so much to say. When they'd met him at the pub, he'd barely strung two sentences together. Then she wondered if he was trying to offer a distraction to cover up for his wife's tardiness.

Had they really walked in on something? The raised voices they'd heard had sounded quite serious. Evie imagined Albert Graham breaking the news to Elizabeth Graham at the last minute and expecting her to have a banquet organized and be ready to welcome their guests...

"Where else have you made movies?" he asked, his tone excited.

Or, Evie thought, nervous. Perhaps even on edge.

Tom and Evie looked at Phillipa who was quick to improvise. "We were recently in India."

"Oh, that must have been a marvelous adventure." As he sat back, he cast his eye at the clock on the mantle and then at the stairs.

"It most certainly was. We tried to capture the essence of tropical woodlands in a studio but, in the end, it was easier to travel there. It was well worth the effort just to film elephants by the roadside, rice paddies straddling mountains and the locals, of course. That's when we decided our next movie would also be filmed away from the studios. After all that heat, we needed a change of scenery and climate. So we came to England."

He gave a vigorous nod. "And how did you settle on our little village?"

"By chance," Phillipa chirped. "We've been traveling all over the country and then we came upon this village. We were instantly in awe of the countryside and buildings. One house, in particular, caught our attention." Phillipa waved in the general direction of Glenda's house. "We saw it as we drove past and then we simply had to stop to have a proper look. A woman lives there." Phillipa rested the tip of her finger on her chin. "What was her name? Tom, do you remember?"

Tom shrugged. "Gladys?"

"Oh, no. I would have remembered that name. I have two cousins named Gladys."

Evie took a sip of her Martini and drawled out, "Glenda, I'm sure of it. I had an aunt named Glenda. She always disapproved of me."

"Yes, that's it." Phillipa frowned. "There was something rather odd about her. For starters, it took some doing to get her to talk to us. She didn't think much of our intentions. Everyone else has been impressed and quite excited, but not Glenda. I find that odd." She looked at Mr. Graham. "Don't you?"

"Yes, rather. She's… She's new to the village," he said as if that would excuse Glenda's fabricated lack of interest.

"Anyhow," Phillipa continued, "Marjorie here has her heart set on that house. We must try to convince Glenda to allow us to film there. Otherwise, I'm afraid Marjorie will lose interest in this village. Do you have any sway with her?"

"With Glenda Fulham?"

"Yes."

Before he could answer, Phillipa said, "Marjorie had the most astonishing suspicion. She thinks Glenda is related to you."

His eyebrows shot up. "She does? Why…" Albert Graham looked at Evie. "What gave you that idea?"

Phillipa answered for her, "She says Glenda's house and your house look the same. And, they do. Don't you think? Marjorie thinks it's a dower house."

Albert Graham chortled. "I suppose the houses were built by the same architect. And, perhaps, at some point, it might have belonged to the estate. Over the years, parcels of land have been sold off along with some buildings…"

"Sold? Is there some way of confirming that? Marjorie loves the history behind the houses."

Mr. Graham drained his glass. "There should be some sort of paperwork around."

"So she's not related to you."

"I can't imagine how she could be. I've never set eyes on her."

Indeed, Evie thought. Glenda hadn't just attended her aunt's funeral, she had actually stayed in Thornbridge for several days.

Albert Graham owned the largest estate near the village and Glenda's aunt had lived practically next door to him. He must surely know everything that went on in the village. It stood to reason that he would have been aware of Glenda's arrival to attend the funeral.

"In any case," Phillipa continued, "I do hope Glenda changes her mind about letting us film in the house." She tilted her head in thought. "There must be a way to find out."

"Find out what?" Albert Graham asked as the butler refilled his glass.

"Find out if Glenda Fulham's house belonged to this estate."

Albert Graham nearly choked on his drink.

"We like to research our projects thoroughly. Marjorie likens it to peeling an onion." Phillipa shrugged. "Getting to all the layers to find out what's lurking underneath it all."

He looked confused. "And what does that have to do with making a movie?"

"It has everything to do with it." Phillipa smiled and continued with her vague explanation. "You'd be surprised how much can be revealed through the eye of a camera lens. We just like to make sure it's there to be revealed." She looked around her. "Take this house…"

"Graham House?"

"Yes, I'm sure there's a long history with several family skeletons hidden in the closet."

He didn't respond and his expression remained puzzled.

"We've been wondering about the architectural style…"

He sat up, his eyes brightening with eagerness as he found himself able to answer something. "Jacobean. Sixteen hundreds."

"Sounds like your family has been around for a long while," Phillipa observed.

He nodded and gestured toward the paintings.

As Phillipa had pointed out, Evie thought, families with long histories had secrets. How far would Mr. Graham go to keep his family's secrets?

Evie pondered the question only to remind herself they needed to focus on Glenda and her past.

However… If she had been born in this village…

Could there be something in her past to link her to the Graham family?

Right in the midst of that thought, she heard the sound of approaching steps. Looking up, Evie saw a woman appear at the top of the stairs. Not young and not old,

Evie thought and guessed she might be somewhere in her late thirties or, perhaps, early forties.

Her hair was styled in the latest fashion, cut quite short and framed around her pale face. Even from a distance, Evie could tell she had vibrant blue eyes. As she came down the stairs, she took in the scene, her face devoid of any expression.

She wore a rose-colored satin dress with long sleeves and a cluster of sparkly jewels in her hair. Her lips were a slash of vibrant red, quite striking against her pale skin and dark hair.

"Apologies for my tardiness," she said when she reached the foot of the stairs. She stood there for a moment as if to give everyone the opportunity to take in the sight of her.

When they all turned, she produced a small smile before approaching. Along the way, she stopped by a table to fix herself a drink, adding an extra splash of gin to her Martini.

Instead of sitting by the chair next to her husband, she went to stand by the fireplace where Tom stood.

"Introductions, darling," Mrs. Graham instructed without looking at her husband.

"Oh, yes… Well, these are the movie people I told you about. That's Mr. Tom…"

"Broadchurch," Tom said.

Evie tried to remember if that had been his chosen name at the pub. Then again, she couldn't remember which family name she had given…

Mrs. Graham expressed her pleasure at meeting Tom and then turned to Evie.

Evie, who still wore her colored spectacles, looked at her over the rim of her glasses and drawled, "Marjorie."

"I'm Phillipa," Phillipa said before being prompted.

Mrs. Graham studied them for a moment and then turned to the butler. "Jones, how far away are we from dinner?" Signaling to her glass, she added, "I'm afraid I need to catch up."

Evie had the impression Mrs. Graham wished to entertain them at her leisure and do so in a thorough state of inebriation.

Suddenly, instead of worrying about Glenda, she found herself intrigued by the unfolding scenario and wondered what insights the evening might provide.

CHAPTER NINETEEN

The dining room, Graham House

*M*rs. Graham did not share her husband's enthusiasm for their guests' endeavors, nor was she impressed by their Hollywood credentials. Mostly, she didn't understand why anyone would be interested in a movie made in a small village or, indeed, why they were so interested in the people living there.

"They want layers," Mr. Graham explained. When she merely shrugged and held her glass out for the butler to refill, he explained, "I'm afraid my wife has no patience for layers of complexities. She finds them annoying. As the local magistrate, she tends to draw a hard line, dismissing all fanciful excuses or ideas."

Mrs. Graham was the magistrate?

Phillipa expressed her surprise.

"Oh, yes. I can't claim to be the first but I am one of a handful of women to be recently appointed."

Phillipa exchanged glances with Evie and Tom before saying, "We've heard a story about a theft but no one seems to have any detailed information. Is it likely to come before you?"

Elizabeth Graham nodded but showed more interest in her meal and her wine than the conversation taking shape or even the three guests her husband had invited.

"We've spoken with Glenda Fulham, the woman accused of theft…"

Elizabeth Graham glanced up from her glass.

"She's the owner of the house we're interested in." With a small nod of encouragement from Evie, Phillipa continued, "Wherever we go, we enjoy hearing strange tales. Glenda Fulham is accused of stealing three French hens. It sounds rather ludicrous. What's your response likely to be?"

Rolling her eyes, Elizabeth Graham drained her wine glass and held it up for the butler to refill again. "It's all a lot of nonsense, I'm sure."

Relieved to hear the admission, Evie hoped Phillipa would prompt her to say more.

"So you'll dismiss it?" Phillipa asked.

"Most likely. Although, I need to remain impartial and hear everyone out."

"We're rather taken with her house and hope to convince Glenda Fulham to allow us to film there. I hope this business doesn't influence her decision."

Elizabeth Graham tipped her head back and laughed. "Are you, by any chance, trying to influence *me*?"

"I wouldn't dream of it." Phillipa gave her a brisk smile.

"However, it really does sound like a bit of fiction." She looked at Tom and Evie before continuing, "We were talking about it earlier. It seems odd to have a witness who didn't bother to report the crime until the chickens were cooked, eaten and their carcasses buried."

"Hens," Elizabeth Graham said. "French hens, to be precise. Duncan Miller is very particular about that."

Phillipa laughed. "The more I think about it, the sillier it all sounds. Three French hens? Who can actually sit down and devour three French hens?"

Amused by Phillipa's reasoning, Albert Graham said, "That does sound odd. But... due process and all that. I'm sure it will all be sorted out in no time. People like to think they'll be heard and taken seriously. This shouldn't affect your movie. Mark my word, Glenda Fulham will be cleared of all wrongdoing. I'm certain of it."

Elizabeth Graham smirked. "My husband is a stickler for the rules but will do anything to maintain the status quo."

Evie waited for Elizabeth Graham to explain. When she didn't, Evie puzzled over the remark. She had no idea what it meant.

Which rules had she been referring to? The rules of the land? The rules of the law or the rules of society and propriety?

Evie then wondered if Elizabeth Graham had meant to mock her husband. She had sensed a hint of derision in her voice and, while Evie hadn't seen her lip curve up in disdain, her tone had suggested she had felt nothing but contempt.

While Evie wanted to know more about Albert Graham's wish to maintain the status quo, Elizabeth

Graham returned her focus to her meal and to drinking while Albert Graham stumbled from one question to the other about the movie business.

At the first opportunity, Phillipa asked, "If Glenda Fulham is not guilty of stealing those French hens, then who is?"

"That's a matter for the police. They'll soon get to the bottom of it all," Albert Graham said and immediately asked if they had met Rudolph Valentino.

With dinner over, Evie assumed Mrs. Graham would lead them through to the drawing room but she wouldn't be parted from her glass of wine.

Feeling they had nothing further to gain by staying, they said they needed to experience the village at the crack of dawn, thanked their hosts for dinner and left.

Tom waited until he'd driven past the gates to say, "That was rather awkward."

Evie agreed.

Tom shook his head. "A strange couple and a strange evening. I fail to see the point to it all."

"I hope Millicent and Edmonds had better luck." Evie huffed out her frustration. "I'm sorry I couldn't be of any help, Phillipa. My disguise comes with certain limitations, preventing me from showing any kind of enthusiasm or being chatty." In hindsight, Evie thought she should have chosen a character with a more argumentative trait. Perhaps even disagreeable. At least, that characteristic might have provoked more responses from their hosts.

"Mrs. Graham must have a fiery temper," Phillipa said. "Do you think they were arguing about us?"

"Heavens, I hope not. They could not have chosen a worst moment. If we were the focus of their clash, it's bad form to leave it until the last minute when your guests are about to arrive. Mr. Graham issued the invitation yesterday. They've had ample time to quarrel."

"It sounded like a violent shouting match," Tom said. "I'm surprised she didn't smash something."

Evie snorted. "Why do you assume the woman would resort to throwing something?"

Shrugging, Tom said, "Violence by proxy."

"Women are too smart to resort to physical violence," Phillipa declared. "We use words instead. Perhaps, on occasion, we might employ an object for emphasis."

"Do you speak from experience?" he asked, his tone filled with curiosity.

"I've written a character with a snappy temper. She always employs reason but the end of her tether is never too far away."

Despite engaging in conversation, they were all alert and attentive, watching the road. Although, as always, Tom drove with care.

"All the lights are out at Glenda's house," Phillipa observed.

"Thank goodness for that. We can rest easy tonight." Although, Evie still wondered what Glenda had been doing. Clearly something that had required all the house lights to be turned on. She had only recently moved into the house, so perhaps she'd been looking for something she'd misplaced.

Evie turned to Phillipa. "By the way, how on earth did it occur to say we'd been curious to know if Glenda was related to the Graham family?"

"I was struck by inspiration," Phillipa said. "We'd been talking about finding some sort of connection and fixating on the architectural similarities between the two houses. Did you happen to notice Albert Graham's reaction?"

Evie stared ahead into the darkness. "I think he tried to dismiss it as odd. To be perfectly honest, I can't really remember. All that time, I sat there watching Elizabeth Graham and almost feeling in awe of the woman. I've never encountered such behavior from a hostess. She wasn't just disinterested, I thought she looked rather bored with our presence. Actually, now that I think about, you might have mentioned the architectural similarities as well as our suspicions about Glenda being related to the Graham family before Elizabeth Graham made her entrance." Evie hummed. "I'm afraid I'm now obsessing with Elizabeth Graham's behavior."

"Countess, you have a low tolerance for rudeness."

"I won't argue with that." Evie laughed. "Oh, I think I'm about to entertain one of my wild suppositions."

Phillipa clapped. "Do share."

"I'm trying to understand the couple's unusual behavior." Evie thought about everyone, including themselves, playing roles and pretending to be someone they weren't. "What if they pretended to have a fight just as we arrived?"

"Why would they do that?"

"Because… let me think… Oh, they had an agenda."

"That actually makes sense," Phillipa said. "The villagers at the pub want to impress us so we'll choose their village to film our movie. We want to fool everyone into believing we are actually making a movie and Mr. and Mrs. Graham, well, as you said, they have an agenda."

"The problem with my wild ideas is that they rarely

have any sound reasoning. Why would Mr. and Mrs. Graham pretend they'd had an argument?"

"To distract us?" Phillipa suggested.

"And to throw us off the scent." Evie shook her head. "But that would mean they're hiding something and I can't begin to imagine what that might be. This really doesn't help our cause. We already have too many unanswered questions." Evie stretched and yawned. "It's been a long day and I can't wait to rest my head on the pillow. With any luck, I'll be able to get some sleep tonight." Remembering her struggles the previous night, Evie groaned. "Although, I doubt Millicent and Edmonds have changed their sleeping arrangements."

Phillipa laughed. "Millicent has been doing such a wonderful job pretending to be someone else, she should have pretended she'd had an argument with Edmonds and asked for separate rooms. I'll suggest it tomorrow."

"That still leaves tonight," Evie murmured.

They drove past the church in time to see the lights being turned off in the dining room.

"I suppose that means Millicent and Edmonds have already returned."

Tom brought the motor car to a stop outside the pub just as the last customer was leaving.

"It's nearly ten o'clock. The barkeeper must have been waiting for us to return."

"Would anyone care for a nightcap?" Tom asked.

"Yes, please," Phillipa said.

"Not for me, thank you. I have some sleep to catch up on."

Evie left Tom and Phillipa in the pub and made her way upstairs.

She considered knocking on the adjoining door to see if Millicent had learned anything of interest from the vicar, but she really needed to sleep.

When she finally climbed into bed, she closed her eyes and tried to empty her mind by focusing on her breathing.

Then she listened for any sounds coming from the room next door. So far, she didn't hear anything. She imagined it took Edmonds a couple of hours of uncomfortable sleeping before he started moaning and groaning.

Plumping up her pillow, she tried to empty her mind again only to find herself wondering if Glenda had attended her aunt's wedding in 1885.

She would have been twenty...

"That's young for a nanny," she murmured. "What experience had she had at that age?"

Not much, she thought.

"And, if she did attend her aunt's wedding, why didn't Glenda say something about being familiar with the village?" Evie murmured. "In fact, she might have mentioned her aunt and mother had been born here."

Had keeping her life private come naturally to her or had she nurtured the habit over the years to discourage people from snooping around for information?

It took a special talent to evade questions and Glenda excelled at it.

When she felt her eyes growing heavy, Evie decided they would stay one more day. At least until Elizabeth Graham dismissed the charges against Glenda. Once the person responsible for trying to make Glenda's life difficult realized they wouldn't get away with such nonsense, they were likely to give up the endeavor.

"She calls herself Fulham," Evie whispered. From the moment she'd first heard this remark, it had taken up residence in her mind, waiting for her to either make a connection or dismiss it.

It suggested a change of name. Why else had the man phrased it the way he had?

Evie knew they would have to return to the church and make further inquiries. Glenda's aunt had been born here so it stood to reason Glenda's mother had also been born here. If Glenda's mother had married in this parish, there might be a record of Glenda's birth. Then, they would know for sure if Glenda had changed her name. "Oh, here's a possibility…" Evie nibbled the edge of her lip. "What if Glenda had married young? Fulham could be her married name." The thought almost had the effect of a splash of icy cold water on her face.

Instead of playing around with the idea, she spent the next few minutes distracting herself with thoughts of returning to Halton House.

Her last thought before finally drifting off to sleep was of Henrietta, Sara and Toodles, all dressed up in their respective roles as ghosts.

CHAPTER TWENTY

Eight maids a-milking

The next morning

*J*f Edmonds had experienced another torturous night, Evie did not know it. She had slept right through the night and, thankfully, had woken up feeling refreshed.

Whether nor not it meant anything, she decided to take it as a good omen.

After last night's dinner, Evie felt more confident about the outcome of Glenda's troubles. Once the magistrate dismissed the ridiculous charge of theft, they could return home.

Evie stood at the door to her room, ready to make her way down to breakfast. The thought made her stop and wonder if they would need to remind Glenda she had been invited to attend the Christmas festivities at Halton House.

"That is definitely a bridge to cross some other day." As she opened the door, she remembered the five gold rings...

They hadn't heard anything about anyone accusing Glenda...

Grumbling, she stepped out into the hallway and met Phillipa as she rushed out of her room.

"Did you hear?" Phillipa asked.

"Edmonds?" Smiling, Evie shook her head. "I must have been too tired."

"No, I meant the commotion."

"What commotion?"

"Outside. I've spent the last half hour watching people running about in a state of panic. I thought you might have been doing the same."

"Heavens, no. I didn't hear anything. I've been busy thinking. I should have known my good night's rest was too good to be true."

"Maybe the barkeeper will know something by now," Phillipa suggested.

They hurried down and found Tom standing by the fireplace, talking with the barkeeper.

Instead of joining them, Phillipa and Evie headed straight for a table near the front window.

"I'm sure we'll hear about the news soon enough." Evie glanced out the window and saw a woman rushing by. She stopped and was joined by another woman. "Oh, dear.

I have the sudden urge to rush to Glenda's house and make sure she's all right."

"News appears to be spreading quickly." Phillipa pointed to a group of people who had congregated across the street. "It was interesting to watch from upstairs. One woman stopped to pass on the information. She then hurried off only to stop and look around as if deciding whom to approach next. I actually saw her knocking on a door. That's when I decided to find out more. I'm sure she's gone from house to house, spreading her news."

Shaking her head, Evie said, "I can't even begin to imagine what might have happened during the night." In the next breath, she said, "I only hope it has nothing to do with Glenda having all the lights on at her house last night. What about you? Can you think of anything?"

"There have already been two thefts," Phillipa said. "It's possible there's been another one. Or, since Glenda hasn't been apprehended for the theft of the French hens, another crime has been committed. Something serious enough to require prompt action."

"Anyone would be forgiven for thinking the spirit of goodwill has gone out of fashion," Evie complained as she looked toward the fireplace. "What can they be talking about? Tom is right. Patience is not one of my strong suits."

Someone ran past the window. A second later, they ran back.

"Was that Millicent?" Phillipa asked. "I only saw a blur, but there was something familiar about the woman."

The front door opened and Millicent rushed inside and headed straight for the door leading to the stairs. Along the way, she noticed Tom and the barkeeper. That slowed her down long enough for Edmonds to rush inside the pub and catch up with her. Noticing Evie and Phillipa, he reached for Millicent and tugged her back.

"Oh, heavens," Millicent exclaimed and hurried toward their table. "I was in such a hurry to get here, I missed the entrance."

"Mrs. Fletcher, has something happened?" Evie asked.

"Yes, oh, heavens, yes, something has happened." To her credit, Millicent remembered to refer to Edmonds by his fake name. "Edward and I were out on our early morning constitutional, when a woman stopped us and told us the news."

Tom joined them, saying, "The barkeeper is about to start on breakfast. What's all the excitement about?"

Instead of telling him about her news, Millicent asked, "Doesn't he have a cook?"

Evie huffed out, "Mrs. Fletcher, you were about to tell us some news."

"Oh, yes." Millicent sat down. "A body's been found."

"What?" Evie half rose out of her chair. "Who? Where? When?"

"No one knows who. They only know the milkmaids found him."

"It's a man?"

Millicent nodded. "I suppose I should have started with that. Anyhow, the milkmaids were making their way along Old Salter Lane and toward a farm, later than usual because the cows don't produce much milk at this time of year. Most of them also work in a tapestry workshop, which reminds me, I should like to look at their work. Anyhow, there were four of them and, along the way, they met up with four more milkmaids, that's when they encountered the man, face down in a ditch."

"And that's why they couldn't identify him?" Evie asked.

Millicent shook her head. "Two of them ran off to fetch the constable and the others were too scared to look. Now they are under instructions not to say anything."

"Whereabouts is this ditch?" Phillipa asked.

Millicent leaned forward and whispered, "Right opposite Glenda's house."

Evie thought this couldn't possibly be a coincidence. She turned to Tom. "Does the barkeeper know about this?"

"No. We were talking about pies. He does a lot of the cooking and baking and I wanted him to share his recipe…" He signaled toward the front door. "But I think he's about to find out."

A woman stormed in. Evie couldn't be sure but she thought it was the same woman who had spread the news about the five gold rings being stolen.

When she didn't see the barkeeper, she called out his name and he emerged from the kitchen.

As she delivered her message, Evie watched his reaction. He frowned and nodded a couple of times. Then, he looked away, toward the door. Almost as if trying to picture the scene. Or, perhaps, trying to piece together the events.

Or, like Evie, he was tossing about some questions.

When had he died?

Had he died from natural causes?

Or, had his death been caused by nefarious means?

And, if so, who had killed him?

Evie nudged Tom. "What if the woman has more information about the man's identity? Tom, go and find out what she's told him. Tell him we've heard about the incident and wondered if he knew more."

Tom waited until the woman left and then approached the barkeeper.

Calling for patience, Evie turned to Edmonds. "How did you sleep last night?"

"I fared better. We found some quilts in the wardrobe and fashioned a mattress out of them."

Millicent adjusted her padding and whispered, "Someone ought to pay Glenda a visit. She must know something."

"That's a very good idea." However, Evie thought, this incident changed everything. This death could be another attempt to implicate Glenda and, as Phillipa had pointed out, this could be an effort to accuse her of a more serious crime.

Now, more than ever, they needed to find out all they could about Glenda's past.

Evie turned to Phillipa. "It looks like you might be right about a third attempt to throw suspicion on Glenda. I'm sure everyone's fingers are itching to point in her direction. That means we're back where we started. Why? Why make Glenda the target? What does the person responsible stand to gain?" Evie gave a pensive nod. "Perhaps that's what we should be focusing on. What happens if the theft charges, along with this new crime, are taken seriously? Glenda will go to prison." A trail of worst-case scenarios spun around in her mind.

Phillipa cringed.

"What?" Evie asked.

"Have you considered the possibility…"

"Absolutely not. Glenda cannot possibly be guilty."

"You think she doesn't have it in her," Phillipa said.

Evie hesitated. What did she really know about Glenda?

Lowering her voice to a whisper, Phillipa said, "You are emotionally invested and will only accept one outcome."

Evie couldn't argue with that, not even if she wanted to. Henrietta and Sara had trusted Glenda to look after Nicholas and they knew about her past. That meant they had chosen to ignore it…

Evie gasped.

"What?" Phillipa asked.

"There is something about Glenda we don't know about. It can't be anything too serious because Henrietta and Sara both chose to ignore it."

What if Glenda had committed some sort of infraction in her youth and had owned up to it during her interview. Sara valued honesty above all else and she might have decided to take Glenda's honesty into account.

Then again…

What if Glenda's past transgression had been dormant all these years. Evie imagined the compulsion to steal could be controlled or somehow inhibited. But it could always resurface.

Shaking her head, she tried to dismiss the suspicion.

"Oh," Evie suddenly exclaimed. "What if someone in the village knew about her past and decided to take advantage of it?"

"By committing a crime she might be accused of

because of her previous crime…" Phillipa floundered.

"Yes." Evie nodded. "A crime similar to something she might have committed in the past. Something such as theft."

Phillipa's voice filled with disbelief. "But now we're talking about murder. At least, I think we might well be talking about murder. If we're lucky, that man died of natural causes."

Tom returned. "He knows as much as we do. Are we having breakfast?"

"Who can eat at a time like this?" Evie stood up. "We should drive up to Glenda's house. We can use curiosity as our excuse."

"Or we could wait for the dust to settle," Tom suggested. "I doubt we'll learn much more than we already know."

Evie looked out the window. She wished they'd checked on Glenda before continuing on to Graham House. "I suppose now there's been a death, the local constabulary will have to call in the detectives."

"Let's hope it's not someone we know," Tom said. "At this point, Detective Inspector O'Neill might become quite suspicious of us."

Evie sat down again. "You're right. We should wait to see what happens. We'll only get in the way. Meanwhile, we could roll up our sleeves and start digging." She smiled at Tom. "I'm sure we'll be spared the awkwardness of encountering Detective Inspector O'Neill. He's not the only detective around." Evie gave a firm nod. "Once we've had breakfast, we'll head over to the church. Since my character, Marjorie, doesn't do much talking, Phillipa can say she's intrigued by old records. Or maybe there are ancestors she wishes to look for. I'm sure she'll think of something."

"You could all just talk at once," Millicent suggested. "The vicar tends to get a bit fuddled."

"That's right. I almost forgot. How was your dinner last night?" Evie asked.

Millicent told them about choir practice and how only half the choir had turned up. When the vicar heard they were looking for a house and were considering settling in the area, he invited them to dinner. He and his wife spent most of the night talking about the merits of the village. "He warned us to act quickly because houses were usually snatched up. I feel guilty lying to a vicar, but it's all for the greater good." Millicent continued by saying that when she mentioned the thefts, they brushed it all aside.

"They didn't blame Glenda?" Evie asked.

Millicent shook her head. "I even tried to bait him into saying something negative about her but he wouldn't be drawn into it."

So the vicar hadn't been involved in excluding Glenda from the choir.

Millicent looked up in thought. "Oh, the vicar also said the magistrate wouldn't put up with any nonsense."

"It's Mrs. Graham," Phillipa told her.

"A woman? That's rather progressive for a small village. If not for the thefts and this new incident, I might actually want to move here," Millicent declared. "Oh, I just remembered something else he said. I mentioned how Edward and I... I mean, Edmonds and I, felt ever so dreadful about missing out on the house and he said Mr. Miller probably felt the same way about Glenda's house."

"Duncan Miller? The owner of the French hens?"

"Yes. Apparently, he'd had his heart set on buying it after Glenda's aunt died."

Could that be the connection they'd been looking for? What if Duncan Miller killed his own chickens and made it look as if they'd been stolen? Had he hoped to cause enough trouble for Glenda to convince her to sell the house and move on?

The barkeeper served their breakfast, his eyebrows drawn down either in concentration or because he found himself in a dark mood.

Evie held up a piece of bacon and murmured, "This new incident certainly adds layers to the village." She glanced at the barkeeper and found him smiling at her.

When he returned to the kitchen, Phillipa said, "You've cheered him up."

"Yes, however, as you said yesterday, we'll have to steal away in the dead of night. When he finds out we're not here to make a movie, he's going to be very disappointed and now I'm feeling rather guilty about it." She stared at her piece of bacon and, after a moment, she murmured, "William Brown."

"What about him?" Tom asked.

"We should have a word with him. He lives in the farm across the lane from Glenda's house. Perhaps he knows something." Evie glanced at Millicent.

"Edward and I will be visiting the vicar."

Edmonds' frown suggested he didn't look forward to the visit. When he nodded and smiled, Evie realized he must have had a brief lapse and forgotten he was actually Edward.

Leaning in, he asked, "Why are we visiting the vicar?"

"Remember, you think you might have some family

here going way back and you want to have a look at the parish register."

Impressed, Evie smiled. Only moments before she had suggested the same plan for Phillipa.

Edmonds looked confused. "I do?"

"Never mind. It will be better if I say I'm looking for my ancestors. You're bound to forget who you are." Millicent finished her breakfast and stood up, saying, "I should go up and put away the quilts before the maid goes in to tidy up. We wouldn't want people getting the wrong ideas."

Seeing the barkeeper within hearing, Edmonds raised his voice and said, "It's no one's business if we've had a quarrel and you forced me to sleep on the floor."

Realizing what had happened, Millicent spat out, "My mother warned me about you."

Edmonds grumbled, "Yes, well, I wish your mother had bothered to warm me about your snappy temper."

Huffing out a breath, Millicent swung away and stormed out of the pub. A moment later, she came back inside. "I'm going upstairs and don't you dare follow me, Mr. Fletcher. At least, not until you decide to remember your manners."

Phillipa dug around her pocket. She turned to Evie and asked, "I don't suppose you brought your handbag?"

"Why do you ask?"

"I wanted to borrow your notebook. I'm sure I can use this for my next play." Leaning forward, she said to Edmonds, "Have you ever considered acting?"

Tom whispered, "Countess, if you're not careful, you might lose your chauffeur and your new secretary to the stage."

CHAPTER TWENTY-ONE

*E*vie stood by the window looking out. To be more precise, she stood on a chair and was leaning as far as she could to the left so she could gain a vantage point and see the roof on Glenda's house.

The sight of smoke curling out of Glenda's chimney set her at ease and stopped her from entertaining any scenario which didn't include Glenda sitting by the fireplace, enjoying a book or a cup of tea, preferably both.

Stepping down from the chair, she glanced down at the street to see if anyone had noticed her. She would have been a curious sight, indeed.

Tom had been charged with finding out when Glenda's case would be presented to the magistrate, something they should have established the previous evening.

Evie assumed Mrs. Graham would remain true to her word and dismiss the charge of theft but, until she did, they would have to continue to snoop around. Although, they couldn't remain in Thornbridge any longer than they had to. If asked, Henrietta would no doubt say they had already overstayed their welcome.

While Evie would not readily admit it, she knew she would agree with Henrietta. As she'd often said, delving into other people's private lives did not come naturally to her.

The only reason she had ever become involved in several investigations was because she had happened to notice something peculiar and not because she had gone out of her way to intrude in other people's lives.

Phillipa had been right in saying she was emotionally invested. However, Evie would suggest she had also been compelled by a sense of right and wrong.

When she knew a person to be honest, she could hardly stand by and watch her being accused of theft.

Checking her reflection in the mirror, she adjusted her dark spectacles so she could see above them.

Millicent or, rather, Mrs. Fletcher, had publicly sorted out her differences with Mr. Fletcher and they had both trekked out again for a long walk before going to the church where Millicent would do her best to obtain information about Glenda's mother. With any luck, that should be enough to lead them to Glenda's birth records. As suggested, Fulham might not be Glenda's real name, but it could end up being her married name, which would be news to Evie who'd always thought she'd been single.

Phillipa had remained downstairs, scribbling away some notes for her play.

"At least one of us has been inspired," Evie murmured and turned toward the door just as someone knocked on it.

"It's me."

Opening the door a fraction, she frowned at Tom. "You changed your knock."

"What?"

"The way you knock. You usually do a single, no nonsense rap. This was more of a thud."

"Are you all right?" he asked.

"Yes, why do you ask?"

"Because you sound strange. Are you going to let me in?"

Nodding, Evie stepped aside. "I think we should go to London."

Tom looked and sounded confused. "Now?"

"Straight after Christmas. We obviously can't go any sooner."

He studied her for a moment. "I see... What you're really saying is that you wish to distance yourself from all this but you have commitments to see to first. So you will delay running away."

"Mr. Winchester, are you laughing at me?"

"Yes, I am. And I understand the reason why you wish to run away. You're simply frustrated with Glenda and Henrietta. They have both been uncooperative and stubbornly secretive, and now you wish to have some distance from everyone who annoys you."

Hearing him say it made Evie come to her senses. She'd faced worse obstacles. Indeed, wherever there was some sort of crime, she would inevitably encounter even worse hurdles and barriers.

"I might as well get used to it. It's the uncertainty of it all I can't stand," she said, her voice barely a murmur. She knew and understood her world, but the last few days had cast doubt on everything because no one was behaving the way they should. "Did you find out anything from the barkeeper?"

Tom continued studying her and then nodded. "The magistrate will hear the charges today."

"And does he know anything new? No, I don't suppose he does, otherwise, you would have mentioned it." Evie lifted her chin. "I'm so cross with Glenda, I have a good mind not to attend the hearing." She knew she would offer her support in any way she could. Growling with frustration, she said, "I can't believe the dead man hasn't been identified yet."

"It doesn't surprise me," Tom said. "The local constabulary has blocked the road leading to Glenda's house. I suppose they want to keep the crime scene fresh."

"Blocked the road?"

"That's what the barkeeper said."

If they wanted to see Glenda, they would have to be creative. "The properties along Old Salter Lane all back into the Graham's land." Evie looked at Tom. "If we want to see Glenda, we could drive along the road leading to the Graham house and approach Glenda's house from there." She looked down at the floor and noticed she'd been tapping her foot. "Yes, that's what we should do."

Tom helped her into her coat. Slipping her dark spectacles back into place, she gave a firm nod. "We should go now. Glenda is still at home."

"How do you know?"

"I have my ways... Anyhow, with any luck, she'll let us drive her. Actually, where does the magistrate hear cases?"

"Next to the constabulary. It's around the corner from the pub, at the end of the street."

"Do you think the villagers will attend?" she asked as they walked down the narrow stairs.

"I'd be surprised if they didn't," Tom said. "Actually, I'd be surprised if they did. Everyone must be acquainted with Mrs. Grahams' attitude toward time wasting accusations. They're bound to know the case will be dismissed."

"We don't really know that for sure."

Downstairs, they found Phillipa standing in front of the fire.

"There you are. I was about to go up and fetch you."

Evie nodded. "Well, we're ready to leave now."

They filed out of the pub and made their way to the motor car. As it had been a rather frosty night, Tom had to spend some time warming the engine. Meanwhile, Evie and Phillipa discussed the morning's events. Once they were on their way, they fell silent.

The streets had once again emptied of people. To her delight, Evie found the absence of villagers helped clear her head of all the clutter and, for the first time since their arrival, she didn't hold a single annoying thought in her mind.

Unfortunately, the sense of calm didn't last.

Evie broke the silence by saying, "Marjorie Evans' husband."

Tom slowed down. "What about him?"

"When Millicent found out he'd worked as a clerk in a law office, I'd been surprised his earnings had been enough to buy the house. Also, he'd been an orphan so, I assumed he hadn't inherited anything, but that's not necessarily the case. Oh... Oh..." Evie fell silent.

"What? For heaven's sake, Countess, we're not privy to

your thoughts. If you have something to say, then spit it out."

"Did anyone notice a law office in the village?" Evie asked.

"I think I remember seeing a bronze plaque on a door. Let me think..." Phillipa closed her eyes. "Oh, yes. Around the corner from the pub, there's a haberdashery store and next door, there is a law office. You can see it from the corner of the street."

"Do you want me to turn around and drive back to the village?" Tom asked.

"No, we have to drive Glenda to the magistrate's..." Evie growled. "In any case, we can't barge in and ask questions about someone who might have worked for them. Why would someone in the moving pictures business want to do that?"

"I believe Lotte manages to ask anything she likes by changing her disguises to suit her purposes," Tom said. "A titled lady might be able to push her way in and demand answers."

Evie lowered her shoulders. "I didn't bring any suitable clothes."

"Let this be a lesson," Tom whispered. "Anyhow, what do you want to find out there?"

Evie looked out the window and toward the Graham estate. "It seems most petty squabbles are over properties. When I heard Mr. Evans had been an orphan, I assumed the absence of parents meant there hadn't been any money." A silly assumption on her part. Seth, the current Earl of Woodridge, had been orphaned when both his parents had died and he stood to inherit the entire Woodridge estate.

"You're now thinking he inherited the funds to purchase the house?" Tom asked.

"Only a person of means could afford such a house," Evie reasoned. "If we could clarify this one point, then… we could clear the way to focus on something else."

Tom brought the motor car to a stop. The Graham House estate stood on one side and the back of the Old Salter Lane properties on the other.

Evie looked toward Glenda's property and realized they would have to trudge through a wooded area.

Opening the passenger door, Tom said, "I'd like to suggest we focus on Glenda."

"We never stopped. The process of elimination can be useful. We can't just assume Mr. Evans managed to buy the house on his clerk's salary. It's a valuable property, I'm sure it is."

"And you're now thinking someone had their eye on it and probably still does?"

Evie nodded. "We already know Duncan Miller wanted to purchase the property. Millicent found that out when she had dinner with the vicar and his wife." As they walked toward Glenda's house, Evie added, "What if no one knew about Glenda's existence? If Marjorie Evans died without anyone to inherit, I assume the house would have been sold. We've been focusing on the obvious. Glenda and her mysterious past. This persecution might have nothing to do with her personally and everything to do with her house."

"You think someone is trying to drive her away?"

"It's possible." She looked up. "I've lost sight of Glenda's house."

"We're on a slight slope. I'm sure it will come into view again soon." Tom led the way, saying, "Continue."

"Continue?" Evie snorted. "You assume I've been entertaining a riot of ideas." Losing her footing, she grabbed hold of Tom's arm. "Oh, wait a moment... I've just remembered something else. Millicent said Glenda's aunt had been living in Bath. As in, that's the address noted in the parish register. We know her husband was from Thornbridge. So how did they meet?"

"Marjorie Evans was born here. Maybe they knew each other from before and met up in later life." Tom glanced at her. "You did say she was forty."

"Yes, that's a possibility." Evie found herself thinking about Anthony Evans' job again. "What if... Let me think... Oh, what if they didn't know each other. Oh..."

"What?"

"I lost my train of thought. Or, rather, my idea disintegrated before it could take shape."

"You were trying to join the dots and they refused to meet?" Tom asked.

"Maybe Evie was trying to say Anthony Evans, in his capacity as a clerk working in a law office, came across some interesting information about Marjorie and..." Phillipa shrugged. "That's as far as I got."

Evie nodded. "You read my mind. That's quite a feat since my mind is a muddle."

Phillipa encouraged her, "Let's play with the idea. We assumed Marjorie met Anthony Evans and when she married him they moved into the house which we assume he purchased. What if Marjorie already owned the house?" Smiling, Phillipa added, "What if Anthony Evans was a scoundrel, discovered Marjorie owned a house and pursued her for that very reason."

"I think Evie is about to say we really need to call on the solicitor's office," Tom said. "They're bound to have information about the ownership of the property. We should, at least, establish that before we start labeling people scoundrels."

"Information they won't divulge," Evie warned.

Tom growled. "That wouldn't be a problem if you had brought your fancy clothes."

Evie stopped.

"Now what?"

"I just remembered something else. Right before Marjorie married, she lived in the village and stayed at the pub where she worked. We could ask the barkeeper about her. He might know something about the house."

"You mean, *I* can ask him," Tom said.

Grinning, Evie nodded. "You've been very helpful, Tom. Anyway, if we can get the information from the barkeeper, we don't have to worry about the solicitor." She pointed ahead. "I see Glenda's house. The property looks even larger from the back. It must be worth a pretty penny."

"Which again raises the question," Tom said. "How did a simple clerk afford to buy such a property."

"Yes, but it also makes the property quite appealing."

"To someone else?" Phillipa asked. "At least we have several avenues to pursue."

"Yes. Oh…" Evie groaned. "I think I might be wrong in suspecting Anthony Evans of finding information about the owner of the house through his job. For a moment there, I thought he might have discovered Marjorie owned the house and he pursued her because of that. But if she owned the house, why did she stay at the pub?"

Tom stopped and looked at her. "Yes, you're right. Your mind is muddled. I didn't understand anything you just said."

"Evie thinks Anthony Evans discovered Marjorie owned a substantial piece of property but that might not be the case because when Marjorie returned to Thornbridge she stayed at the pub. Now that I think about it, I really like Evie's story about Anthony finding out Marjorie owned the house. If I wrote a play about it, I'd have him traveling to Bath to accidentally bump into her and woe her into marriage."

"Oh, I see."

Evie frowned. "Why did you understand the story better when Phillipa told it?"

"She explained it better."

"She had no trouble understanding me," Evie complained.

Tom laughed. "She told the story with confidence. Whereas you, my dear Countess, hesitated and doubted yourself."

"I might need to engage Phillipa to interpret my thoughts." Evie pointed ahead to Glenda's house. "Of course, Glenda could answer all our questions, but she won't, stubborn woman."

They continued on in silence. When they reached the house, they walked to the front door and stood there looking out toward the lane.

"According to Millicent, the body was found in a ditch directly opposite Glenda's house. I don't see anyone out there. If the police blocked the road, you'd think they would have someone standing guard over the immediate crime scene," Evie reasoned and looked at Tom. "Do you need Phillipa to interpret what I just said?"

"I understood you perfectly well this time," he muttered.

"Brace yourself, here's another thought," Evie mused. Glancing at Tom, she said, "I'll try to be clear and concise. All the people we saw running around the village today spreading the news about the body means the man was not from the village. No one seemed to know his name."

Tom nodded.

"So he must be someone who either doesn't live in the village or he lives right here on Old Salter Lane. And, since the police blocked the road, no one's been able to find out who's missing."

"We know William Brown, the farmer, and then there's the owner of the French hens, Duncan Miller," Tom said. "We didn't see either one in the village. I'm sure there are more men living in the lane... So it could be someone we haven't encountered."

"I hope it's not the farmer, William Brown." Earlier, she had suggested having a chat with the him. He might have noticed Glenda's lights on. Indeed, he might have seen or heard something...

Evie looked at her watch and turned toward the front door. "We should make our way to the magistrate's."

"Would you like me to do the honors?" Tom went ahead and knocked on the front door.

"The curtain shifted," Phillipa whispered.

When the door remained closed, Evie muttered, "She's pretending she's not at home."

"Shall I knock again?" Tom asked. "Or, would that make it awkward."

Evie pressed her lips together. Emitting a soft growl, she stepped forward and banged her fisted hand on the door. "Glenda. Open up. We know you're in there."

Tom's eyes widened slightly. "Well, that definitely makes it awkward."

"Only if she doesn't open the door." Evie tapped her foot and fisted her hand again.

"Countess, you'll bruise your hand or, worse, break a bone."

The door opened and Glenda stepped forward. "Lady Woodridge. I thought I heard someone at the door."

She looked calm and composed. Almost as if she didn't have a care in the world.

Lifting her chin, Evie said, "We're here to accompany you."

Pressing her hand to her chest, Glenda asked, "Where?"

"To see the magistrate."

"Why would I want to see the magistrate?"

Evie scratched around for some patience but found none for this particular game of avoidance.

"Your hearing is scheduled for today, Glenda. You must attend. Have you organized your legal defense?" Belatedly, Evie realized she should have asked this before.

"There's no need for any of that, my lady."

"I'm not sure you understand, Glenda. You must attend today."

She shook her head. "No, actually, there's no need for it."

"Why? Has it been postponed?"

Glenda nodded. "Dismissed."

"What? That's... That's wonderful news. How did it come about?"

"The accuser is dead."

It took a full minute for Evie to understand her meaning. "The accuser?"

Glenda smiled. "Duncan Miller."

CHAPTER TWENTY-TWO

Nine drummers drumming

*E*vie climbed into the passenger seat and stared into the distance. "Duncan Miller, dead."

Settling in beside her, Phillipa asked, "Do you think Glenda killed him?"

Evie's eyes widened with shock. "What? How could you say that?"

Phillipa shrugged. "He might have gone a step too far in trying to get her house. In fact, he might have made up the story about the stolen French hens. When that didn't work, he confronted her. They argued, then they fought and Glenda saw her chance to finally rid herself of her accuser."

Evie gaped at her. "Did you make all that up just now?"

"You're biased. Otherwise, you would have painted a similar picture."

"No, I'm not biased. I simply don't believe Glenda to be capable of cold-blooded murder. It goes against her character."

"It might have been a convenient accident," Phillipa suggested. "I'm picturing Duncan Miller confronting her and pointing an accusatory finger at her. When she didn't respond, he prodded her with his accusatory finger. Glenda warned him not to prod her. He went ahead and prodded her again. That hit a raw nerve and incensed Glenda into retaliating. Let's call it a trigger. Something that's been dormant all her life. A little Pandora's box. She went ahead and pushed him. Caught by surprise, he lost his footing, fell and broke his neck or hit his head on a stone."

"Are you quite finished tearing Glenda's reputation to shreds? She is incapable of violence."

"Be reasonable, Evie. The average person is incapable of violence until they are provoked."

Evie huffed. "Fine. I'll concede the point. If pushed too far, anyone could act out of character."

Tom got them on their way, driving in silence. Something Evie found unusual.

After Glenda told them the charge of theft had been dismissed, they'd tried to find out what Glenda knew about the death but she'd told them the police had instructed her not to say anything. Although, she had, at least, identified the victim.

"Why the secrecy?"

"What are you referring to?" Phillipa asked.

"Duncan Miller's death." Shaking her head, Evie said, "I wish we'd made an effort to see the crime scene for ourselves the moment we heard the news."

After speaking with Glenda, they'd wandered over to the edge of the road but hadn't gone any further for fear of disturbing the scene. Not that they'd been able to see a scene, as such.

The ground and ditch beyond the road hadn't looked disturbed. If he had been killed, there would have been something to suggest a struggle but Evie hadn't seen a single blade of grass out of place.

"Of course, there's a simple explanation for that," Evie murmured. "The incident might have happened further along the road." She glanced at Tom and noticed his jaw muscles clenching and unclenching. "Tom, you've been very quiet. Did you notice something?" If he had, Evie thought, he would have said something.

"I'm trying to remember if you had any theories about Duncan Miller."

Evie gasped.

"What?"

"No new theories but I just thought of something. Do you remember Elizabeth Graham saying her husband liked to maintain the status quo?"

Tom nodded.

"At the time, I didn't quite understand why she said it or what she'd been referring to." Off-the-cuff remarks, Evie thought, could be quite revealing.

"And now you do?" he asked.

"Not really. I just wonder how far Albert Graham would go to maintain the status quo. We only met him briefly and formed opinions about him based on our observations. His wife's remark could help us understand him better."

Phillipa clasped her hands on her lap. "What if the status quo is another secret?"

"I hope not. We have enough of those as it is. But you might be right. I just can't begin to imagine what secret Albert Graham would want to guard." After a moment, Evie added, "I wish we knew what time Duncan Miller died."

"If he died after ten last night, Albert Graham could be the killer," Phillipa suggested. "He could have waited until we left and then gone out to kill him."

"Why?" Evie asked.

"Because Duncan Miller was making trouble and disrupting the status quo."

"That actually makes sense." Evie nibbled the edge of her lip. "However, his wife also said he's a stickler for the law."

Tom cleared his throat.

"What?" Evie prompted.

He shrugged. After a moment, he said, "I can't actually believe Glenda didn't see or hear anything."

Evie had no idea how to respond to that. She was tempted to say it was Glenda's nature to keep quiet about other people's business but she couldn't bring herself to say so. If Glenda knew something or saw something, it might be in her best interest to keep quiet about it.

"We saw the house lights on," Phillipa reminded them. "That was just after sunset. Maybe that's when it happened."

"That would rule out Albert Graham because he was home arguing with his wife." Evie knew it was preposterous to suspect the Grahams. What possible reason would they have for killing Duncan Miller?

"Evie's right," Tom said. "It would help to know what time Duncan Miller died. However, we can't really jump to conclusions and assume he was killed."

Evie sat back and considered the problem. They needed to establish a time of death but they couldn't approach the police, certainly not in their current disguises. The local constabulary wouldn't investigate the death. They must have reported the incident to the nearest constabulary with a detective.

Theorizing was all well and good but, at some point, they needed something more solid to go on with. Then again, Glenda's problem had been resolved and they no longer had a reason to linger.

When they arrived in the village, they found it practically deserted. "Where is everyone?"

"I imagine they're all taking a break from watching us," Phillipa suggested. "Actually, I'm surprised they didn't follow us."

Climbing out of the motor car, they made their way to the pub where they hoped to meet up with Millicent and Edmonds. However, when they walked in, they found the pub empty.

Evie shivered. "This is strange."

When they didn't see Millicent or Edmonds, Evie went upstairs and knocked on the connecting door to her room. Moments later, she returned downstairs. "They're not here. Shall we go look for them?"

Stepping outside, they looked up and down the street.

"Does anyone have any thoughts about this?" Evie asked.

Tom shook his head. "I'm still only entertaining one

thought and it's about Duncan Miller. We really can't assume someone killed him."

"That only leaves one other option. He died of natural causes but that would make his death a coincidence." And, Evie thought, experience had shown her things rarely happened by chance. Certainly not when a crime was involved. "Do you think it's nothing but bad timing?"

"What I think doesn't matter," he said.

"Yes, I suppose we shouldn't jump to conclusions just to suit our theories. Even if, at times, it helps." Evie stopped and, gaping, she looked around.

Phillipa laughed. "Did you spot someone peering through the window?"

"No... Do you hear that?" Evie looked up and down the street. When she didn't see anything, she hurried up to the corner. "Someone is beating a drum."

Tom and Phillipa caught up with her.

Phillipa shrugged. "I don't see anyone."

"Yes, but do you hear it?"

"Oh, yes. It sounds like a couple of drums."

Relieved to know someone else could hear the sound, Evie said, "It might be the village band but where's the drumming coming from?"

"The church?" Tom suggested.

They hurried along to the end of the next street and toward the church.

Sounding confused, Evie said, "Now I'm hearing a piper."

Tom agreed. "More drums and more pipers. But I can't tell where the sound is coming from."

"And where is everyone?" Evie now sounded frustrated. "What is going on in this village?" She stopped and looked in every direction. "Living at Halton House, I've become accustomed to bizarre behavior and strange occurrences. This should make me feel right at home, but it doesn't."

Phillipa swung around and pointed to the end of the other street. "I see a drummer."

A man playing a drum emerged from around the corner. He was joined by another one and… another one.

"There are nine drummers." Looking toward the opposite street, Phillipa again pointed. "There's a piper coming from the opposite street."

"Do you think it's a parade?" Evie turned to Tom. "Did the barkeeper mention anything about this?"

"No."

They stood in the corner, each one looking in a different direction.

"I can see nine drummers," Phillipa said. "And ten pipers."

Evie tugged Tom's sleeve. "There's a woman headed this way and she's dancing." She wore a bright, fancy dress that resembled something out of the previous era. Suddenly, there were eleven women dancing and headed toward the drummers and pipers.

People were now emerging from their houses and standing by their doors to watch the procession.

"Oh, look," Phillipa exclaimed. "It's a bunch of men and they're leaping."

Evie counted them. "I see twelve of them." And they were all dressed formally. "They look like titled gentlemen."

Phillipa laughed, "Twelve lords a-leaping?"

"It might be some sort of Christmas festival."

"They're coming this way," Tom said.

People were now jostling for the best vantage point from which to watch the procession.

"Do we recognize anyone?" Evie asked. As she watched the group, she studied people's faces for any tell-tale signs.

"Countess? Are you looking for a murderer among them?"

"I might be."

As the parade reached them, Phillipa asked, "What do we do now? Do we follow them?"

Evie was about to say it would be a good idea to do so when the people on parade all stopped and, as if by mutual agreement, they dispersed, each one headed in a different direction.

Tom slipped his hands inside his pockets and whistled under his breath. "Well, I suppose that's that. What do we do now?"

"Now that the unexpected interruption has gone away? We're still looking for Millicent and Edmonds. They must be at the church." Not bothering to make sense of the scene or read anything into it, Evie led the way, her hurried steps suddenly slowing down.

"What is it now, Countess?"

She glanced over her shoulder just in case the ladies dancing or lords a-leaping appeared again. "I'm sure I'm grasping at straws. I'm thinking about the solicitor again. Millicent and Edmonds could go to the solicitor's office. They could say they are looking for a house in this village and… Oh, I don't know. What sort of questions does one normally ask when buying a house? Do you think people need to consult with a solicitor?" Hearing the panic in her voice, Evie scooped in a breath. "As I said, I'm grasping at straws."

Frowning, Tom asked, "What exactly do you hope Millicent will discover there?"

Evie cringed. Millicent had already experienced a loss of confidence when she'd suggested she speak with the vicar. Asking her to do this might send her running home. "The house. I'd like to know if Marjorie owned it or if it was purchased after her marriage. Please don't ask me why I want to know this, I just do."

"Countess."

"Yes?"

"We now know Glenda won't be prosecuted for the theft. Do you think we should start thinking about returning to Halton House?"

"Go home? Empty-handed and with even more unanswered questions than when we first came here? Absolutely not."

He gave her an incredulous look. "At some point, we will have to return."

"Yes, of course. But not right this minute." If she had been engaged to solve this mystery through Lotte's lady detective agency, she would be facing utter failure. "Have we heard anyone else mention the five gold rings? No, we haven't, but that's not to say the matter has been resolved."

Phillipa pointed ahead. "Here they come."

Millicent and Edmonds walked toward them.

Sighing, Evie caved in and decided they should abandon their efforts to learn the truth.

Deep in conversation, Millicent and Edmonds had their eyes on the ground and didn't see them until they almost collided with them.

Evie was about to make the announcement when Millicent flapped her arms.

"Oh, milady... I mean, Marjorie." Millicent looked around and mouthed an apology.

Eager to ask if they had learned anything new but still mindful of not being overheard, Evie suggested, "Let's walk and talk."

Edmonds nudged Millicent. "Well, go on. Tell them. If you don't, I will."

"It's not your place."

"Mrs. Fletcher!"

Millicent mouthed another apology. "We searched the parish register and we found nothing."

"Nothing?"

"Absolutely no record of Marjorie's sister or Glenda." Before Evie could respond, Millicent added, "We searched back and found all the records, birth, marriage and death, for Marjorie's parents."

"Glenda's grandparents?"

"Yes, and we confirmed that Marjorie was christened in this parish."

Evie tipped her head back and stared up at the sky. "No, I'm not going to suggest Marjorie's sister was born and christened somewhere else even if my imagination is prompting me to do so."

Millicent exchanged a knowing look with Edmonds. "According to the vicar, Marjorie's parents both worked at Graham House and we all know how those grand houses can be with their servants, working them to the bone and grudgingly giving them half a day, if they're lucky, but only when it suits them. Not to mention the pittance they pay."

When Evie looked at Millicent with incredulity, Edmonds gave Millicent a discreet nudge with his elbow.

"Well, not all houses, of course... I mean... Never mind all that. I doubt very much they moved away, had a baby, and then returned." Brightening, Millicent continued, "It's rather a puzzle. How can Marjorie not have a sister when we know she did because she had a niece, Glenda?"

"That could be the secret Glenda, Henrietta and Sara don't want you to know about," Phillipa suggested.

"Countess?"

"I... I'm speechless." Speechless and in denial. Evie turned to Millicent. "Did the vicar know anything about the death?"

"He didn't mention it and I forgot to ask because I became obsessed with Marjorie Evans not having a sister. I hope you believe me when I say I searched every entry."

Evie nodded and glanced at Phillipa. "I believe you're the first one to have mentioned it."

"Mentioned what?"

"Illegitimacy."

CHAPTER TWENTY-THREE

"**I**s it too early for a drink?" Phillipa asked when they returned to the pub.

"Your nose is red from the cold," Tom said. "I think you would benefit from a drink. I'll organize it."

"Thank you." Phillipa went to stand in front of the fireplace, her hands spread out to capture some of the warmth.

Evie joined her while Millicent brought some chairs from a nearby table.

"Are we going to talk about it?" Millicent asked.

"I'm not sure that we should. No one ever talks about illegitimacy. I'm feeling rather stunned but I want to be perfectly clear. If this is Glenda's secret, then it should remain that way. It certainly doesn't change how I feel about her." Thanking Millicent for getting the chairs, Evie drew in a long breath and sat down.

"It makes sense," Phillipa said.

"Yes, it does. At least, that part of the mystery makes sense. However, the only proof we have is the lack of information in the parish register. We don't have the resources to search the records in Bath." If they had been liaising with Detective Inspector O'Neill, they might have suggested it. Although, the information would not have been relevant to the case so she would have needed a solid argument to convince the detective to look into it.

Falling silent, Evie mulled over the rest of the questions they had been entertaining.

Looking slightly confused, Millicent asked, "Are we to assume Marjorie Evans was Glenda's mother?"

Evie looked at her without blinking. After a moment, she laughed. "Millicent, I wish I knew. Actually, I don't really want to know. Henrietta was right. Some things are best left buried in the past. Of course, I'll say it again, this doesn't change the way I feel about Glenda. She still has my full support."

Millicent smiled. "So you're no longer angry with her?"

"Oh, yes, I am rather cross with her because she's been stubbornly private. However, her behavior is understandable. Everyone is entitled to their privacy."

Returning from the bar, Tom set down a tray on the edge of the table and poured everyone a glass of brandy. "The barkeeper is busy in the kitchen and said to help ourselves." Going to stand by the fireplace, he asked, "How are the theories coming along?"

"They're not, Tom. We're too stunned to respond. In fact, my imagination has been stifled by the shock."

"Countess, I've never known you to be so sensitive."

"This has nothing to do with being sensitive. A part of me has already rationalized the need to keep the information private. I understand why Glenda wouldn't want it to become public knowledge."

In the past, they had jumped to conclusions and had, more often than not, been correct.

This would be the biggest assumption to date. While it made sense, there might be a perfectly acceptable reason for the lack of birth records. Just because Marjorie Evans' sister was not registered in this parish didn't mean she hadn't been born.

Yes, there had to be a perfectly good explanation.

Then again…

They might be on the right track.

Taking a sip of her drink, Evie sat back and gazed at the fireplace. "Marjorie Evans might have met someone in Bath and then she fell pregnant. Or…" Evie fell silent and entertained several possibilities she couldn't quite bring herself to voice.

"What?" Tom demanded.

Looking up, she settled for the one option which sounded feasible. "It's possible she was already in the family way when she left here." That meant someone in the village could be Glenda Fulham's father.

Millicent looked over her shoulder toward the bar and then lowered her voice to say, "Or, Glenda could have been stolen. I've heard horror stories about babies being stolen. Marjorie Evans might have been a baby thief, but that theory is too harsh." Brightening, Millicent added, "Some women have been known to abandon their unwanted babies. Maybe Marjorie found a baby on her doorstep and decided to keep it."

"I won't deny it," Evie said, "it's a viable theory." Looking at her glass, she shook her head. "Regardless of how Glenda came into this world, we now have no reason to remain in Thornbridge. The charge of theft has been dismissed and it seems no one has made a fuss about the gold rings." They had only been concerned about Glenda's wellbeing. Now, peace had been restored.

"Countess? Shall we start packing?"

She was about to say yes when the prospect of returning home without knowing the full story stopped her. "How long does it take for a detective to arrive on the scene of a crime?"

Grinning, Tom said, "I'd be more interested to know how long it would take you to extract information out of the detective once he arrives."

"You have a point. Not all detectives are as receptive as the ones we know." She happened to glance toward the bar in time to catch the barkeeper looking at them, his eyes narrowed, giving them a look that appeared to be full of suspicion. "Tom..."

"Yes, I'll go have a word with him."

"Ask him about the gold rings. Oh, and the parade."

When Edmonds joined Tom, Millicent whispered, "I think Edmonds finds this entire situation rather confusing. I don't blame him and he doesn't like the name Edward. He said if we ever have to do this again, I should choose another name. He's fond of the name George. He says it has a regal sound to it."

Setting the glass down, Evie stretched her hands out to warm them. "If the police had found anything suspicious about Duncan Miller's death, a detective would have been dispatched here straightaway. I suppose the local doctor will examine the body and decide if there is anything suspicious about the death."

"I hope he died of natural causes," Millicent said. "I should hate to think someone in the village is guilty of murder. We've already missed out on one house, it would be dreadful if we find a house here. We'll have to pass up on it. I'd be too worried about living in a village with a murderer."

It took a moment for Evie to realize they were no longer alone. Several people had come into the pub and Millicent had taken the initiative to step into character.

"I'm sure you have no need to worry, Mrs. Fletcher." Evie stood up. "I'm going upstairs to freshen up." And, Evie thought, to collect her thoughts.

When she entered her room, she walked to the window and looked out toward Glenda's house.

From the start, Glenda's behavior had been odd. "Almost as if she's determined to stand her ground, no matter what," Evie murmured.

She had dismissed the accusation of theft as a prank and...

"She said she was determined to stay in Thornbridge."

Evie remembered Glenda sounding quite set on staying on despite feeling out of place. She had spoken about the village being different from what she knew, saying it just didn't feel like home.

"But she is determined." Evie gave a firm nod. "It's almost as if she's drawn battle lines."

"Who?"

Evie swung around and found Millicent and Phillipa standing at the door. "Oh, I didn't hear you come in."

"We knocked. We thought you wanted us to come up," Millicent said. "I'm sure you gave us the signal."

Had she?

"You winked," Millicent explained. "Well, Phillipa thinks you winked while I actually thought your eye twitched."

"Oh…" That probably had nothing to do with sending a signal and everything to do with having developed a nervous twitch, she thought. "Just as well you did come up. I'm afraid I've been dwelling to the point of brooding over Glenda's behavior. I am almost convinced she is up against something or someone and it has nothing to do with settling into a new life and finding everything different to what she is accustomed to."

Millicent and Phillipa looked puzzled.

"When Glenda told us about Duncan Miller's death, she didn't show any emotions. Actually, she smiled." Pushing out a hard breath, Evie's shoulders lowered. "It means something. Her response to the news of a death is so odd, it has to be significant."

"Did she look relieved?" Millicent asked.

"No, Glenda didn't express any emotions. Not even relief." Everyone knew her to be a caring person. She'd never been overly emotional but when a person she knew or someone she was merely acquainted with died, she'd always expressed some sort of sympathy.

"And now I'm thinking we didn't ask about having all the house lights on the previous night." Evie tapped her foot. "Oh, I do wish I'd remembered to ask. She might have given something away."

Phillipa nodded. "As Tom said, she must have seen or heard something." Phillipa folded her arms and looked down at the floor for a moment. "I'm now thinking that if we're right about our suspicions and she is illegitimate, then her odd behavior might be excused. She might have felt threatened by your curiosity, thinking one question would lead to another."

"You think she's been afraid of me finding out about her past?"

Phillipa shrugged. "It's possible. I'm only guessing. However, I'm referring to the moment she told us of Duncan Miller's death. I understand what you mean by Glenda not expressing emotions. At the very least, she might have said something about his family or friends. Instead, she ended the conversation. Maybe she didn't want to give you the opportunity to ask more questions."

Looking out the window, Evie hoped Glenda didn't have anything to do with Duncan Miller's death. She stepped back and tried to distract herself with other thoughts.

"The status quo." She glanced over her shoulder. "Phillipa, did you notice anything about Albert Graham when you said we thought Glenda might be related to the Graham family?"

"I think he might have scoffed at the idea. Wait a minute... There might have been a moment of hesitation or maybe he answered too quickly." She shook her head. "I'm afraid I can't remember."

Evie nodded. "That can be a problem. When you see or hear something, you later remember it differently. Memories begin to vary. I think, as time goes by, memories become vague and we fill in the gaps."

Millicent huffed, "That sounds rather complex. I'm not sure I follow."

"It's simple. You've been listening to me. If someone asked you about my mood, what would you say?"

Millicent lowered her eyes and, peering at her, she whispered, "I'd rather not say."

"You won't get into trouble, Millicent," Evie assured her.

"Let me think… you tapped your foot so you must be feeling frustrated and you've jumped from one theory to another. By now, you must be quite confused. I believe I would say you were at the end of your tether."

"My point, Millicent, is that you skipped over some details and meshed together the foot tapping and my frustration. I'm sure I had other reactions. If you were to relate this moment again, you might tell it all differently, adding or leaving out some parts."

"Oh, I see. Yes, I do rather enjoy embellishing stories. I might throw in a few exclamations. By the time I've told the tale a few times, I might even have you screaming."

Had Albert Graham hesitated, floundering with indecision as the question thrown at him came too close to the truth, or had he jumped in with a swift denial?

"From the start, I found him unable to relax but that might have been because of his argument—" Evie broke off.

"What?" Phillipa asked.

Millicent put her finger to her lip. "She's come up with a theory, I'm sure of it, and she needs time to sort it all out in her mind."

"Something else has been bothering me." Evie took a couple of steps and then stopped. "The argument Albert Graham had with his wife."

"What about it?" Phillipa asked.

"I seem to remember it differently now." Evie tried to mentally step back and view everything that had happened with a critical eye. Past experience told her everything happened for a reason. "We arrived at the Graham's house and, as the butler took our coats, we heard raised voices."

When Phillipa nodded, Evie smiled. "That's just it. We didn't."

"What?" Phillipa looked thoroughly confused.

"That's the part I remember differently. Like you, I thought we heard raised voices. On our way back to the pub, we talked about Albert Graham having an argument with his wife. Now, however, I don't think we heard voices. I am convinced we only heard one voice. Think about it. Try to remember the moment."

Phillipa closed her eyes and her eyebrows expressed her emotions, drawing down in concentration and then rising in astonishment. "My goodness. You're right. I thought back to that moment and I could hear him shouting. Then, my mind filled in the gap with a woman's voice but she wasn't shouting. Elizabeth Graham has a husky voice that doesn't rise above a murmur. We only heard him shouting. But what does it mean?"

Evie replayed the moment in her mind. "As the butler took our coats, I'm sure he started to say Mr. Graham will be with you..."

Phillipa exclaimed, "That confirms it. The butler knew Albert Graham was in the next room by himself."

Evie nodded. "I think he put on a performance for us."

"But why?" Phillipa asked.

Evie swung toward the window. "We've all been putting on a performance to dupe people into thinking we're someone other than who we really are. In his case... we have to wonder why he would pretend to have an argument with his wife. What purpose did it serve?" Evie stopped and gaped. "Oh."

"She's got it," Millicent clapped.

Evie turned to face them. "Elizabeth Graham wasn't there but he wanted us to believe she was."

"What?" both Millicent and Phillipa exclaimed.

Evie paced around the room. "He heard us arrive or he might even have seen us arrive. Then, he timed it so that when we were in the hall being attended to by the butler, he started talking in a loud voice."

"He definitely shouted," Phillipa said. "And I distinctly remember the tone of his voice rising and falling. Mostly rising to a high pitch. Then again, I might be dramatizing the moment."

Evie nodded. "It all happened within seconds. Not even a minute, I'm sure. But it was long enough for us to assume there had been two people arguing. After all, if you hear one person raising their voice, it stands to reason there would be another person at the receiving end."

The door to her room opened and Tom walked in, followed by Edmonds.

When Edmonds closed the door, Tom said, "The detective has arrived. He's downstairs, about to have luncheon."

CHAPTER TWENTY-FOUR

A deluge of questions swamped her mind. Evie heard Tom say the detectives had arrived but she couldn't move past the idea they had just been discussing.

Had Albert Graham really pretended to have an argument with his wife?

If Elizabeth Graham hadn't been in the room, arguing with him, where had she been?

Closing her eyes, Evie remembered noticing the lights on at Glenda's house.

"Is it possible?" she whispered.

Could the two incidents be related?

What if Duncan Miller had died at about that time?

What if Elizabeth Graham had something to do with his death and her husband had tried to cover up her absence?

Evie rearranged the pieces of information they had and imagined Duncan Miller disrupting the status quo with his allegations of theft.

She saw him going too far and confronting Glenda.

Closing her eyes for a moment, Evie suddenly saw everyone in the village playing a role. The confrontation could have been reported to Elizabeth Graham, who then rushed to restore the peace and, in the process, accidentally killed Duncan Miller.

Evie shivered.

Yes... but...

Would the false accusation made against Glenda disrupt Albert Graham's status quo? Would he care if someone made false accusations against Glenda?

Opening her eyes, she stared at Tom without blinking. "Did the barkeeper know anything about the stolen gold rings?"

"Yes, he had plenty to say about the subject. The woman is always claiming someone stole her rings," Tom said. "She thinks everyone is intent on stealing from her."

"What about the parade?" Evie couldn't help wondering if that had been a distraction.

"It's an annual event. The villagers have been arguing about the lack of practice for weeks, with some saying they do the same parade every year so there is no need to practice because everyone knows what to do. Yesterday, they decided to have an impromptu dress rehearsal before the parade in a few days' time to prove the point." Tom frowned. "Countess, did you hear what I said a moment ago. There is a detective downstairs."

Evie folded her arms and tapped her foot. "Yes, I heard you. Ordinarily, I wouldn't hesitate but I just don't see how we can engage with him. If anyone has an idea, I'd love to hear it."

"Milady, you could let him know you are a lady detective," Millicent suggested.

"And run the risk of being told to mind my own business?" Evie shuddered. She could picture the scene in her mind. She would approach the detective and mention her friendship with Detective Inspector O'Neill. She imagined that would count in her favor. However, she knew some men where not receptive to the idea of outsiders, specially meddling females. Then again, they were living in interesting times, with women beating a path toward male domains and excelling at their otherwise male dominated roles. "We need to be strategic. Otherwise, we risk annoying him."

"Would you like me to have a word with him?" Tom asked. "Break the ice, so to speak."

Clearing his throat, Edmonds stepped forward. "Or, we could suggest you have some vital information but you're concerned about becoming involved in a local matter." He shrugged. "He might agree to meet with you in private, well away from prying eyes and ears."

Evie brightened. "Dangle a bait? That's a very good idea, Edmonds." While she didn't want to impede the detective's investigation, it would help greatly to know if a time of death had been established. "Once we have a time, we can start crossing names off the list."

"Did I miss something, milady?" Millicent asked. "To which list are you referring to?"

"Let me rephrase that. Once we know what time Duncan Miller died, we can place everyone and dismiss them as suspects." Shrugging, Evie added, "I still hope Duncan Miller died of natural causes." Even without solid proof, it seemed Glenda's attitude toward not sharing information had to do with the question of her birth. Evie would gladly leave it at that and return to Halton House. However, Glenda might not realize it, but she might be in danger of becoming a suspect in a man's death.

Edmonds had a whispered conversation with Millicent who then urged him to speak up.

Clearing his throat, he asked, "Does this mean you want us to approach the detective and set up a meeting?"

She nodded. "Perhaps you and Tom can go down. Meanwhile... Oh, I know. Phillipa, Millicent and I could go to the church. That would be a quiet place to meet and, for the benefit of anyone watching us, we could make it look like a chance encounter."

Millicent bounced on her toes. "This is exciting. I can't wait to tell Caro about my first official case. I mean... Lady Evans. Although, she will always be Caro to me."

Evie put on her coat and gloves. "We shouldn't look too suspicious going to the church."

As they made their way out of the pub, they saw Tom and Edmonds sitting down with the detective.

Tom glanced up and gave a small nod. Evie imagined he would wait several minutes before telling the detective about their suspicions.

"There's a little cottage two lanes away from the church. I hear the owners might wish to move closer to their family in Kent," Millicent said, once again taking the initiative and playing her role to the hilt. "I told Edward it would be lovely to keep chickens and he said I can keep anything I want so long as I don't expect him to collect eggs or wring necks." Once outside, Millicent looked around and then whispered, "He really did say that, which makes me pity the poor woman who marries him."

When they came up to the church, Millicent hurried on and went through the little gate first. Stopping, she turned to them. "It's a small parish church sitting about forty people, perhaps fifty at a squeeze. It's quite old and it's actually recorded in the Domesday Book."

"I'm sure we'll be impressed, Millicent."

Easing the door open, Millicent peered inside. "There's no one here," she said in a hushed tone. "I'm sure the vicar won't mind if we have a look around. The Graham family have their own pews," Millicent whispered.

"And memorial plaques," Phillipa pointed to one of the walls. Walking up to it, she read, "Charles Graham, died in 1905. That must be Albert Graham's father."

Evie stared at the plaque under it. "Reginal Graham. 1885."

They all stared at it.

Evie was about to state the obvious when they heard the door open. They all turned and saw a man walking in.

He wore a suit and, standing still for a moment, he removed his hat.

"That must be the detective," Millicent whispered. "Why do I suddenly feel the urge to flee or step back and hide behind you?"

"Probably because we are all about to be told to mind our own business," Evie said.

The man walked toward them in no particular hurry.

He wore a brown suit with a blue tie sitting slightly askew. Evie imagined him tugging at it and not bothering to rearrange it properly. Despite looking at ease, Evie thought he must have left the pub in a hurry because he didn't wear an overcoat.

When he reached them, he studied them for a moment. "Which one of you is the lady detective?"

Both Phillipa and Millicent looked at Evie, prompting the detective to also look at her.

Evie smiled and thanked him for agreeing to meet with them.

"I understand you have some information you wish to share."

Instead of answering him, Evie posed a question of her own. "Are you here to investigate Duncan Miller's death?"

He nodded.

Evie nodded in return. "We have information but it might only be relevant if the time of death coincides with what we saw."

"Time of death?"

"Yes, you must surely know by now. I assume the local doctor has examined the body."

He looked at her for a moment, his expression blank. Evie thought he would do very well in a game of poker.

"If you saw something, it is your duty to report it to the police."

Evie gave him a knowing smile. "We don't wish to interfere or bother the police with information that might be irrelevant." Her gaze fell on his tie and she had to fight the urge to straighten it. When she noticed a smudge of dirt on his collar, she had to stop herself from reaching out and wiping it off. On closer inspection, she realized his coat didn't fit properly. It looked too tight around the arms and shoulders.

Finally, he answered, "Yesterday evening. Sometime before midnight or thereabouts."

"Thereabouts? Could the time be closer to ten in the evening?"

"Perhaps."

"Or even earlier."

He hesitated and then nodded. "Yes, that's possible."

Evie stopped herself from tapping away her frustration. "What's the cause of death?"

"Head wound. He fell and hit his head." The detective shifted. "Now, what's this information you have?"

He fell and hit his head? The detective had made it sound like an accident. "Did you find signs of a struggle?"

His eyes narrowed.

Evie persevered. "Do you think someone pushed him?"

"The investigation is... still continuing. Now, about your information..."

"I'm not really sure it is relevant, after all. Just to be sure, could you tell us where exactly he died?"

"Directly opposite the Fulham house."

They had looked at the scene and hadn't seen anything. "From what we understand, he was found in a ditch."

The detective didn't hesitate, giving Evie the impression he merely wanted to get to the information she had. "That's correct."

Evie frowned. She'd never met a detective so willing to give away so much information. "I think we might be wrong. Did you say the body was found directly opposite the house?"

He nodded.

"Oh, dear... We're obviously mistaken. We thought he

had died on the road leading to the Graham house. I'm so sorry, detective. We seem to have wasted your time, after all."

As Evie turned to leave, the detective asked, "What exactly did you see?"

Evie lowered her voice. "We thought we saw a man running across the field. He was carrying a bundle. Actually, we might have witnessed someone in the act of poaching. I'm sure that's not something you'd be interested in." She apologized profusely. "We won't waste any more of your time."

Responding to Evie's prompt, Millicent and Phillipa followed her and hurried out of the church. Instead of returning to the pub, Evie led them toward the back of the church and the churchyard.

Trying to keep up with Evie, Millicent said, "Phillipa doesn't want to ask but I'm too curious to wait for you to decide to tell us. What happened?"

Evie stopped by the first grave she came up to and looked back. The detective hadn't followed them.

"Well…" Evie cast her gaze around the churchyard and searched for the largest gravestone. "What happened? I'm not sure," Evie admitted. "I only know that man was an impostor."

It took a moment for Millicent and Phillipa to express their surprise, "What?"

"When I first saw him, I accepted the fact he was a detective. He wore a suit and we were expecting a man in a suit. Then, during our stilted conversation, I managed to place him." Evie smiled. "I've seen him in the pub."

"Are you sure?" Phillipa asked.

"When we first arrived, there were only a couple of

people sitting near the fireplace. Then, over the last couple of days, more and more people came to the pub. We assume they were all interested to see what the movie makers were doing. At times, I studied faces but, mostly, I just glanced around. I couldn't tell you how many times I saw him in the pub. I only know I recognized him and he wasn't wearing a suit. Like most of the villagers walking in, he wore his winter coat and a cap."

"The detective is not a detective?" Millicent asked. "Are you absolutely sure?"

"If I had any doubts before, I certainly don't now. A real detective would have insisted I tell him everything I know. Indeed, he would have followed us."

Evie smiled. Every theory they had entertained suddenly made sense. "I think the entire village has been conspiring."

"The entire village?" both Phillipa and Millicent exclaimed.

Evie nodded. "We all saw how quickly they banded together to impress the Hollywood movie makers."

They nodded.

"It's quite clear they would all do anything for their village."

Again, they nodded.

"What if one man threatened to rock the boat?"

"Duncan Miller?" Millicent asked.

"It's only a theory and the only way to prove that theory would be to talk with Glenda." Something Evie knew wouldn't happen. She didn't see the point in approaching Glenda who would, no doubt, remain silent.

Millicent's eyes widened. "And you think the entire village is responsible for killing Duncan Miller?"

"I wouldn't go so far as to say that…"

"What do you mean, milady?"

"I'm basing my theory on Glenda's reaction. Or, rather, her lack of reaction when she told us the news about Duncan Miller. She didn't even flinch. She smiled. That's such an uncharacteristic response, I can't help but read into it."

"I hope this doesn't work against me, milady, but I'm still struggling to understand."

"Millicent, I no longer believe Duncan Miller has been killed or even that he died. In fact, I'm sure if we go to his house, we will find him, probably sitting by the fireplace. If he's not there, he might be hiding somewhere."

Looking at Millicent, Evie knew her new secretary was on the verge of shedding tears of frustration.

"If I think about it too much, it will begin to sound complicated. I believe Duncan Miller has been silenced and I suspect Elizabeth Graham had a hand in it. If I am right, this is a masterful ruse. It all started with the accusation of theft and it might have ended there. However, something else happened."

"What?"

"We came to Thornbridge."

"Are you saying this is all our fault?" Millicent wailed.

Evie gave Millicent a reassuring pat on her arm. "Not exactly, but I suspect we set something in motion. We know the villagers have been trying to impress us by showing their village would be the ideal place to make our movie."

"You think they pretended someone killed Duncan Miller just to add another layer and make the village interesting?"

Evie nodded. "It's possible Duncan Miller tried to confront Glenda, hence the lights we saw on at her house. I believe someone decided to use the incident to their advantage. Quite possibly, Elizabeth Graham. She's a magistrate, so she might have used her influence to end the provocation and talk Duncan Miller into pretending he'd been killed." That scenario would fit in well with Elizabeth Graham's delayed arrival. "But there is something else... Our very presence threatened the status quo and I think I know what that is now."

"This is about the mysterious status quo?" Phillipa asked.

Nodding, Evie breathed a sigh of relief. "It has to do with Glenda's parentage. I'm sure of it." Evie's gaze skated over the headstones until she spotted the most elaborate one in the churchyard. "1885."

"Oh," Millicent exclaimed. "That's the date on the plaque we were looking at when the fake detective arrived."

"Yes. Albert Graham's grandfather."

Millicent whispered, "Are we going to assume the date of his death has some significance?"

"How can we not? It's right there, in front of us. 1885. Carved into the headstone and the plaque inside. The year Marjorie returned to Thornbridge and went to live in a house we know she couldn't afford. The same year Albert Graham's grandfather died and—" Evie's explanation was interrupted when a motor car came to an abrupt stop nearby.

They all turned toward the road and saw a man approaching, his steps hurried.

Albert Graham.

"I believe we might finally get some answers. Either that or Albert Graham is going to try to reinforce the lie. After all, he wants to maintain the status quo."

"Quickly, before he reaches us. What are you talking about?"

"He's protecting his family name from scandal."

CHAPTER TWENTY-FIVE

The churchyard

*A*lbert Graham walked at a brisk pace, his expression serious. Tipping his hat, he greeted them. The man who had, at first, come across as lacking in confidence had an air of directness when he spoke. "It seems you had a clash with the detective investigating Duncan Miller's death."

Had the man pretending to be a police officer reported to Albert Graham?

Evie wanted to know why they felt it was essential for them to believe Duncan Miller had died. Did they simply want him out of the picture or were they correct in thinking they'd taken advantage of the scenario and used it in their favor?

Albert Graham, looking more confident than he had

271

before, leaned in and lowered his voice to say, "I know who you are, Lady Woodridge."

That came as a surprise. She didn't want to think Glenda had given her identity away...

Also, Evie thought, it could pose problems in future investigations. How effective would she be as a lady detective if someone always managed to recognize her?

"My wife recognized you and we know you enjoy snooping around."

Taking a step forward, Millicent warned, "Mind what you say to her ladyship."

Before the encounter could turn into a clash, Evie smiled, "You're quite correct in saying I enjoy snooping around. Does that bother you, Mr. Graham? I suppose it would, if you had something to hide. Perhaps your family's reputation." She suspected that had been his priority all along. To keep the facts hidden and maintain the status quo which, in this case, would be the family's respectability.

His cheeks reddened and his lips pressed together.

Evie leaned forward and whispered, "Or you might be preoccupied with keeping a certain person's paternity secret. I wonder what we would discover if we delve enough. Perhaps a secret will, bequeathing a house to a certain person after his death. Quite generous, I think, but not as generous as making provisions—"

His eyes bulged. "Keep your voice down."

Evie stifled a gasp. Phillipa had raised the question about Nanny Fulham's early retirement. They hadn't given it too much thought, so the question had remained unanswered.

A timeline of events took shape in her mind. It

included Marjorie's departure from Thornbridge and eventual return in 1885, the same year Glenda had taken up her position as nanny.

If they were right and Glenda was Marjorie's daughter, it was quite possible the father had provided financial support for them to live in Bath until his death.

"Why the secrecy, Mr. Graham? I imagine the entire village knows about it."

He sputtered, "That's no reason to go about telling all and sundry."

Evie took that as confirmation. Once again, Phillipa had been right about Glenda being related to the Graham family.

Folding her arms, she asked him a direct question, "Mr. Graham, where is Duncan Miller?"

He growled under his breath. "If I tell you, will you leave this village?"

He was alive!

Evie decided she might question herself but she would never doubt her instincts again. But why had they created an elaborate deception? As a way to distract them? Getting rid of the person threatening Glenda removed the immediate problem. Had they decided to fake Duncan Miller's death before discovering her true identity or after?

Evie held his gaze for as long as she dared. "I assume I don't need to worry about Glenda Fulham coming to any harm or being the target of more malicious accusations?"

"You have my word."

"Do I?"

"Yes, of course," he snapped.

"I'm not entirely convinced. You see, I understand the

role Duncan Miller played. He merely wanted to chase Glenda away so that he could purchase the house. However, I am confused about the villagers. It seems some of them don't really care for Glenda's presence. That strikes me as odd because no one has really said anything bad about her. Yet she was discouraged from joining the choir."

His teeth gritted. "They sided with Duncan Miller... If Glenda Fulham wishes to participate, then I'm sure the way will be clear for her."

It seemed as though he didn't know the answer himself. "Do I have your word on that?"

His gaze slid over to the prominent headstone. "Yes."

Glancing at Millicent, Evie saw her look of confusion. Knowing her secretary would want to hear a full explanation, Evie stepped forward and said, "May I have a word with you in private?"

Albert Graham agreed with a stiff nod.

Excusing herself, she led the way back inside the church.

Ten minutes later, they emerged.

Evie smiled. "I look forward to reading Glenda's letters. I'm sure they'll be full of praise for the village that has welcomed her with open arms."

He looked from one to the other and, huffing, he swung away and left.

Evie drew in a long breath and released it as a sigh.

"Why do I feel that conversation was replete with unspoken words?" Phillipa asked.

Millicent's cheeks puffed out. "What Phillipa means to say is that we require an explanation. I only followed half of the conversation."

Evie walked over to the headstone and read the inscription, "Noblesse oblige."

Phillipa and Millicent exchanged a look of frustration.

"His grandfather, Reginald Graham, took his responsibilities seriously. That was his motto. Nanny Fulham retired young because she was provided for by her father. Albert Graham just confirmed it. And, yes, her father was his grandfather, Reginald Graham."

Millicent gasped. "Are you saying Reginald Graham and Marjorie…"

"Yes, and that's why Marjorie left the village and only returned after he died in 1885. They had a liaison."

"But… Marjorie married another man," Millicent said.

"Yes, that came up in the conversation I just had with Albert Graham. As accepting as Reginald Graham was of his responsibilities, he wouldn't marry her. Social barriers being what they were and still are, it almost goes without saying. However, he provided for her and she left and moved to Bath where she had Glenda."

"But why did Glenda work as a nanny?" Millicent asked.

Evie shrugged. "According to Albert Graham, when Marjorie, Glenda's mother, inherited the house, Glenda decided she would make her own way in the world. He didn't go into details and he probably doesn't know the full reason why she made that decision. We can only assume she had her pride. Then, when her services as a nanny were no longer required, the Graham family talked her into accepting a living allowance so she wouldn't continue working as a nanny. It seemed they didn't wish to run the risk of someone, anyone finding out her real identity, especially if she went to work in another grand house. In any case, Albert Graham said his grandfather had made provisions and it was his duty to ensure his will was fulfilled. Despite her reservations, she accepted the money. The issue didn't come up again until Marjorie died and left the house to Glenda. He offered to buy the house from her but she refused. She must have had a change of heart about her illegitimacy. When we spoke about her having the option to sell the house, she said something about it being the first house she'd owned... I suppose she saw it as gaining some sort of legitimacy." Evie shook her head. "I really don't wish to push her for more information. I can only assume she has come to terms with her parentage and has decided to turn a blind eye to the fact the house had once belonged to her father."

Millicent nodded. "Glenda can be pragmatic. She must have realized she couldn't change the circumstances of her past."

Phillipa frowned. "I don't understand why they had to pretend to kill poor Duncan Miller."

Evie laughed. "He had one too many drinks and decided to confront Glenda. We were right in thinking Albert Graham faked the argument with his wife. She went out to talk sense into Duncan Miller and she used her power as the magistrate to threaten him."

"So when Albert Graham says he wants to keep the status quo, he means he wants to pretend..." Millicent scrunched up her nose. "No, it still doesn't make sense."

"The fact his grandfather was Glenda's father is common knowledge but no one talks about it and that's the way Albert Graham wants to keep it," Evie explained.

"What about Glenda's name? Is it really Fulham?"

Evie smiled. "She made it up when she went to work as a nanny."

Millicent looked heavenward. "My goodness, these last few days have been exhausting, trying to keep up the pretense and remembering all our lies. How on earth does he do it?"

Evie glanced toward the road and saw Tom and Edmonds walking toward the church. Her shoulders rose and fell. "I'm going to have to explain everything again."

CHAPTER TWENTY-SIX

Halton House

Saying goodbye to Glenda turned into a lesson in diplomacy. Glenda pretended nothing had happened and Evie played along, adding how much she had enjoyed the visit.

One burning question remained unanswered. Evie employed all her willpower to stop herself from asking how Glenda had secured a cottage at Halton House. With any luck, she might eventually get the information out of Henrietta. If she didn't, Evie would be satisfied to think Henrietta and Sara had both decided to offer Glenda shelter and say no more on the subject.

Just as she'd been about to remind Glenda about her standing invitation to spend Christmas at Halton House, a villager arrived, bringing a large basket to welcome Glenda to Thornbridge and to extend an invitation for the village's Christmas festivities, which included luncheon at Graham House. It seemed Albert Graham was eager to provide proof of his promise to make Glenda feel right at home.

Millicent remarked, "I believe you have instilled fear into Mr. Graham, milady."

As they returned to the pub to collect their luggage, Evie scooped in a breath. "Now to face the barkeeper's disappointment. Tom…"

"Yes, Countess. I'll take care of pacifying him."

An hour later, they were ready to make their way back to Halton House.

Before parting ways, Millicent giggled. "I've never seen anyone go to so much trouble to keep up appearances. I wonder if they have allowed Duncan Miller to walk free from his untimely death?"

Just then, Phillipa remembered to tell Millicent she should visit the local dressmaker to have a new set of garments made. "You're a secretary now, Millicent. Of course, Evie will be more than happy to provide you with new clothes."

Millicent looked at Evie who confirmed it with a nod.

Gaping, Millicent stepped back and continued stepping back until she reached the motor car and climbed in.

"Oh, dear. Phillipa, I believe you have triggered another episode with Millicent."

"I'm sure she's just overjoyed by the prospect of getting new clothes," Phillipa said.

"You don't know the half of it. She's been having the strangest reactions to good news. She will lose her power of speech and then wake us all up in the middle of the night…"

Tom shook his head. "That's what comes of spoiling your servants."

Evie grinned. "Millicent is my secretary now and don't you forget it or she will remind you."

"Have you given any thought to what awaits you at Halton House?" Tom asked.

Evie ran through the long list of things she needed to do, including the hiring of a new lady's maid. Then, she remembered they had left Henrietta, Sara and Toodles rehearsing their play... "Oh, dear. I suppose I will have to brace myself. Although, I'm sure by now they will have sorted out their respective roles and polished their performance to a high sheen. Yes, indeed. I'm sure we're in for a treat." Feeling relieved to be headed back home, Evie said, "I'm glad we didn't have to investigate a murder." As Tom got them on their way, Evie added, "I suggest we say no more about the matter."

Tom glanced at her, "What if they ask?"

"We'll dismiss their curiosity by saying it's not our tale to tell."

Evie sat back, closed her eyes and drifted off to sleep...

———

Driving past the gates, Halton House came into view. "I hope there's a sumptuous luncheon waiting for us. I'm famished."

"Did you telephone ahead?" Phillipa asked.

"Oh, dear. It completely slipped my mind." She smiled and climbed out of the motor car, saying, "Sara is quite sensible. I trust she kept the peace."

As no one came to open the door, they let themselves in.

Relieved to be home, Evie smiled and removed her gloves. She didn't want to think about the last few days. For now, she would allow herself to be swept along by the festive season...

Tom cleared his throat. "Um... Countess..."

Evie stopped and looked up. Her smile wavered.

Phillipa stopped right beside her. Startled, she gasped.

"Henrietta, will you please stop flapping your arms. You're making it worse," Sara exclaimed.

Tom leaned in and whispered, "Are you seeing what I'm seeing?"

Henrietta wore a long gossamer gown with a train attached to it. Narrowing her eyes, Evie could just make out a harness around Henrietta's waist. The rope attached to it was being held by several footmen standing on the balcony, their faces showing the exertion of their efforts.

"Henrietta," Sara snapped. "They can't hold on if you keep moving like that. Stand still and be careful or you'll bring the Christmas tree down."

"That's the problem. I'm not standing, I'm hovering," Henrietta wailed.

"Well, this was your idea and you were determined to sweep onto the stage. Do try to cooperate."

"I'm not sure I want to anymore. I didn't realize I would be dangling so high up. Why aren't they lowering me?"

Sara's arms shot out. "Because you're stuck. Now, please stop moving. Edgar and Toodles will be along shortly."

Sounding dejected, Henrietta said, "It didn't look this complicated."

Sara sighed. "How long ago did you see that performance at the *Moulin Rouge*? Forty years ago?"

"Thirty-two years ago, and I remember the act as if I had seen it only yesterday. The woman swept across the stage like a will-o'-the-wisp"

Sara scoffed. "And how old was she?"

"Age should not be a deterrent. I thought we decided we were going to do this properly."

Phillipa whispered, "How old is Henrietta."

Evie blinked and shook her head in disbelief. "She refuses to say, but she's definitely old enough to know better. Definitely over seventy."

"Henrietta, whatever you do, do not lean forward," Sara warned. "Or look down."

"I can't imagine seeing this in any other household," Phillipa said. "If Millicent and Edmonds don't hurry up, they will be disappointed to have missed seeing this."

Snapping out of her stupor, Evie stepped forward. "Sara."

"Oh, oh, dear," Sara exclaimed. "You're back."

"Sara, how could you let this happen?" Evie chided.

Sara smiled. "It's perfectly safe. We tested the rope with twice her weight, not that she would reveal her weight. Anyhow, that's when we encountered a problem. The footmen pulled too hard and she suddenly... whooshed up. Luckily, the rope caught on something."

"You mean to say—"

"Evangeline! Don't look up, you'll spoil the surprise."

"Henrietta, you can't possibly be serious."

"Oh, but it's perfectly safe."

Edgar rushed through a side door carrying one end of a ladder with Toodles carrying the other end.

"What took you so long?" Henrietta complained as she flapped her arms.

"Countess. *Countess.*"

"What?" Evie was jolted awake.

"You fell asleep. We're here."

"Here?"

"Halton House and, you'll be pleased to know, it's still standing."

Evie brushed her hands across her face and looked toward the porticoed entrance. Edgar stood at attention with two footmen flanking him.

"Where's the ladder?" Evie asked.

"What?"

"Oh, oh, heavens. I had the most outrageous dream. Henrietta was dangling from the ceiling…"

"What?"

"And Edgar and Toodles dashed to her rescue, carrying a ladder. You were there." Evie turned to Phillipa. "And you were there. I wish you hadn't woken me up. Now I'll never know how they managed to get her down."

***

Printed in Great Britain
by Amazon